# SHATTER ME

# SHATTER ME

## TAHEREH MAFI

**HARPER**

*An Imprint of HarperCollinsPublishers*

Dress designer: Alex London
Styling: Katherine Erwin
Hair & makeup: Arturo Swayze

Library of Congress Cataloging-in-Publication Data
Mafi, Tahereh.
Shatter me / Tahereh Mafi. — 1st ed.
          p.     cm.
    Summary: Ostracized or incarcerated her whole life,
seventeen-year-old Juliette is freed on the condition that she
use her horrific abilities in support of The Reestablishment, a
postapocalyptic dictatorship, but Adam, the only person ever
to show her affection, offers hope of a better future.
    ISBN 978-0-06-208548-1 (trade bdg.)
    ISBN 978-0-06-211420-4 (international edition)
    [1. Science fiction. 2. Ability—Fiction. 3. Love—
Fiction. 4. Soldiers—Fiction. 5. Dictatorship—Fiction.]
I. Title.
PZ7.M2695Sh 2011                                    2011019370
[Fic]—dc23                                                CIP
                                                           AC

Typography by Ray Shappell
11 12 13 14 15   CG/BV   10 9 8 7 6 5 4 3 2 1

First Edition

*For my parents, and for my husband,*
*because when I said I wanted to touch the moon*
*you took my hand, held me close,*
*and taught me how to fly.*

*Two roads diverged in a wood, and I—*
*I took the one less traveled by,*
*and that has made all the difference.*

—ROBERT FROST, "The Road Not Taken"

# ONE

I've been locked up for 264 days.

I have nothing but a small notebook and a broken pen and the numbers in my head to keep me company. 1 window. 4 walls. 144 square feet of space. 26 letters in an alphabet I haven't spoken in 264 days of isolation.

6,336 hours since I've touched another human being.

"You're getting a ~~cellmate~~ roommate," they said to me.

"~~We hope you rot to death in this place~~ For good behavior," they said to me.

"~~Another psycho just like you~~ No more isolation," they said to me.

They are the minions of The Reestablishment. The initiative that was supposed to help our dying society. The same people who pulled me out of my parents' home and locked me in an asylum for something outside of my control. No one cares that I didn't know what I was capable of. That I didn't know what I was doing.

I have no idea where I am.

I only know that I was transported by someone in a white van who drove 6 hours and 37 minutes to get me here. I know I was handcuffed to my seat. I know I was strapped to my chair. ~~I know my parents never bothered to~~

say good-bye. I know I didn't cry as I was taken away.

I know the sky falls down every day.

The sun drops into the ocean and splashes browns and reds and yellows and oranges into the world outside my window. A million leaves from a hundred different branches dip in the wind, fluttering with the false promise of flight. The gust catches their withered wings only to force them downward, forgotten, left to be trampled by the soldiers stationed just below.

There aren't as many trees as there were before, is what the scientists say. They say our world used to be green. Our clouds used to be white. Our sun was always the right kind of light. But I have very faint memories of that world. I don't remember much from before. The only existence I know now is the one I was given. An echo of what used to be.

I press my palm to the small pane of glass and feel the cold clasp my hand in a familiar embrace. We are both alone, both existing as the absence of something else.

I grab my nearly useless pen with the very little ink I've learned to ration each day and stare at it. Change my mind. Abandon the effort it takes to write things down. Having a cellmate might be okay. Talking to a real human being might make things easier. I practice using my voice, shaping my lips around the familiar words unfamiliar to my mouth. I practice all day.

I'm surprised I remember how to speak.

I roll my little notebook into a ball I shove into the wall. I sit up on the cloth-covered springs I'm forced to sleep on.

I wait. I rock back and forth and wait.

I wait too long and fall asleep.

My eyes open to 2 eyes 2 lips 2 ears 2 eyebrows.

I stifle my scream my urgency to run the crippling horror gripping my limbs.

"You're a b-b-b-b—"

"And you're a girl." He cocks an eyebrow. He leans away from my face. He grins but he's not smiling and I want to cry, my eyes desperate, terrified, darting toward the door I'd tried to open so many times I'd lost count. They locked me up with a boy. A boy.

Dear God.

They're trying to kill me.

They've done it on purpose.

To torture me, to torment me, to keep me from sleeping through the night ever again. His arms are tatted up, half sleeves to his elbows. His eyebrow is missing a ring they must've confiscated. Dark blue eyes dark brown hair sharp jawline strong lean frame. ~~Gorgeous~~ Dangerous. Terrifying. Horrible.

He laughs and I fall off my bed and scuttle into the corner.

He sizes up the meager pillow on the spare bed they shoved into the empty space this morning, the skimpy mattress and threadbare blanket hardly big enough to support his upper half. He glances at my bed. Glances at his bed.

Shoves them both together with one hand. Uses his foot to push the two metal frames to his side of the room.

Stretches out across the two mattresses, grabbing my pillow to fluff up under his neck. I've begun to shake.

I bite my lip and try to bury myself in the dark corner.

He's stolen my bed my blanket my pillow.

I have nothing but the floor.

I will have nothing but the floor.

I will never fight back because I'm too petrified too paralyzed too paranoid.

"So you're—what? Insane? Is that why you're here?"

~~I'm not insane.~~

He props himself up enough to see my face. He laughs again. "I'm not going to hurt you."

~~I want to believe him~~ I don't believe him.

"What's your name?" he asks.

~~None of your business. What's your name?~~

I hear his irritated exhalation of breath. I hear him turn over on the bed that used to be half mine. I stay awake all night. My knees curled up to my chin, my arms wrapped tight around my small frame, my long brown hair the only curtain between us.

I will not sleep.

I cannot sleep.

I cannot hear those screams again.

4

# TWO

It smells like rain in the morning.

The room is heavy with the scent of wet stone, upturned soil; the air is dank and earthy. I take a deep breath and tiptoe to the window only to press my nose against the cool surface. Feel my breath fog up the glass. Close my eyes to the sound of a soft pitter-patter rushing through the wind. Raindrops are my only reminder that clouds have a heartbeat. That I have one, too.

I always wonder about raindrops.

I wonder about how they're always falling down, tripping over their own feet, breaking their legs and forgetting their parachutes as they tumble right out of the sky toward an uncertain end. It's like someone is emptying their pockets over the earth and doesn't seem to care where the contents fall, doesn't seem to care that the raindrops burst when they hit the ground, that they shatter when they fall to the floor, that people curse the days the drops dare to tap on their doors.

I am a raindrop.

~~My parents emptied their pockets of me and left me to evaporate on a concrete slab.~~

The window tells me we're not far from the mountains

and definitely near the water, but everything is near the water these days. I just don't know which side we're on. Which direction we're facing. I squint up at the early morning light. Someone picked up the sun and pinned it to the sky again, but every day it hangs a little lower than the day before. It's like a negligent parent who only knows one half of who you are. It never sees how its absence changes people. How different we are in the dark.

A sudden rustle means my cellmate is awake.

I spin around like I've been caught stealing food again. That only happened once and my parents didn't believe me when I said it wasn't for me. I said I was just trying to save the stray cats living around the corner but they didn't think I was human enough to care about a cat. Not me. Not ~~something~~ someone like me. But then, they never believed anything I said. That's exactly why I'm here.

Cellmate is studying me.

He fell asleep fully clothed. He's wearing a navy blue T-shirt and khaki cargo pants tucked into shin-high black boots.

I'm wearing dead cotton on my limbs and a blush of roses on my face.

His eyes scan the silhouette of my structure and the slow motion makes my heart race. I catch the rose petals as they fall from my cheeks, as they float around the frame of my body, as they cover me in something that feels like the absence of courage.

Stop looking at me, is what I want to say.

Stop touching me with your eyes and keep your hands to your sides and please and please and please—

"What's your name?" The tilt of his head cracks gravity in half.

I'm suspended in the moment. I blink and bottle my breaths.

He shifts and my eyes shatter into thousands of pieces that ricochet around the room, capturing a million snapshots, a million moments in time. Flickering images faded with age, frozen thoughts hovering precariously in dead space, a whirlwind of memories that slice through my soul. ~~He reminds me of someone I used to know.~~

One sharp breath and I'm shocked back to reality. ~~No more daydreams.~~

"Why are you here?" I ask the cracks in the concrete wall. 14 cracks in 4 walls a thousand shades of gray. The floor, the ceiling: all the same slab of stone. The pathetically constructed bed frames: built from old water pipes. The small square of a window: too thick to shatter. My hope is exhausted. My eyes are unfocused and aching. My finger is tracing a lazy path across the cold floor.

I'm sitting on the ground where it smells like ice and metal and dirt. Cellmate sits across from me, his legs folded underneath him, his boots just a little too shiny for this place.

"You're afraid of me." His voice has no shape.

My fingers find their way to a fist. "I'm afraid you're wrong."

I might be lying, but that's none of his business.

He snorts and the sound echoes in the dead air between us. I don't lift my head. I don't meet the eyes he's drilling in my direction. I taste the stale, wasted oxygen and sigh. My throat is tight with something familiar to me, something I've learned to swallow.

2 knocks at the door startle my emotions back into place.

He's upright in an instant.

"No one is there," I tell him. "It's just our breakfast." 264 breakfasts and I still don't know what it's made of. It smells like too many chemicals; an amorphous lump always delivered in extremes. Sometimes too sweet, sometimes too salty, always disgusting. Most of the time I'm too starved to notice the difference.

I hear him hesitate for only an instant before edging toward the door. He slides open a small slot and peers through to a world that no longer exists.

"*Shit!*" He practically flings the tray through the opening, pausing only to slap his palm against his shirt. "Shit, *shit*." He curls his fingers into a tight fist and clenches his jaw. He's burned his hand. I would've warned him if he would've listened.

"You should wait at least three minutes before touching the tray," I tell the wall. I don't look at the faint scars gracing my small hands, at the burn marks no one could've taught me to avoid. "I think they do it on purpose," I add quietly.

"Oh, so you're talking to me today?" He's angry. His eyes flash before he looks away and I realize he's more embarrassed than anything else. He's a tough guy. Too tough to make stupid mistakes in front of a girl. Too tough to show pain.

I press my lips together and stare out the small square of glass they call a window. There aren't many animals left, but I've heard stories of birds that fly. Maybe one day I'll get to see one. The stories are so wildly woven these days there's very little to believe, but I've heard more than one person say they've actually seen a flying bird within the past few years. So I watch the window.

There will be a bird today. It will be white with streaks of gold like a crown atop its head. It will fly. There will be a bird today. It will be white with streaks of gold like a crown atop its head. It will fly. There will be a—

His hand.

On me.

2 tips

of 2 fingers graze my cloth-covered shoulder for less than a second and every muscle every tendon in my body is fraught with tension and tied into knots that clench my spine. I stay very still. I don't move. I don't breathe. Maybe if I don't move, this feeling will last forever.

~~No one has touched me in 264 days.~~

Sometimes I think the loneliness inside of me is going to explode through my skin and sometimes I'm not sure if crying or screaming or laughing through the hysteria will solve anything at all. Sometimes I'm so desperate to touch to be touched *to feel* that I'm almost certain I'm going to fall off a cliff in an alternate universe where no one will ever be able to find me.

It doesn't seem impossible.

I've been screaming for years and no one has ever heard me.

"Aren't you hungry?" His voice is lower now, a little worried now.

~~I've been starving for 264 days.~~ "No." The word is little more than a broken breath as it escapes my lips and I turn and I shouldn't but I do and he's staring at me. Studying me. His lips are only barely parted, his limbs limp at his side, his lashes blinking back confusion.

Something punches me in the stomach.

His eyes. Something about his eyes.

~~It's not him not him not him not him not him.~~

I close the world away. Lock it up. Turn the key so tight. Blackness buries me in its folds.

"Hey—"

My eyes break open. 2 shattered windows filling my mouth with glass.

"What is it?" His voice is a failed attempt at flatness, an anxious attempt at apathy.

~~Nothing.~~

I focus on the transparent square wedged between me and my freedom. I want to smash this concrete world into oblivion. I want to be bigger, better, stronger.

~~I want to be *angry angry angry*.~~

I want to be the bird that flies away.

"What are you writing?" Cellmate speaks again.

~~These words are vomit.~~

~~This shaky pen is my esophagus.~~

~~This sheet of paper is my porcelain bowl.~~

"Why won't you answer me?" He's too close too close too close.

No one is ever close enough.

I suck in my breath and wait for him to walk away like everyone else in my life. My eyes are focused on the window and the promise of what could be. The promise of something grander, something greater, some reason for the madness building in my bones, some explanation for my inability to do anything without ruining everything. There will be a bird. It will be white with streaks of gold like a crown atop its head. It will fly. There will be a bird. It will be—

"Hey—"

"You can't touch me," I whisper. I'm lying, is what I don't tell him. He can touch me, is what I'll never tell him. Please touch me, is what I want to tell him.

But things happen when people touch me. Strange things. Bad things.

Dead things.

I can't remember the warmth of any kind of embrace. My arms ache from the inescapable ice of isolation. My own mother couldn't hold me in her arms. My father couldn't warm my frozen hands. I live in a world of nothing.

11

Hello.

World.

You will forget me.


Knock knock.

Cellmate jumps to his feet.

It's time to shower.

# THREE

The door opens to an abyss.

There's no color, no light, no promise of anything but horror on the other side. No words. No direction. Just an open door that means the same thing every time.

Cellmate has questions.

"What the hell?" He looks from me to the illusion of escape. "They're letting us out?"

~~They'll never let us out.~~ "It's time to shower."

"Shower?" His voice loses inflection but it's still threaded with curiosity.

"We don't have much time," I tell him. "We have to hurry."

"Wait, what?" He reaches for my arm but I pull away. "But there's no light—we can't even see where we're going—"

"Quickly." I focus my eyes on the floor. "Take the hem of my shirt."

"What are you talking about—"

An alarm sounds in the distance. A buzzing hums closer by the second. Soon the entire cell is vibrating with the warning and the door is slipping back into place. I grab his shirt and pull him into the blackness beside me. "Don't. Say. Anything."

"Bu—"

"*Nothing*," I hiss. I tug on his shirt and command him to follow me as I feel my way through the maze of the mental institution. ~~It's a home, a center for troubled youth, for neglected children from broken families, a safe house for the psychologically disturbed.~~ It's a prison. They feed us nothing and our eyes never see each other except in the rare bursts of light that steal their way through cracks of glass they pretend are windows. Nights are punctured by screams and heaving sobs, wails and tortured cries, the sounds of flesh and bone breaking by force or choice I'll never know. I spent the first 3 months in the company of my own stench. No one ever told me where the bathrooms and showers were located. No one ever told me how the system worked. No one speaks to you unless they're delivering bad news. No one touches you ever at all. Boys and girls never find each other.

Never but yesterday.

It can't be coincidence.

My eyes begin to readjust in the artificial cloak of night. My fingers feel their way through the rough corridors, and Cellmate doesn't say a word. I'm almost proud of him. He's nearly a foot taller than me, his body hard and solid with the muscle and strength of someone close to my age. The world has not yet broken him. Such freedom in ignorance.

"Wha—"

I tug on his shirt a little harder to keep him from speaking. We've not yet cleared the corridors. I feel oddly protective of him, this person who could probably break me with 2 fingers. He doesn't realize how his ignorance makes him vulnerable. He doesn't realize that they might kill him for no reason at all.

I've decided not to be afraid of him. I've decided his actions are more immature than genuinely threatening. ~~He looks so familiar so familiar so familiar to me.~~ I once knew a boy with the same blue eyes and my memories won't let me hate him.

Perhaps I'd like a friend.

6 more feet until the wall goes from rough to smooth and then we make a right. 2 feet of empty space before we reach a wooden door with a broken handle and a handful of splinters. 3 heartbeats to make certain we're alone. 1 foot forward to edge the door inward. 1 soft creak and the crack widens to reveal nothing but what I imagine this space to look like. "This way," I whisper.

I tug him toward the row of showers and scavenge the floor for any bits of soap lodged in the drain. I find 2 pieces, one twice as big as the other. "Open your hand," I tell the darkness. "It's slimy. But don't drop it. There isn't much soap and we got lucky today."

He says nothing for a few seconds and I begin to worry.

"Are you still there?" I wonder if this was the trap. If this was the plan. If perhaps he was sent to kill me under the cover of darkness in this small space. I never really knew what they were going to do to me in the asylum, I never knew if they thought locking me up would be good enough but I always thought they might kill me. It always seemed like a viable option.

I can't say I wouldn't deserve it.

But I'm in here for something I never meant to do and no one seems to care that it was an accident.

~~My parents never tried to help me.~~

I hear no showers running and my heart stops in place. This particular room is rarely full, but there are usually others, if only 1 or 2. I've come to realize that the asylum's residents are either legitimately insane and can't find their way to the showers, or they simply don't care.

I swallow hard.

"What's your name?" His voice splits the air and my stream of consciousness in one movement. I can feel him breathing much closer than he was before. My heart is racing and I don't know why but I can't control it. "Why won't you tell me your name?"

"Is your hand open?" I ask, my mouth dry, my voice hoarse.

He inches forward and I'm almost scared to breathe. His fingers graze the starchy fabric of the only outfit I'll ever own and I manage to exhale. As long as he's not touching my skin. As long as he's not touching my skin. As long as he's not touching my skin. This seems to be the secret.

My thin T-shirt has been washed in the harsh water of this building so many times it feels like a burlap sack against my skin. I drop the bigger piece of soap into his hand and tiptoe backward. "I'm going to turn the shower on for you," I explain, anxious not to raise my voice lest others should hear me.

"What do I do with my clothes?" His body is still too close to mine.

I blink 1,000 times in the blackness. "You have to take them off."

He laughs something that sounds like an amused breath. "No, I know. I meant what do I do with them while I shower?"

"Try not to get them wet."

He takes a deep breath. "How much time do we have?"

"Two minutes."

"Jesus, why didn't you say somethi—"

I turn on his shower at the same time I turn on my own and his complaints drown under the broken bullets of the barely functioning spigots.

My movements are mechanical. I've done this so many times I've already memorized the most efficient methods of scrubbing, rinsing, and rationing soap for my body as well as my hair. There are no towels, so the trick is trying not to soak any part of your body with too much water. If you do you'll never dry properly and you'll spend the next week nearly dying of pneumonia. I would know.

In exactly 90 seconds I've wrung my hair and I'm slipping back into my tattered outfit. My tennis shoes are the only things I own that are still in fairly good condition. We don't do much walking around here.

Cellmate follows suit almost immediately. I'm pleased that he learns quickly.

"Take the hem of my shirt," I instruct him. "We have to hurry."

His fingers skim the small of my back for a slow moment and I have to bite my lip to stifle the intensity. I nearly stop in place. No one ever puts their hands anywhere near my body.

I have to hurry forward so his fingers will fall back. He stumbles to catch up.

When we're finally trapped in the familiar 4 walls of claustrophobia, Cellmate won't stop staring at me.

I curl into myself in the corner. He still has my bed, my blanket, my pillow. I forgive him his ignorance, but perhaps it's too soon to be friends. Perhaps I was too hasty in helping him. Perhaps he really is only here to make me miserable. But if I don't stay warm I will get sick. My hair is too wet and the blanket I usually wrap it in is still on his side of the room. Maybe I'm still afraid of him.

I breathe in too sharply, look up too quickly in the dull light of the day. Cellmate has draped 2 blankets over my shoulders.

1 mine.

1 his.

"I'm sorry I'm such an asshole," he whispers to the wall. He doesn't touch me and I'm ~~disappointed~~ happy he doesn't. ~~I wish he would.~~ He shouldn't. No one should ever touch me.

"I'm Adam," he says slowly. He backs away from me

18

until he's cleared the room. He uses one hand to push my bed frame back to my side of the space.

Adam.

Such a nice name. Cellmate has a nice name.

It's a name I've always liked but I can't remember why.

I waste no time climbing onto the barely concealed springs of my mattress and I'm so exhausted I can hardly feel the metal coils threatening to puncture my skin. I haven't slept in more than 24 hours. *Adam is a nice name* is the only thing I can think of before exhaustion cripples my body.

# FOUR

I am not insane. I am not insane. I am not insane. I am not insane. I am not insane. I am not insane. I am not insane. I am not insane. I am not insane. I am not insane. I am not insane. I am not insane. I am not insane. I am not insane. I am not insane. I am not insane. I am not insane. I am not insane. I am not insane. I am not insane. I am not insane. I am not insane. I am not insane. I am not insane. I am not insane. I am not insane. I am not insane. I am not insane. I am not insane. I am not insane. I am not insane. I am not insane. I am not insane. I am not insane. I am not insane. I am not insane. I am not insane. I am not insane. I am not insane. I am not insane. I am not insane. I am not insane. I am not insane. I am not insane. I am not insane. I am not insane. I am not insane. I am not insane. I am not insane. I am not insane. I am not insane. I am not insane. I am not insane. I am not insane. I am not insane. I am not insane. I am not insane. I am not insane. I am not insane. I am not insane. I am not insane. I am not insane. I am not insane. I am not insane. I am not insane. I am not insane. I am not insane. I am not insane. I am not insane. I am not insane. I am not insane. I am not insane. I am not insane. I am not insane. I am not insane. I am not insane. I am not insane. I am not insane. I am not insane. I am not insane. I am not insane. I am not insane. I am not insane.

Horror rips my eyelids open.

My body is drenched in a cold sweat, my brain swimming in unforgotten waves of pain. My eyes settle on circles of black that dissolve in the darkness. I have no idea how long I've slept. I have no idea if I've scared my cellmate with my dreams. Sometimes I scream out loud.

Adam is staring at me.

I'm breathing hard and I manage to heave myself upright. I pull the blankets closer to my body only to realize I've stolen his only means for warmth. It never even occurred to me that he might be freezing just as much as I am. I'm shivering in place but his body is unflinching in the night, his silhouette a strong form against the backdrop of black. ~~I have no idea what to say.~~ There's nothing to say.

"The screams never stop in this place, do they?"

~~The screams are only the beginning.~~ "No," I mouth almost mutely. A faint blush flushes my face and I'm happy it's too dark for him to notice. He must have heard my cries.

Sometimes I wish I never had to sleep. Sometimes I think that if I stay very, very still, if I never move at all, things will change. I think if I freeze myself I can freeze the pain. Sometimes I won't move for hours. I will not move an inch.

If time stands still nothing can go wrong.

"Are you okay?" Adam's voice is concerned. I study the balled fists at his sides, the furrow buried in his brow, the tension in his jaw. This same person who stole my bed and my blanket is the same one who went without tonight. So cocky and careless so few hours ago; so careful and quiet right now. It scares me that this place could have broken him so quickly. I wonder what he heard while I was sleeping.

I wish I could save him from the horror.

Something shatters; a tortured cry sounds in the distance. These rooms are buried deep in concrete, walls thicker than the floors and ceilings combined to keep sounds from escaping too far. If I can hear the agony it must be insurmountable. Every night there are sounds I don't hear. Every night I wonder if I'm next.

"You're not insane."

My eyes snap up. His head is cocked, his eyes focused and clear despite the shroud that envelops us. He takes a deep breath. "I thought everyone in here was insane," he continues. "I thought they'd locked me up with a psycho."

I take a sharp hit of oxygen. "Funny. So did I."

1

2

3 seconds pass.

He cracks a grin so wide, so amused, so refreshingly sincere it's like a clap of thunder through my body. Something pricks at my eyes and breaks my knees. I haven't seen a smile in 265 days.

Adam is on his feet.

I offer him his blanket.

He takes it only to wrap it more tightly around my body and something is suddenly constricting in my chest. My lungs are skewered and strung together and I've just decided not to move for an eternity when he speaks.

"What's wrong?"

~~My parents stopped touching me when I was old enough~~ ~~to crawl. Teachers made me work alone so I wouldn't hurt~~ ~~the other children. I've never had a friend. I've never known~~ ~~the comfort of a mother's hug. I've never felt the tenderness~~ ~~of a father's kiss. I'm not insane.~~ "Nothing."

5 more seconds. "Can I sit next to you?"

~~That would be wonderful.~~ "No." I'm staring at the wall again.

He clenches and unclenches his jaw. He runs a hand through his hair and I realize for the first time that he's not wearing a shirt. It's so dark in this room I can only catch the curves and contours of his silhouette; the moon is allowed only a small window to light this space but I watch as the muscles in his arms tighten with every movement and I'm suddenly on fire. Flames are licking at my skin and there's a burst of heat clawing through my stomach. Every inch of his body is raw with power, every surface somehow luminous in the darkness. In 17 years I've never seen anything like him. In 17 years I've never talked to a boy my own age. ~~Because I'm a monster.~~

I close my eyes until I've sewn them shut.

I hear the creak of his bed, the groan of the springs as he sits down. I unstitch my eyes and study the floor. "You must be freezing."

"No." A strong sigh. "I'm actually burning up."

I'm on my feet so quickly the blankets fall to the floor. "Are you sick?" My eyes scan his face for signs of a fever but I don't dare inch closer. "Do you feel dizzy? Do your joints hurt?" I try to remember my own symptoms. I was chained to my bed by my own body for 1 week. I could do nothing more than crawl to the door and fall face-first into my food. I don't even know how I survived.

"What's your name?"

He's asked the same question 3 times already. "You might be sick," is all I can say.

"I'm not sick. I'm just hot. I don't usually sleep with my clothes on."

Butterflies catch fire in my stomach. An inexplicable humiliation is searing my flesh. I don't know where to look.

A deep breath. "I was a jerk yesterday. I treated you like crap and I'm sorry. I shouldn't have done that."

I dare to meet his gaze.

His eyes are the perfect shade of cobalt, blue like a blossoming bruise, clear and deep and decided. His jaw is set and his features are carved into a careful expression. He's been thinking about this all night.

"Okay."

"So why won't you tell me your name?" He leans forward and I freeze.

I thaw.

I melt. "Juliette," I whisper. "My name is Juliette."

His lips soften into a smile that cracks apart my spine. He repeats my name like the word amuses him. Entertains him. Delights him.

~~In 17 years no one has said my name like that.~~

24

# FIVE

*I don't know when it started.*

*I don't know why it started.*

*I don't know anything about anything except for the screaming.*

*My mother screaming when she realized she could no longer touch me. My father screaming when he realized what I'd done to my mother. My parents screaming when they'd lock me in my room and tell me I should be grateful. For their food. For their humane treatment of this thing that could not possibly be their child. For the yardstick they used to measure the distance I needed to keep away.*

*I ruined their lives, is what they said to me.*

*I stole their happiness. Destroyed my mother's hope for ever having children again.*

*Couldn't I see what I'd done, is what they'd ask me. Couldn't I see that I'd ruined everything.*

*I tried so hard to fix what I'd ruined. I tried every single day to be what they wanted. I tried all the time to be better but I never really knew how.*

*I only know now that the scientists are wrong.*

*The world is flat.*

*I know because I was tossed right off the edge and I've been trying to hold on for 17 years. I've been trying to climb back up for 17 years but it's nearly impossible to beat gravity when no one is willing to give you a hand.*

*When no one wants to risk touching you.*

It's snowing today.

The concrete is icy and stiffer than usual, but I prefer these freezing temperatures to the stifling humidity of summer days. Summer is like a slow-cooker bringing everything in the world to a boil 1 degree at a time. It promises a million happy adjectives only to pour stench and sewage into your nose for dinner. I hate the heat and the sticky, sweaty mess left behind. I hate the lackadaisical ennui of a sun too preoccupied with itself to notice the infinite hours we spend in its presence. The sun is an arrogant thing, always leaving the world behind when it tires of us.

The moon is a loyal companion.

It never leaves. It's always there, watching, steadfast, knowing us in our light and dark moments, changing forever just as we do. Every day it's a different version of itself. Sometimes weak and wan, sometimes strong and full of light. The moon understands what it means to be human.

Uncertain. Alone. Cratered by imperfections.

I stare out the window for so long I forget myself. I hold out my hand to catch a snowflake and my fist closes around the icy air. Empty.

I want to put this fist attached to my wrist right through the window.

Just to feel something.

Just to feel human.

"What time is it?"

My eyes flutter for a moment. His voice pulls me back down to a world I keep trying to forget. "I don't know," I tell him. I have no idea what time it is. I have no idea which day of the week it is, what month we're in, or even if there's a specific season we're supposed to be in.

We don't really have seasons anymore.

The animals are dying, birds don't fly, crops are hard to come by, flowers almost don't exist. The weather is unreliable. Sometimes our winter days hit 92 degrees. Sometimes it snows for no reason at all. We can't grow enough food anymore, we can't sustain enough vegetation for the animals anymore, and we can't feed the people what they need. Our population was dying off at an alarming rate before The Reestablishment took over and they promised us they had a solution. Animals were so desperate for food they were willing to eat anything and people were so desperate for food they were willing to eat poisoned animals. We were killing ourselves by trying to stay alive. The weather, the plants, the animals, and our human survival are all inextricably linked. The natural elements were at war with one another because we abused our ecosystem. Abused our atmosphere. Abused our animals. Abused our fellow man.

The Reestablishment promised they would fix things. But even though human health has found a modicum of relief under the new regime, more people have died at the end of a loaded gun than from an empty stomach. It's progressively getting worse.

"Juliette?"

My head snaps up.

His eyes are wary, worried, analyzing me.

I look away.

He clears his throat. "So, uh, they only feed us once a day?"

His question sends both our eyes toward the small slot in the door.

I curl my knees to my chest and balance my bones on the mattress. If I hold myself very, very still, I can almost ignore the metal digging into my skin. "There's no system to the food," I tell him. My finger traces a new pattern down the rough material of the blanket. "There's usually something in the morning, but there are no guarantees for anything else. Sometimes . . . we get lucky." My eyes flick up to the pane of glass punched into the wall. Pinks and reds filter into the room and I know it's the start of a new beginning. The start of the same end. Another day.

~~Maybe I will die today.~~

Maybe a bird will fly today.

"So that's it? They open the door once a day for people to do their business and maybe if we're *lucky* they feed us? That's it?"

The bird will be white with streaks of gold like a crown atop its head. It will fly. "That's it."

"There's no . . . group therapy?" He almost laughs.

"Until you arrived, I hadn't spoken a single word in two hundred sixty-four days."

His silence says so much. I can almost reach out and touch the guilt growing on his shoulders. "How long are you in for?" he finally asks.

~~Forever.~~ "I don't know." A mechanical sound creaks/groans/cranks in the distance. My life is 4 walls of missed opportunities poured into concrete molds.

"What about your family?" There's a serious sorrow in his voice, almost like he already knows the answer to that question.

~~Here is what I know about my parents: I have no idea where they are.~~ "Why are you here?" I talk to my fingers to avoid his gaze. I've studied my hands so thoroughly I know exactly where each bump cut and bruise has ravaged my skin. Small hands. Slim fingers. I curl them into a fist and release them to lose the tension. He still hasn't responded.

I look up.

"I'm not insane," is all he says.

"That's what we all say." I cock my head only to shake it a fraction of an inch. I bite my lip. My eyes can't help but steal glances out the window.

"Why do you keep looking outside?"

I don't mind his questions, I really don't. It's just strange to have someone to talk to. It's strange to have to exert energy to move my lips to form words necessary to explain my actions. No one has cared for so long. No one's watched me closely enough to wonder why I stare out a window. No one has ever treated me like an equal. Then again, he doesn't know ~~I'm a monster~~ my secret. I wonder how long this will last before he's running for his life.

I've forgotten to answer and he's still studying me.

I tuck a piece of hair behind my ear only to change my mind. "Why do you stare so much?"

His eyes are careful, curious. "I figured the only reason they would lock me up with a girl was because you were crazy. I thought they were trying to torture me by putting me in the same space as a psychopath. I thought you were my punishment."

"That's why you stole my bed." To exert power. To stake a claim. To fight first.

He drops his eyes. Clasps and unclasps his hands before rubbing the back of his neck. "Why'd you help me? How'd you know I wouldn't hurt you?"

I count my fingers to make sure they're still there. "I didn't."

"You didn't help me or you didn't know if I'd hurt you?"

"Adam." My lips curve around the shape of his name. I'm surprised to discover how much I love the easy, familiar way the sound rolls off my tongue.

He's sitting almost as still as I am. His eyes are pulled together with a new kind of emotion I can't place. "Yeah?"

"What's it like?" I ask, each word quieter than the one before. "Outside?" ~~In the real world.~~ "Is it worse?"

An ache mars the features of his finely chiseled face. It takes him a few heartbeats to answer. He glances out the window. "Honestly? I'm not sure if it's better to be in here or out there."

I follow his eyes to the pane of glass separating us from reality and I wait for his lips to part; I wait to listen to him speak. And then I try to pay attention as his words bounce around in the haze of my head, fogging my senses, misting my eyes, clouding my concentration.

Did you know it was an international movement? Adam asks me.

No I did not, I tell him. I do not tell him I was dragged from my home 3 years ago. I do not tell him that I was dragged away exactly 7 years after The Reestablishment began to preach and 4 months after they took control of everything. I do not tell him how little I know of our new world.

Adam says The Reestablishment had its hands in every country, ready for the moment to bring its leaders into a position of control. He says the inhabitable land left in the world has been divided into 3,333 sectors and each space is now controlled by a different Person of Power.

Did you know they lied to us? Adam asks me.

Did you know that The Reestablishment said someone had to take control, that someone had to save society, that someone had to restore the peace? Did you know that they said killing all the voices of opposition was the only way to find peace?

Did you know this? is what Adam asks me.

And this is where I nod. This is where I say yes.

This is the part I remember: The anger. The riots. The rage.

My eyes close in a subconscious effort to block out the bad memories, but the effort backfires. Protests. Rallies.

31

Screams for survival. I see women and children starving to death, homes destroyed and buried in rubble, the countryside a burnt landscape, its only fruit the rotting flesh of casualties. I see dead dead dead red and burgundy and maroon and the richest shade of your mother's favorite lipstick all smeared into the earth.

So much everything all the things dead.

The Reestablishment is struggling to maintain its hold over the people, Adam says. He says The Reestablishment is struggling to fight a war against the rebels who will not acquiesce to this new regime. The Reestablishment is struggling to root itself as a new form of government across all international societies.

And then I wonder what has happened to the people I used to see every day. What's become of their homes, their parents, their children. I wonder how many of them have been buried in the ground.

How many of them were murdered.

"They're destroying everything," Adam says, and his voice is suddenly a solemn sound in the silence. "All the books, every artifact, every remnant of human history. They're saying it's the only way to fix things. They say we need to start fresh. They say we can't make the same mistakes of previous generations."

2

knocks

at the door and we're both on our feet, abruptly startled back into this bleak world.

Adam raises an eyebrow at me. "Breakfast?"

"Wait three minutes," I remind him. We're so good at masking our hunger until the knocks at the door cripple our dignity.

They starve us on purpose.

"Yeah." His lips are set in a soft smile. "I wouldn't want to burn myself." The air shifts as he steps forward.

I am a statue.

"I still don't understand," he says, so quietly. "Why are you here?"

"Why do you ask so many questions?"

He leaves less than a foot of space between us and I'm 10 inches away from spontaneous combustion. "Your eyes are so deep." He tilts his head. "So calm. I want to know what you're thinking."

"You shouldn't." My voice falters. "You don't even know me."

He laughs and the action gives life to the light in his eyes. "I don't know you."

"No."

He shakes his head. Sits on his bed. "Right. Of course not."

"What?"

"You're right." His breath catches. "Maybe I am insane."

I take 2 steps backward. "Maybe you are."

He's smiling again and I'd like to take a picture. I'd like to stare at the curve of his lips for the rest of my life. "I'm not, you know."

"But you won't tell me why you're here," I challenge.

"And neither will you."

I fall to my knees and tug the tray through the slot. Something unidentifiable is steaming in 2 tin cups. Adam folds himself onto the floor across from me.

"Breakfast," I say as I push his portion forward.

# SIX

*1 word, 2 lips, 3 4 5 fingers form 1 fist.*

*1 corner, 2 parents, 3 4 5 reasons to hide.*

*1 child, 2 eyes, 3 4 17 years of fear.*

*A broken broomstick, a pair of wild faces, angry whispers, locks on my door.*

*Look at me, is what I wanted to say to you. Talk to me every once in a while. Find me a cure for these tears, I'd really like to exhale for the first time in my life.*

It's been 2 weeks.

2 weeks of the same routine, 2 weeks of nothing but routine. 2 weeks with the cellmate ~~who has come too close to touching me~~ who does not touch me. Adam is adapting to the system. He never complains, he never volunteers too much information, he continues to ask too many questions.

He's nice to me.

I sit by the window and watch the rain and the leaves and the snow collide. They take turns dancing in the wind, performing choreographed routines for unsuspecting masses. The soldiers stomp stomp stomp through the rain, crushing leaves and fallen snow under their feet. Their hands are wrapped in gloves wrapped around guns that could put a bullet through a million possibilities. They don't bother to be bothered by the beauty that falls from the sky. They don't understand the freedom in feeling the universe on their skin. They don't care.

I wish I could stuff my mouth full of raindrops and fill my pockets full of snow. I wish I could trace the veins in a fallen leaf and feel the wind pinch my nose.

Instead, I ignore the desperation sticking my fingers together and watch for the bird I've only seen in my dreams. Birds used to fly, is what the stories say. Before the ozone layer deteriorated, before the pollutants mutated the creatures into something ~~horrible~~ different. They say the weather wasn't always so unpredictable. They say there were birds who used to soar through the skies like planes.

It seems strange that a small animal could achieve anything as complex as human engineering, but the possibility is too enticing to ignore. I've dreamt about the same bird flying through the same sky for exactly 10 years. White with streaks of gold like a crown atop its head.

It's the only dream I have that gives me peace.

"What are you writing?"

I squint up at his strong stature, the easy grin on his face. I don't know how he manages to smile in spite of everything. I wonder if he can hold on to that shape, that special curve of the mouth that changes lives. I wonder how he'll feel in 1 month and I shudder at the thought.

I don't want him to end up like me.

Empty.

"Hey—" He grabs the blanket off my bed and crouches next to me, wasting no time wrapping the thin cloth around my thinner shoulders. "You okay?"

I try to smile. Decide to avoid his question. "Thank you for the blanket."

He sits down next to me and leans against the wall. His shoulders are so close too close ~~never close enough~~. His body heat does more for me than the blanket ever will. Something in my joints aches with an acute yearning, a desperate need I've never been able to fulfill. My bones are begging for something I cannot allow.

~~Touch me.~~

He glances at the little notebook tucked in my hand, at the broken pen clutched in my fist. I close the book and roll it into a little ball. I shove it into a crack in the wall. I study the pen in my palm. I know he's staring at me.

"Are you writing a book?"

"No." No I am not writing a book.

"Maybe you should."

I turn to meet his eyes and regret it immediately. There are less than 3 inches between us and I can't move because my body only knows how to freeze. Every muscle every movement tightens, every vertebra in my spinal column is a block of ice. I'm holding my breath and my eyes are wide, locked, caught in the intensity of his gaze. I can't look away. I don't know how to retreat.

Oh.

God.

His eyes.

I've been lying to myself, determined to deny the impossible.

*I know him I know him I know him I know him*

The boy ~~who does not remember me~~ I used to know.

"They're going to destroy the English language," he says, his voice careful, quiet.

I fight to catch my breath.

"They want to re-create everything," he continues. "They want to redesign everything. They want to destroy anything that could've been the reason for our problems. They think we need a new, universal language." He drops his voice. Drops his eyes. "They want to destroy everything. Every language in history."

"No." My breath hitches. Spots cloud my vision.

"I know."

"No." This I did not know.

He looks up. "It's good that you're writing things down. One day what you're doing will be illegal."

I've begun to shake. My body is suddenly fighting a maelstrom of emotions, my brain plagued by the world I'm losing and pained by this boy who does not remember me. The pen stumbles its way to the floor and I'm gripping the blanket so hard I'm afraid it's going to tear. Ice slices my skin, horror clots my veins. I never thought it would get this bad. I never thought The Reestablishment would take things so far. They're incinerating culture, the beauty of diversity. The new citizens of our world will be reduced to nothing but numbers, easily interchangeable, easily removable, easily destroyed for disobedience.

We have lost our humanity.

I wrap the blanket around my shoulders until I'm cocooned in the tremors that won't stop terrorizing my body. I'm horrified by my lack of self-control. I can't make myself still.

His hand is suddenly on my back.

His touch is scorching my skin through the layers of fabric and I inhale so fast my lungs collapse. I'm caught in colliding currents of confusion, so desperate ~~so desperate so desperate~~ to be close so desperate to be far away. I don't know how to move away from him. ~~I don't want to move away from him.~~

I don't want him to be afraid of me.

"Hey." His voice is soft so soft so soft. His arms are stronger than all the bones in my body. He pulls my swaddled figure close to his chest and I shatter. Two three four fifty thousand pieces of feeling stab me in the heart, melt into drops of warm honey that soothe the scars in my soul. The blanket is the only barrier between us and he pulls me closer, tighter, stronger, until I hear the beats humming deep within his chest and the steel of his arms around my body severs all ties to tension in my limbs. His heat melts the icicles propping me up from the inside out and I thaw I thaw I thaw, my eyes fluttering fast until they fall closed, until silent tears are streaming down my face and I've decided the only thing I want to freeze is his frame holding mine. "It's okay," he whispers. "You'll be okay."

Truth is a jealous, vicious mistress that never ever sleeps, is what I don't tell him. I'll never be okay.

It takes every broken filament in my being to pull away

from him. I do it because I have to. ~~Because it's for his own good.~~ Someone is sticking forks in my back as I trip away. The blanket catches my foot and I nearly fall before Adam reaches out to me again. "Juliette—"

"You can't t-touch me." My breathing is shallow and hard to swallow, my fingers shaking so fast I clench them into a fist. "You can't touch me. You can't." My eyes are trained on the door.

He's on his feet. "Why not?"

"You just can't," I whisper to the walls.

"I don't understand—why won't you talk to me? You sit in the corner all day and write in your book and look at everything but my face. You have so much to say to a piece of paper but I'm standing right here and you don't even acknowledge me. Juliette, *please*—" He reaches for my arm and I turn away. "Why won't you at least *look* at me? I'm not going to hurt you—"

~~You don't remember me. You don't remember that we went to the same school for 7 years.~~

You don't remember me.

"You don't know me." My voice is even, flat; my limbs numb, amputated. "We've shared one space for two weeks and you think you know me but you don't know anything about me. Maybe I *am* crazy."

"You're not," he says through clenched teeth. "You *know* you're not."

"Then maybe it's you," I say carefully, slowly. "Because one of us is."

40

"That's not true—"

"Tell me why you're here, Adam. What are you doing in an insane asylum if you don't belong here?"

"I've been asking you the same question since I got here."

"Maybe you ask too many questions."

I hear his hard exhalation of breath. He laughs a bitter laugh. "We're practically the only two people who are *alive* in this place and you want to shut me out, too?"

I close my eyes and focus on breathing. "You can talk to me. Just don't touch me."

7 seconds of silence join the conversation. "Maybe I want to touch you."

There are 15,000 feelings of disbelief hole-punched in my heart. I'm tempted by recklessness, aching aching aching, desperate forever for what I can never have. I turn my back on him but I can't keep the lies from spilling out of my lips. "Maybe I don't want you to."

He makes a harsh sound. "I disgust you that much?"

I spin around, so caught off guard by his words I forget myself. He's staring at me, his face hard, his jaw set, his fingers flexing by his sides. His eyes are 2 buckets of rainwater: deep, fresh, clear.

Hurt.

"You don't know what you're talking about." I can't breathe.

"You can't just answer a simple question, can you?" He shakes his head and turns to the wall.

My face is cast in a neutral mold, my arms and legs filled

with plaster. I feel nothing. I am nothing. I am empty of everything I will never move. I'm staring at a small crack near my shoe. I will stare at it forever.

The blankets fall to the floor. The world fades out of focus, my ears outsource every sound to another dimension. My eyes close, my thoughts drift, my memories kick me in the heart.

I know him.

I've tried so hard to stop thinking about him.
I've tried so hard to forget his face.
I've tried so hard to get those blue blue blue eyes out of my head but I know him I know him I know him it's been 3 years since I last saw him.
I could never forget Adam.
But he's already forgotten me.

# SEVEN

*I remember televisions and fireplaces and porcelain sinks. I remember movie tickets and parking lots and SUVs. I remember hair salons and holidays and window shutters and dandelions and the smell of freshly paved driveways. I remember toothpaste commercials and ladies in high heels and old men in business suits. I remember mailmen and libraries and boy bands and balloons and Christmas trees.*

*I remember being 10 years old when we couldn't ignore the food shortages anymore and things got so expensive no one could afford to live.*

Adam is not speaking to me.

Maybe it's for the best. Maybe there was no point hoping he and I could be friends, maybe it's better he thinks I don't like him than that I like him too much. He's hiding a lot of something that might be pain, but his secrets scare me. He won't tell me why he's here. Though I don't tell him much, either.

~~And yet and yet and yet~~.

Last night the memory of his arms around me was enough to scare away the screams. The warmth of a kind embrace, the strength of firm hands holding all of my pieces together, the relief and release of so many years' loneliness. This gift he's given me I can't repay.

Touching Juliette is nearly impossible.

I'll never forget the horror in my mother's eyes, the torture in my father's face, the fear etched in their expressions. Their child ~~was~~ is a monster. Possessed by the devil. Cursed by darkness. Unholy. An abomination. Drugs, tests, medical solutions failed. Psychological cross-examinations failed.

*She is a walking weapon in society,* is what the teachers said. *We've never seen anything like it,* is what the doctors said. *She should be removed from your home,* is what the police officers said.

~~No problem at all, is what my parents said.~~ I was 14 years old when they finally got rid of me. When they stood back and watched as I was dragged away for a murder I didn't know I could commit.

Maybe the world is safer with me locked in a cell. Maybe Adam is safer if he hates me. He's sitting in the corner with his fists in his face.

I never wanted to hurt him.

I never wanted to hurt the only person who never wanted to hurt me.

The door crashes open and 5 people swarm into the room, rifles pointed at our chests.

Adam is on his feet and I'm made of stone. I've forgotten to inhale. I haven't seen so many people in so long I'm momentarily stupefied. I should be screaming.

"HANDS UP, FEET APART, MOUTHS SHUT. DON'T MOVE AND WE WON'T SHOOT YOU."

I'm still frozen in place. I should move, I should lift my arms, I should spread my feet, I should remember to breathe. Someone is cutting off my neck.

The one barking orders slams the butt of his gun into my back and my knees crack as they hit the floor. I finally taste oxygen and a side of blood. I think Adam is yelling but there is an acute agony ripping through my body unlike anything I've experienced before. I'm utterly immobilized.

"What don't you understand about keeping your mouth SHUT?" I squint sideways to see the barrel of the gun 2 inches away from Adam's face.

"GET UP." A steel-toed boot kicks me in the ribs, fast, hard, hollow. I'm swallowing nothing but the strangled gasps choking my body. "I said GET UP." Harder, faster, stronger, another boot in my gut. I can't even cry out.

~~Get up, Juliette. Get up. If you don't, they'll shoot Adam.~~

I heave myself up to my knees and fall back on the wall behind me, stumbling forward to catch my balance. Lifting my hands is more torture than I knew I could endure. My organs are dead, my bones are cracked, my skin is a sieve, punctured by pins and needles of pain. They've finally come to kill me.

That's why they put Adam in my cell.

Because I'm leaving. Adam is here because I'm leaving, because they forgot to kill me on time, because my moments are over, because my 17 years were too many for this world. They're going to kill me.

I always wondered how it would happen. ~~I wonder if this will make my parents happy.~~

Someone is laughing. "Well aren't you a little shit?"

I don't even know if they're talking to me. I can hardly focus on keeping my arms upright.

"She's not even crying," someone adds. "The girls are usually begging for mercy by now."

The walls are beginning to bleed into the ceiling. I wonder how long I can hold my breath. I can't distinguish words I can't understand the sounds I'm hearing the blood is rushing through my head and my lips are 2 blocks of concrete I can't crack open. There's a gun in my back and I'm tripping forward. The floors are falling up. My feet are dragging in a direction I can't decipher.

I hope they kill me soon.

# EIGHT

It takes me 2 days to open my eyes.

There's a tin of water and a tin of food set off to the side and I inhale the cold contents with trembling hands, a dull ache creaking through my bones, a desperate drought suffocating my throat. Nothing seems to be broken, but one glance under my shirt proves the pain was real. The bruises are discolored blossoms of blue and yellow, torture to touch and slow to heal.

Adam is nowhere.

I am alone in a block of solitude, 4 walls no more than 10 feet in every direction, the only air creeping in through a small slot in the door. I've just begun to terrorize myself with my imagination when the heavy metal door slams open. A guard with 2 rifles strung across his chest looks me up and down.

"Get up."

This time I don't hesitate.

I hope Adam, at least, is safe. I hope he doesn't come to the same end I do.

"Follow me." The guard's voice is thick and deep, his gray eyes unreadable. He looks about 25 years old, blond hair cropped close to the crown, shirtsleeves rolled up to his shoulders, military tattoos snaking up his forearms just like Adam's.

Oh.

God.

No.

Adam steps into the doorway beside the blond and gestures with his weapon toward a narrow hallway. "Move."

~~Adam is pointing a gun at my chest,~~

~~Adam is pointing a gun at my chest.~~

Adam is pointing a gun at my chest.

His eyes are foreign to me, glassy and distant, far, far away.

I am nothing but novocaine. I am numb, a world of nothing, all feeling and emotion gone forever.

I am a whisper that never was.

Adam is a soldier. ~~Adam wants me to die.~~

I stare at him openly now, every sensation amputated, my pain a distant scream disconnected from my body. My feet move forward of their own accord; my lips remain shut because there will never be words for this moment.

Death would be a welcome release from these earthly joys I've known.


I don't know how long I've been walking before another blow to my back cripples me. I blink against the brightness of light I haven't seen in so long. My eyes begin to tear and I'm squinting against the fluorescent bulbs illuminating the large space. I can hardly see anything.

"Juliette Ferrars." A voice detonates my name. There's a heavy boot pressed into my back and I can't lift my head to distinguish who's speaking to me. "Weston, dim the lights and release her. I want to see her face." The command is cool and strong like steel, dangerously calm, effortlessly powerful.

The brightness is reduced to a level I'm able to tolerate. The imprint of a boot is carved into my back but no longer settled on my skin. I lift my head and look up.

I'm immediately struck by his youth. He can't be much older than me.

It's obvious he's in charge of something, though I have no idea what. His skin is flawless, unblemished, his jawline sharp and strong. His eyes are the palest shade of emerald I've ever seen.

He's beautiful.

His crooked smile is calculated evil.

He's sitting on what he imagines to be a throne but is nothing more than a chair at the front of an empty room. His suit is perfectly pressed, his blond hair expertly combed, his soldiers the ideal bodyguards.

I hate him.

"You're so stubborn." His green eyes are almost translucent. "You never want to cooperate. You wouldn't even play nice with your cellmate."

I flinch without intending to. The burn of betrayal blushes up my neck.

Green Eyes looks unexpectedly amused and I'm suddenly

mortified. "Well isn't that interesting." He snaps his fingers. "Kent, would you step forward, please."

My heart stops beating when Adam comes into view. ~~Kent. His name is Adam Kent.~~

I am aflame from head to toe. Adam flanks Green Eyes in an instant, but only offers a curt nod of his head as a salute. Perhaps the leader isn't nearly as important as he thinks.

"Sir," he says.

So many thoughts are tangling in my head I can't untie the insanity knotting itself together. I should've known. I'd heard rumors of soldiers living among the public in secret, reporting to the authorities if things seemed suspicious. Every day people disappeared. No one ever came back.

Though I still can't understand why Adam was sent to spy on me.

"It seems you made quite an impression on her."

I squint closer at the man in the chair only to realize his suit has been adorned with tiny colored patches. Military mementos. His last name is etched into the lapel: Warner.

Adam says nothing. He doesn't look in my direction. His body is erect, 6 feet of ~~gorgeous~~ lean muscle, his profile strong and steady. The same arms that held my body are now holsters for lethal weapons.

"You have nothing to say about that?" Warner glances at Adam only to tilt his head in my direction, his eyes dancing in the light, clearly entertained.

Adam clenches his jaw. "Sir."

"Of course." Warner is suddenly bored. "Why should I expect you to have something to say?"

"Are you going to kill me?" The words escape my lips before I have a chance to think them through and someone's gun slams into my spine all over again. I fall to the floor with a broken whimper, wheezing into the filthy floor.

"That wasn't necessary, Roland." Warner's voice is saturated with mock disappointment. "I suppose I'd be wondering the same thing if I were in her position." A pause. "Juliette?"

I manage to lift my head.

"I have a proposition for you."

# NINE

I'm not sure I'm hearing him correctly.

"You have something I want." Warner is still staring at me.

"I don't understand," I tell him.

He takes a deep breath and stands up to pace the length of the room. Adam has not yet been dismissed. "You are kind of a pet project of mine." Warner smiles to himself. "I've studied your records for a very long time."

I can't handle his pompous, self-satisfied strut. I want to break the grin off his face.

Warner stops walking. "I want you on my team."

"What?" A broken whisper of surprise.

"We're in the middle of a *war*," he says a little impatiently. "Maybe you can put the pieces together."

"I don't—"

"I know your secret, Juliette. I know why you're in here. Your entire life is documented in hospital records, complaints to authorities, messy lawsuits, public demands to have you locked up." His pause gives me enough time to choke on the horror caught in my throat. "I'd been considering it for a long time, but I wanted to make sure you weren't *actually* psychotic. Isolation wasn't exactly a good indicator, though you did fend for yourself quite well."

He offers me a smile that says I should be grateful for his praise. "I sent Adam to stay with you as a final precaution. I wanted to make sure you weren't volatile, that you were capable of basic human interaction and communication. I must say I'm quite pleased with the results."

Someone is ripping my skin off.

"Adam, it seems, played his part a little too excellently. He is a fine soldier. One of the best, in fact." Warner spares him a glance before smiling at me. "But don't worry, he doesn't know what you're capable of. Not yet, anyway."

I claw at the panic, I swallow the agony, I beg myself not to look in his direction but I fail ~~I fail I fail~~. Adam meets my eyes in the same split second I meet his but he looks away so quickly I'm not sure if I imagined it.

~~I am a monster.~~

"I'm not as cruel as you think," Warner continues, a musical lilt in his voice. "If you're so fond of his company I can make this"—he gestures between myself and Adam— "a permanent assignment."

"No," I breathe.

Warner curves his lips into a careless grin. "Oh *yes*. But be careful, pretty girl. If you do something . . . *bad* . . . he'll have to shoot you."

There are wire cutters carving holes in my heart. Adam doesn't react to anything Warner says.

He is doing a job.

I am a number, a mission, an easily replaceable object; I am not even a memory in his mind.

I am nothing.

I didn't expect his betrayal to bury me so deep.

"If you accept my offer," Warner interrupts my thoughts, "you will live like I do. You will be one of *us*, and not one of *them*. Your life will change forever."

"And if I do not accept?" I ask, catching my voice before it cracks in fear.

Warner looks genuinely disappointed. His hands are clasped together in dismay. "You don't really have a choice. If you stand by my side you will be rewarded." He presses his lips together. "But if you choose to disobey? Well . . . I think you look rather lovely with all your body parts intact, don't you?"

I'm breathing so hard my frame is shaking. "You want me to torture people for you?"

His face breaks into a brilliant smile. "That would be wonderful."

The world is bleeding.

I don't have time to form a response before he turns to Adam. "Show her what she's missing, would you?"

Adam answers a beat too late. "Sir?"

"That is an order, soldier." Warner's eyes are trained on me, his lips twitching with suppressed amusement. "I'd like to break this one. She's a little too feisty for her own good."

"You can't touch me," I spit through clenched teeth.

"Wrong," he singsongs. He tosses Adam a pair of black gloves. "You're going to need these," he says with a conspiratorial whisper.

"You're a monster." My voice is too even, my body filled with a sudden rage. "Why don't you just *kill* me?"

"That, my dear, would be a waste." He steps forward and I realize his hands are carefully sheathed in white leather gloves. He tips my chin up with one finger. "Besides, it'd be a shame to lose such a pretty face."

I try to snap my neck away from him but the same steel-toed boot slams into my spine and Warner catches my face in his grip. I suppress a scream. "Don't struggle, love. You'll only make things more difficult for yourself."

"I hope you rot in hell."

Warner flexes his jaw. He holds up a hand to stop someone from shooting me, kicking me in the spleen, cracking my skull open, I have no idea. "You're a fighter for the wrong team." He stands up straight. "But we can change that. Adam," he calls. "Don't let her out of your sight. She's your charge now."

"Yes, sir."

# TEN

Adam puts on the gloves but he doesn't touch me. "Let her up, Roland. I'll take it from here."

The boot disappears. I struggle to my feet and stare at nothing. I won't think about the horror that awaits me. Someone kicks in the backs of my knees and I nearly stumble to the ground. "Get *going*," a voice growls from behind. I look up and realize Adam is already walking away. I'm supposed to be following him.

Only once we're back in the familiar blindness of the asylum hallways does he stop walking.

"Juliette." ~~One soft word and my joints are made of air.~~

I don't answer him.

"Take my hand," he says.

"I will never," I manage between broken bites of oxygen. "Not ever."

A heavy sigh. I feel him shift in the darkness and soon his body is too close so disarmingly close to mine. His hand is on my lower back and he's guiding me through the corridors toward an unknown destination. Every inch of my skin is blushing. I have to hold myself upright to keep from falling backward into his arms.

The distance we're walking is much longer than I expected. When Adam finally speaks I suspect we're close to the end. "We're going to go outside," he says near my ear. I have to ball my fists to control the thrills tripping my heart. I'm almost too distracted by the feel of his voice to understand the significance of what he's saying. "I just thought you should know."

An audible intake of breath is my only response. I haven't been outside in almost a year. I'm painfully excited but I haven't felt natural light on my skin in so long I don't know if I'll be able to handle it. I have no choice.

The air hits me first.

Our atmosphere has little to boast of, but after so many months in a concrete corner even the wasted oxygen of our dying Earth tastes like heaven. I can't inhale fast enough. I fill my lungs with the feeling; I step into the slight breeze and clutch a fistful of wind as it weaves its way through my fingers.

Bliss unlike anything I've ever known.

The air is crisp and cool. A refreshing bath of tangible nothing that stings my eyes and snaps at my skin. The sun is high today, blinding as it reflects the small patches of snow keeping the earth frozen. My eyes are pressed down by the weight of the bright light and I can't see through more than two slits, but the warm rays wash over my body like a jacket fitted to my form, like the hug of something greater than a human. I could stand still in this moment forever. For one infinite second I feel free.

Adam's touch shocks me back to reality. I nearly jump out of my skin and he catches my waist. I have to beg my bones to stop shaking. "Are you okay?" His eyes surprise

57

me. They're the same ones I remember, blue and bottom-less like the deepest part of the ocean. His hands are ~~gentle so gentle~~ around me.

"I don't want you to touch me," I lie.

"You don't have a choice." He won't look at me.

"I always have a choice."

He runs a hand through his hair and swallows the noth-ing in his throat. "Follow me."

We're in a blank space, an empty acre filled with dead leaves and dying trees taking small sips from melted snow in the soil. The landscape has been ravaged by war and neglect and it's still the most beautiful thing I've seen in so long. The stomping soldiers stop to watch as Adam opens a car door for me.

It's not a car. It's a tank.

I stare at the massive metal body and attempt to climb my way up the side when Adam is suddenly behind me. He hoists me up by the waist and I gasp as he settles me into the seat.

Soon we're driving in silence and I have no idea where we're headed.

I'm staring out the window at everything.

I'm eating and drinking and absorbing every infinitesi-mal detail in the debris, in the skyline, in the abandoned homes and broken pieces of metal and glass sprinkled in the scenery. The world looks naked, stripped of vegetation and warmth. There are no street signs, no stop signs; there is no need for either. There is no public transportation. Everyone knows that cars are now manufactured by only one company and sold at a ridiculous rate.

Very few people are allowed a means of escape.

~~My parents~~ The general population has been distributed across what's left of the country. Industrial buildings form the spine of the landscape: tall, rectangular metal boxes stuffed full of machinery. Machinery intended to strengthen the army, to strengthen The Reestablishment, to destroy mass quantities of human civilization.

Carbon/Tar/Steel

Gray/Black/Silver

Smoky colors smudged into the skyline, dripping into the slush that used to be snow. Trash is heaped in haphazard piles everywhere, patches of yellowed grass peeking out from under the devastation.

Traditional homes of our old world have been abandoned, windows shattered, roofs collapsing, red and green and blue paint scrubbed into muted shades to better match our bright future. Now I see the compounds carelessly constructed on the ravaged land and I begin to remember. I remember how these were supposed to be temporary. I remember the few months before I was locked up when they'd begun building them. These small, cold quarters would suffice just until they figured out all the details of this new plan, is what The Reestablishment had said. Just until everyone was subdued. Just until people stopped protesting and realized that this change was *good* for them, *good* for their children, *good* for their future.

I remember there were rules.

No more dangerous imaginations, no more prescription

medications. A new generation comprised of only healthy individuals would sustain us. The sick must be locked away. The old must be discarded. The troubled must be given up to the asylums. Only the strong should survive.

Yes.

Of course.

No more stupid languages and stupid stories and stupid paintings placed above stupid mantels. No more Christmas, no more Hanukkah, no more Ramadan and Diwali. No talk of religion, of belief, of personal convictions. Personal convictions were what nearly killed us all, is what they said.

Convictions priorities preferences prejudices and ideologies divided us. Deluded us. Destroyed us.

Selfish needs, wants, and desires needed to be obliterated. Greed, overindulgence, and gluttony had to be expunged from human behavior. The solution was in self-control, in minimalism, in sparse living conditions; one simple language and a brand-new dictionary filled with words everyone would understand.

These things would save us, save our children, save the human race, is what they said.

Reestablish Equality. Reestablish Humanity. Reestablish Hope, Healing, and Happiness.

SAVE US!

JOIN US!

REESTABLISH SOCIETY!

The posters are still plastered on the walls.

The wind whips their tattered remains, but the signs are determinedly fixed, flapping against the steel and concrete structures they're stuck to. Some are still pasted to poles sprung right out of the ground, loudspeakers now affixed at the very top. Loudspeakers that alert the people, no doubt, to the imminent dangers that surround them.

But the world is eerily quiet.

Pedestrians pass by, ambling along in the cold, frigid weather to do factory work and find food for their families. Hope in this world bleeds out of the barrel of a gun.

No one really cares for the concept anymore.

People used to want hope. They wanted to think things could get better. They wanted to believe they could go back to worrying about gossip and holiday vacations and going to parties on Saturday nights, so The Reestablishment promised a future too perfect to be possible and society was too desperate to disbelieve. They never realized they were signing away their souls to a group planning on taking advantage of their ignorance. Their fear.

Most civilians are too petrified to protest but there are others who are stronger. There are others who are waiting for the right moment. There are others who have already begun to fight back.

I hope it's not too late to fight back.

I study every quivering branch, every imposing soldier, every window I can count. My eyes are 2 professional pickpockets, stealing everything to store away in my mind.

I lose track of the minutes we trample over.

We pull up to a structure 10 times larger than the asylum and suspiciously central to civilization. From the outside it looks like a bland building, inconspicuous in every way but its size, gray steel slabs comprising 4 flat walls, windows cracked and slammed into the 15 stories. It's bleak and bears no marking, no insignia, no proof of its true identity.

Political headquarters camouflaged among the masses.

The inside of the tank is a convoluted mess of buttons and levers I'm at a loss to operate, and Adam is opening my door before I have a chance to identify the pieces. His hands are in place around my waist and my feet are now firmly on the ground but my heart is pounding so fast I'm certain he can hear it. He hasn't let go of me.

I look up.

His eyes are tight, his forehead pinched, his lips ~~his lips his lips~~ are 2 pieces of frustration forged together.

I step backward and 10,000 tiny particles shatter between us. He drops his eyes. He turns away. He inhales and 5 fingers on one hand form a fickle fist. "This way." He nods toward the building.

I follow him inside.

# ELEVEN

I'm so prepared for unimaginable horror that the reality is almost worse.

Dirty money is dripping from the walls, a year's supply of food wasted on marble floors, hundreds of thousands of dollars in medical aid poured into fancy furniture and Persian rugs. I feel the artificial heat pouring in through air vents and think of children screaming for clean water. I squint through crystal chandeliers and hear mothers begging for mercy. I see a superficial world existing in the midst of a terrorizing reality and I can't move.

I can't breathe.

So many people must've died to sustain this luxury. So many people had to lose their homes and their children and their last 5 dollars in the bank for promises promises promises so many promises to save them from themselves. They *promised* us—The Reestablishment promised us hope for a better future. They said they would fix things, they said they would help us get back to the world we knew— the world with movie dates and spring weddings and baby showers. They said they would give us back our homes, our health, our sustainable future.

But they stole everything.

They took everything. ~~My life. My future. My sanity. My freedom.~~

They filled our world with weapons aimed at our foreheads and smiled as they shot 16 candles right through our future. They killed those strong enough to fight back and locked up the freaks who failed to live up to their utopian expectations. ~~People like me.~~

Here is proof of their corruption.

My skin is cold-sweat, my fingers trembling with disgust, my legs unable to withstand ~~the waste the waste the waste~~ the selfish waste in these 4 walls. I'm seeing red everywhere. The blood of bodies spattered against the windows, spilled across the carpets, dripping from the chandeliers.

"Juliette—"

I break.

I'm on my knees, my body cracking from the pain I've swallowed so many times, heaving with sobs I can no longer suppress, my dignity dissolving in my tears, the agony of this past week ripping my skin to shreds.

I can't ever breathe.

I can't catch the oxygen around me and I'm dry-heaving into my shirt and I hear voices and see faces I don't recognize, wisps of words wicked away by confusion, thoughts scrambled so many times I don't know if I'm even conscious anymore.

I don't know if I've officially lost my mind.

I'm in the air. I'm a bag of feathers in his arms and he's breaking through soldiers crowding around for a glimpse of the commotion and for a moment I don't want to care that I shouldn't want this so much. I want to forget that I'm supposed to hate him, that he betrayed me, that he's working for the same people who are trying to destroy the very little that's left of humanity and my face is buried in the soft material of his shirt and my cheek is pressed against his chest and he smells like strength and courage and the world drowning in rain. I don't want him to ~~ever ever ever~~ ever let go of my body. I wish I could touch his skin, I wish there were no barriers between us.

Reality slaps me in the face.

Mortification muddles my brain, desperate humiliation clouds my judgment; red paints my face, bleeds through my skin. I clutch at his shirt.

"You can kill me," I tell him. "You have guns—" I'm wriggling out of his grip and he tightens his hold around my body. His face shows no emotion but a sudden strain in his jaw, an unmistakable tension in his arms. "You can just *kill me*—" I plead.

"*Juliette.*" His voice is solid with an edge of desperation. "*Please.*"

I'm numb again. Powerless all over again. Melting from within, life seeping out of my limbs.

We're standing in front of a door.

Adam takes a key card and swipes it against a black pane of glass fitted into the small space beside the handle, and the stainless steel door slides out of place. We step inside.

We're all alone in a new room.

"Please ~~don't let go of me~~ put me down," I tell him.

There's a queen-size bed in the middle of the space, lush carpet gracing the floors, an armoire flush against the wall, light fixtures glittering from the ceiling. The beauty is so tainted I can't stand the sight of it. Adam gentles me onto the soft mattress and takes a small step backward.

"You'll be staying here for a while, I think," is all he says.

I squeeze my eyes shut. I don't want to think about the inevitable torture awaiting me. "Please," I tell him. "I'd like to be left alone."

A deep sigh. "That's not exactly an option."

"What do you mean?" I spin around.

"I have to watch you, Juliette." He says my name like a whisper. ~~My heart my heart my heart.~~ "Warner wants you to understand what he's offering you, but you're still considered . . . a threat. He's made you my assignment. I can't leave."

~~I don't know whether to be thrilled or horrified.~~ I'm horrified. "You have to live with me?"

"I live in the barracks on the opposite end of this building. With the other soldiers. But, yeah." He clears his throat. He's not looking at me. "I'll be moving in."

There's an ache in the pit of my stomach that's gnawing on my nerves. I want to hate him and judge him and scream forever but I'm failing because all I see is an 8-year-old boy who doesn't remember that he used to be the kindest person I ever knew.

I don't want to believe this is happening.

I close my eyes and curl my head into my knees.

"You have to get dressed," he says after a moment.

I pop my head up. I blink at him like I can't understand what he's saying. "I am dressed."

He clears his throat again but tries to be quiet about it. "There's a bathroom through here." He points. I see a door connected to the room and I'm suddenly curious. I've heard stories about people with bathrooms in their bedrooms. I guess they're not exactly *in* the bedroom, but they're close enough. I slip off the bed and follow his finger. As soon as I open the door he resumes speaking. "You can shower and change in here. The bathroom . . . it's the only place there are no cameras," he adds, his voice trailing off.

*There are cameras in my room.*

Of course.

"You can find clothes in there." He nods to the armoire. He suddenly looks uncomfortable.

"And you can't leave?" I ask.

He rubs his forehead and sits down on the bed. He sighs. "You have to get ready. Warner will be expecting you for dinner."

*"Dinner?"* My eyes are the size of the moon.

Adam looks grim. "Yeah."

"He's not going to hurt me?" I'm ashamed at the relief in my voice, at the unexpected tension I've released, at the fear I didn't know I was harboring. "He's going to give me dinner?" ~~I'm starving my stomach is a tortured pit of starvation I'm so hungry so hungry so hungry~~ I can't even imagine what real food must taste like.

Adam's face is inscrutable again. "You should hurry. I can show you how everything works."

I don't have time to protest before he's in the bathroom and I've followed him inside. The door is still open and he's standing in the middle of the small space with his back to me and I can't understand why. "I already know how to use the bathroom," I tell him. ~~I used to live in a regular home. I used to have a family.~~

He turns around very, very slowly and I begin to panic. He finally lifts his head but his eyes are darting in every direction. When he looks at me his eyes narrow; his forehead is tight. His right hand curls into a fist and his left hand lifts one finger to his lips. He's telling me to be quiet.

Every organ in my body falls to the floor.

I knew something was coming but I didn't know it'd be Adam. I didn't think he'd be the one to hurt me, to torture me, to make me wish for death more than I ever have before. I don't even realize I'm crying until I hear the whimper and feel the silent tears stream down my face and I'm ~~ashamed so ashamed~~ so ashamed of my weakness but a part of me doesn't care. I'm tempted to beg, to ask for mercy, to steal his gun and shoot myself first. Dignity is the only thing I have left.

He seems to register my sudden hysteria because his eyes snap open and his mouth falls to the floor. "No, God, Juliette—I'm not—" He swears under his breath. He pumps his fist against his forehead and turns away, sighing heavily, pacing the length of the small space. He swears again.

He walks out the door and doesn't look back.

# TWELVE

5 full minutes under piping hot water, 2 bars of soap both smelling of lavender, a bottle of shampoo meant only for my hair, and the touch of soft, plush towels I dare to wrap around my body and I begin to understand.

They want me to forget.

They think they can wash away my memories, my loyalties, my priorities with a few hot meals and a room with a view. They think I am so easily purchased.

Warner doesn't seem to understand that I grew up with nothing and I didn't hate it. I didn't want the clothes or the perfect shoes or the expensive anything. I didn't want to be draped in silk. All I ever wanted was to reach out and touch another human being not just with my hands but with my heart. I saw the world and its lack of compassion, its harsh, grating judgment, and its cold, resentful eyes. I saw it all around me.

I had so much time to listen.

To look.

To study people and places and possibilities. All I had to do was open my eyes. All I had to do was open a book— to see the stories bleeding from page to page. To see the memories etched onto paper.

I spent my life folded between the pages of books.

In the absence of human relationships I formed bonds with paper characters. I lived love and loss through stories threaded in history; I experienced adolescence by association. My world is one interwoven web of words, stringing limb to limb, bone to sinew, thoughts and images all together. I am a being comprised of letters, a character created by sentences, a figment of imagination formed through fiction.

They want to delete every point of punctuation in my life from this earth and I don't think I can let that happen.

I slip back into my old clothes and tiptoe into the bedroom only to find it abandoned. Adam is gone even though he said he would stay. I don't understand him I don't understand his actions I don't understand my disappointment. I wish I didn't love the freshness of my skin, the feel of being perfectly clean after so long; I don't understand why I still haven't looked in the mirror, why I'm afraid of what I'll see, why I'm not sure if I'll recognize the face that might stare back at me.

I open the armoire.

It's bursting with dresses and shoes and shirts and pants and clothing of every kind, colors so vivid they hurt my eyes, material I've only ever heard of, the kind I'm almost afraid to touch. The sizes are perfect too perfect.

*They've been waiting for me.*

The sky is raining bricks right into my skull.

I've been neglected abandoned ostracized and dragged from my home. I've been poked prodded tested and thrown in a cell. I've been studied. I've been starved. I've been tempted with friendship only to be left betrayed and trapped into this nightmare I'm expected to be grateful for. My parents. My teachers. Adam. Warner. The Reestablishment. I am expendable to all of them.

They think I'm a doll they can dress up and twist into prostration.

But they're wrong.

"Warner is waiting for you."

I spin around and fall back against the armoire, slamming it closed in the craze of panic clutching my heart. I steady myself and fold away my fear when I see Adam standing at the door. His mouth moves for a moment but he says nothing. Eventually he steps forward so forward until he's close enough to touch.

He reaches past me to reopen the door hiding the things I'm embarrassed to know exist. "These are all for you," he says without looking at me, his fingers touching the hem of a purple dress, a rich plum color good enough to eat.

"I already have clothes." My hands smooth out the wrinkles in my dirty, ragged outfit.

He finally decides to look at me, but when he does his eyebrows trip, his eyes blink and freeze, his lips part in surprise. I wonder if I've washed off a new face for myself and I flush, hoping he's not disgusted by what he might see. I don't know why I care.

He drops his gaze. Takes a deep breath. "I'll be waiting outside."

~~I stare at the purple dress with Adam's fingerprints~~ I study the inside of the armoire for only a moment before I abandon it. I comb anxious fingers through my wet hair and steel myself.

I am no one's property.

And I don't care what Warner wants me to look like.

I step outside and Adam stares at me for a small second. He rubs the back of his neck and says nothing. He shakes his head. He starts walking. He doesn't touch me and I shouldn't notice but I do. I have no idea what to expect I have no idea what my life will be like in this new place and I'm being nailed in the stomach by every exquisite embellishment, every lavish accessory, every superfluous painting, molding, lighting, coloring of this building. I hope the whole thing catches fire.

I follow Adam down a long carpeted corridor to an elevator made entirely of glass. He swipes the same key card he used to open my door and we step inside. I didn't even realize we'd taken an elevator to get up this many floors. I realize I must've made a horrible scene when I arrived and I'm almost happy.

I hope I disappoint Warner in every possible way.

The dining room is big enough to feed thousands of orphans. Instead, there are 7 banquet tables draped across the room, blue silk spilling across the tabletops, crystal vases bursting with orchids and stargazer lilies, glass bowls filled with gardenias. ~~It's enchanting~~. I wonder where they got the flowers from. They must not be real. I don't know how they could be real. I haven't seen real flowers in years.

Warner is positioned at the table directly in the middle, seated at the head. As soon as he sees ~~me~~ Adam he stands up. The entire room stands in turn.

I realize almost immediately that there is an empty seat on either side of him and I don't intend to stop moving but I do. I take quick inventory of the attendees and can't count any other women.

Adam brushes the small of my back with 3 fingertips and I'm startled out of my skin. I hurry forward and Warner beams at me. He pulls out the chair on his left and gestures for me to sit down. I do.

I try not to look at Adam as he sits across from me.

"You know . . . there are clothes in your armoire, my dear." Warner sits down beside me; the room reseats itself and resumes a steady stream of chatter. He's turned almost entirely in my direction but somehow the only presence I'm aware of is directly across from me. I focus on the empty plate 2 inches from my fingers. I drop my hands in my lap. "And you don't have to wear those dirty tennis shoes any-more," Warner continues, stealing another glance before pouring something into my cup. It looks like water.

~~I'm so thirsty I could inhale a waterfall.~~

I hate his smile.

Hate looks just like everybody else until it smiles. Until it spins around and lies with lips and teeth carved into the semblance of something too passive to punch.

"Juliette?"

I inhale too quickly. A stifled cough is ballooning in my throat.

His glassy green eyes glint in my direction.

"Are you not hungry?" Words dipped in sugar. His gloved hand touches my wrist and I nearly sprain it in my haste to distance myself from him.

~~I could eat every person in this room.~~ "No, thank you."

He licks his bottom lip into a smile. "Don't confuse stupidity for bravery, love. I know you haven't eaten anything in days."

Something in my patience snaps. "I'd really rather die than eat your food and listen to you call me *love*," I tell him.

Adam drops his fork.

Warner spares him a swift glance and when he looks my way again his eyes have hardened. He holds my gaze for a few infinitely long seconds before he pulls a gun out of his jacket pocket. He fires.

The entire room screams to a stop.

My heart is flapping wings against my throat.

I turn my head very, very slowly to follow the direction of Warner's gun only to see he's shot some kind of meat right through the bone. The platter of food is slightly steaming across the room, the meal heaped less than a foot away from the guests. He shot it without even looking. He could've killed someone.

It takes all of my energy to remain very, very still.

Warner drops the gun on my plate. The silence gives

it space to clatter around the universe and back. "Choose your words very wisely, Juliette. One word from me and your life here won't be so easy."

I blink.

Adam pushes a plate of food in front of me; the strength of his gaze is like a white-hot poker pressed against my skin. I look up and he cocks his head the tiniest millimeter. His eyes are saying *Please*.

I pick up my fork.

Warner doesn't miss a thing. He clears his throat a little too loudly. He laughs with no humor as he cuts into the meat on his plate. "Do I have to get Kent to do all my work for me?"

"Excuse me?"

"It seems he's the only one you'll listen to." His tone is breezy but his jaw is unmistakably set. He turns to Adam. "I'm surprised you didn't tell her to change her clothes like I asked you to."

Adam sits up straighter. "I did, sir."

"I like my clothes," I tell him. I'd like to punch you in the eye, is what I don't tell him.

Warner's smile slides back into place. "No one asked what *you* like, love. Now eat. I need you to look your best when you stand beside me."

# THIRTEEN

Warner insists on accompanying me to my room.

After dinner Adam disappeared with a few of the other soldiers. He disappeared without a word or glance in my direction and I don't have any idea what to anticipate. At least I have nothing to lose but my life.

"I don't want you to hate me," Warner says as we make our way toward the elevator. "I'm only your enemy if you want me to be."

"We will always be enemies." My voice is cracked into chips of ice. The words melt on my tongue. "I will never be what you want me to be."

Warner sighs as he presses the button for the elevator. "I really think you'll change your mind." He glances at me with a small smile. A shame, really, that such striking looks should be wasted on such a miserable human being. "You and I, Juliette—together? We could be unstoppable."

I will not look at him though I feel his gaze touching every inch of my body. "No, thank you."

We're in the elevator. The world is whooshing past us and the walls of glass make us a spectacle to every person on every floor. There are no secrets in this building.

He touches my elbow and I pull away. "You might reconsider," he says softly.

"How did you figure it out?" The elevator dings open but I'm not moving. I finally turn to face him because I can't contain my curiosity. I study his hands, so carefully sheathed in leather, his sleeves thick and crisp and long. Even his collar is high and regal. He's dressed impeccably from head to toe and covered everywhere except his face. Even if I wanted to touch him I'm not sure I'd be able to. He's protecting himself.

From me.

"Perhaps a conversation for tomorrow night?" He cocks a brow and offers me his arm. I pretend not to notice it as we walk off the elevator and down the hall. "Maybe you could wear something nice."

"What's your first name?" I ask him.

We're standing in front of my door.

He stops. Surprised. Lifts his chin almost imperceptibly. Focuses his eyes on my face until I begin to regret my question. "You want to know my name."

I don't do it on purpose, but my eyes narrow just a bit. "Warner is your last name, isn't it?"

He almost smiles. "You want to know my name."

"I didn't realize it was a secret."

He steps forward. His lips twitch. His eyes fall, his lips draw in a tight breath. He drops a gloved finger down the apple of my cheek. "I'll tell you mine if you tell me yours," he whispers, too close to my neck.

I inch backward. Swallow hard. "You already know my name."

He's not looking at my eyes. "You're right. I should

rephrase that. What I meant to say was I'll tell you mine if you show me yours."

"What?" I'm breathing too fast too suddenly.

He begins to pull off his gloves and I begin to panic. "Show me what you can do."

My jaw is too tight and my teeth have begun to ache. "I won't touch you."

"That's all right." He tugs off the other glove. "I don't exactly need your help."

"No—"

"Don't worry." He grins. "I'm sure it won't hurt *you* at all."

"No," I gasp. "No, I won't—I can't—"

"Fine," Warner snaps. "That's fine. You don't want to hurt me. I'm so utterly flattered." He almost rolls his eyes. Looks down the hall. Spots a soldier. Beckons him over. "Jenkins?"

Jenkins is swift for his size and he's at my side in a second.

"Sir." He bows his head an inch even though he's clearly Warner's senior. He can't be more than 27; stocky, sturdy, packed with bulk. He spares me a sidelong glance. His brown eyes are warmer than I'd expect them to be.

"I'm going to need you to accompany Ms. Ferrars back downstairs. But be warned: she's incredibly uncooperative and will try to break free from your grip." He smiles too slowly. "No matter what she says or does, soldier, you cannot let go of her. Are we clear?"

Jenkins' eyes widen; he blinks, his nostrils flare, his fingers flex at his sides. He takes a short breath. Nods.

Jenkins is not an idiot.

I start running.

I'm bolting down the hallway and running past a series of stunned soldiers too scared to stop me. I don't know what I'm doing, why I think I can run, where I think I could possibly go. I'm straining to reach the elevator if only because I think it will buy me time. I don't know what else to do.

Warner's commands are bouncing off the walls and exploding in my eardrums. He doesn't need to chase me. He's getting others to do the work for him.

Soldiers are lining up before me.

Beside me.

Behind me.

I can't breathe.

I'm spinning in a circle of my own stupidity, panicked, pained, petrified by the thought of what I'm going to do to Jenkins against my will. What he will do to me against his will. What will happen to both of us despite our best intentions.

"Seize her," Warner says softly. Silence has stuffed itself into every corner of this building. His voice is the only sound in the room.

Jenkins steps forward.

My eyes are flooding and I squeeze them shut. I pry them open. I blink back at the crowd and spot a familiar face. Adam is staring at me, horrified.

Shame has covered every inch of my body.

Jenkins offers me his hand.

My bones begin to buckle, snapping in synchronicity with the beats of my heart. I crumble to the floor, folding into myself like a flimsy crepe. My arms are so painfully bare in this ragged T-shirt.

"Don't—" I hold up a tentative hand, pleading with my eyes, staring into the face of this innocent man. "Please don't—" My voice breaks. "You don't want to touch me—"

"I never said I did." Jenkins's voice is deep and steady, full of regret. Jenkins who has no gloves, no protection, no preparation, no possible defense.

"That was a direct order, soldier," Warner barks, trains a gun at his back.

Jenkins grabs my arms.

*NO NO NO*

I gasp.

My blood is surging through my veins, rushing through my body like a raging river, waves of heat lapping against my bones. I can hear his anguish, I can feel the power pouring out of his body, I can hear his heart beating in my ear and my head is spinning with the rush of adrenaline fortifying my being.

I feel alive.

I wish it hurt me. I wish it maimed me. I wish it repulsed me. I wish I hated the potent force wrapping itself around my skeleton.

But I don't. My skin is pulsing with someone else's life and I don't hate it.

I hate myself for enjoying it.

I enjoy the way it feels to be brimming with more life and hope and human power than I knew I was capable of. His pain gives me a pleasure I never asked for.

And he's not letting go.

But he's not letting go because he can't. Because I have to be the one to break the connection. Because the agony incapacitates him. Because he's caught in my snares.

Because I am a Venus flytrap.

And I am lethal.

I fall on my back and kick at his chest, willing him away from me, willing his weight off of my small frame, his limp body collapsed against my own. I'm suddenly screaming and struggling to see past the sheet of tears obscuring my vision; I'm hiccupping, hysterical, horrified by the frozen look on this man's face, his paralyzed lips wheezing gasps through his lungs.

I break free and stumble backward. The sea of soldiers parts behind me. Every face is etched in astonishment and pure, unadulterated fear. Jenkins is lying on the floor and no one dares approach him.

"Somebody help him!" I scream. "Somebody *help* him! He needs a doctor—he needs to be taken—he needs—he— oh God—what have I done—"

"Juliette—"

"DON'T TOUCH ME—DON'T YOU DARE TOUCH ME—"

Warner's gloves are back in place and he's trying to hold me together, he's trying to smooth back my hair, he's trying to wipe away my tears and I want to murder him.

"Juliette, you need to calm down—"

"HELP HIM!" I cry, falling to my knees, my eyes glued to the figure lying on the floor. The other soldiers are finally creeping closer, cautious as though he might be contagious. "Please—you have to help him! *Please*—"

"Kent, Curtis, Soledad—TAKE CARE OF THIS!" Warner shouts to his men before scooping me up into his arms.

I'm still kicking when the world goes black.

# FOURTEEN

The ceiling is fading in and out of focus.

My head is heavy, my vision is blurry, my heart is strained. There is a distinct flavor of panic lodged somewhere underneath my tongue and I'm fighting to remember where it came from. I try to sit up and can't understand why I was lying down.

Someone's hands are on my shoulders.

"How are you feeling?" Warner is peering down at me.

Suddenly my memories are burning in my eyes and Jenkins' face is swimming in my consciousness and I'm swinging my fists and screaming for Warner to get away from me and struggling to wriggle out of his grip but he just smiles. Laughs a little. Gentles my hands down beside my torso.

"Well, at least you're awake," he sighs. "You had me worried for a moment."

I try to control my trembling limbs. "Get your hands away from me."

He waves sheathed fingers in front of my face. "I'm all covered up. Don't worry."

"I *hate* you."

"So much passion." He laughs again. He looks so calm,

so genuinely amused. He stares at me with eyes softer than I ever expected them to be.

I turn away.

He stands up. Takes a short breath. "Here," he says, reaching for a tray on a small table. "I brought you food."

I take advantage of the moment to sit up and look around. I'm lying on a bed draped in damask golds and burgundies the darkest shade of blood. The floor is covered in thick, rich carpet the color of a setting summer sun. It's warm in this room. It's the same size as the one I occupy, its furniture standard enough: bed, armoire, side tables, chandelier glittering from the ceiling. The only difference is there's an extra door in this room and there's a candle burning quietly on a small table in the corner. I haven't seen fire in so many years I've lost count. I have to stifle an impulse to reach out and touch the flame.

I prop myself up against the pillows and try to pretend I'm not comfortable. "Where am I?"

Warner turns around holding a plate with bread and cheese on it. His other hand is gripping a glass of water. He looks around the room as if seeing it for the first time. "This is my bedroom."

If my head weren't splitting into pieces I'd be tempted to run. "Take me to my own room. I don't want to be here."

"And yet, here you are." He sits at the foot of the bed, a few feet away. Pushes the plate in front of me. "Are you thirsty?"

I don't know if it's because I can't think straight or if

it's because I'm genuinely confused, but I'm struggling to reconcile Warner's polarizing personalities. Here he is, offering me a glass of water after he forced me to torture someone. I lift my hands and study my fingers as if I've never seen them before. "I don't understand."

He cocks his head, inspecting me as though I might've seriously injured myself. "I only asked if you were thirsty. That shouldn't be difficult to understand." A pause. "Drink this."

I take the glass. Stare at it. Stare at him. Stare at the walls.

I must be insane.

Warner sighs. "I'm not sure, but I think you fainted. And I think you should probably eat something, though I'm not entirely sure about that, either." He pauses. "You've probably had too much exertion your first day here. My mistake."

"Why are you being nice to me?"

The surprise on his face surprises me even more. "Because I care about you," he says simply.

"You *care* about me?" The numbness in my body is beginning to dissipate. My blood pressure is rising and anger is making its way to the forefront of my consciousness. "I almost killed Jenkins because of you!"

"You didn't kill—"

"Your soldiers beat me! You keep me here like a prisoner! You threaten me! You threaten to kill me! You give me no freedom and you say you *care* about me?" I nearly throw the glass of water at his face. "You are a *monster!*"

Warner turns away so I'm staring at his profile. He clasps his hands. Changes his mind. Touches his lips. "I am only trying to help you."

"Liar."

He seems to consider that. Nods, just once. "Yes. Most of the time, yes."

"I don't want to be here. I don't want to be your experiment. Let me go."

"No." He stands up. "I'm afraid I can't do that."

"Why not?"

"Because I can't. I just—" He tugs at his fingers. Clears his throat. His eyes touch the ceiling for a brief moment. "Because I need you."

"You need me to kill people!"

He doesn't answer right away. He walks to the candle. Pulls off a glove. Tickles the flame with his bare fingers. "You know, I am very capable of killing people on my own, Juliette. I'm actually very good at it."

"That's disgusting."

He shrugs. "How else do you think someone my age is able to control so many soldiers? Why else would my father allow me to take charge of an entire sector?"

"Your *father?*" I sit up, suddenly curious in spite of myself.

He ignores my question. "The mechanics of fear are simple enough. People are intimidated by me, so they listen when I speak." He waves a hand. "Empty threats are worth very little these days."

I squeeze my eyes shut. "So you kill people for power."

"As do you."

"How *dare* you—"

He laughs, loud. "You're free to lie to yourself, if it makes you feel better."

"I am not lying—"

"Why did it take you so long to break your connection with Jenkins?"

My mouth freezes in place.

"Why didn't you fight back right away? Why did you allow him to touch you for as long as he did?"

My hands have begun to shake and I grip them, hard. "You don't know anything about me."

"And yet you claim to know me so well."

I clench my jaw, not trusting myself to speak.

"At least I'm honest," he adds.

"You just agreed you're a liar!"

He raises his eyebrows. "At least I'm honest about being a liar."

I slam the glass of water on the side table. Drop my head in my hands. Try to stay calm. Take a steadying breath. "Well," I rasp, "why do you need me, then? If you're such an excellent murderer?"

A smile flickers and fades across his face. "One day I'll introduce you to the answer to that question."

I try to protest but he stops me with one hand. Picks up a piece of bread from the plate. Holds it under my nose. "You hardly ate anything at dinner. That can't possibly be healthy."

I don't move.

He drops the bread on the plate and drops the plate beside the water. Turns to me. Studies my eyes with such intensity I'm momentarily disarmed. There are so many things I want to say and scream but somehow I've forgotten all about the words waiting patiently in my mouth. I can't make myself look away.

"Eat something." His eyes abandon me. "Then go to sleep. I'll be back for you in the morning."

"Why can't I sleep in my own room?"

He gets to his feet. Dusts off his pants for no real reason. "Because I want you to stay here."

"But why?"

He barks out a laugh. "So many questions."

"Well if you'd give me a straight answer—"

"Good night, Juliette."

"Are you going to let me go?" I ask, this time quietly, this time timidly.

"No." He takes 6 steps into the corner with the candle. "And I won't promise to make things easier for you, either." There is no regret, no remorse, no sympathy in his voice. He could be talking about the weather.

"You could be lying."

"Yes, I could be." He nods, as if to himself. Blows out the candle.

And disappears.

I try to fight it
I try to stay awake
I try to find my head but I can't.

I collapse from sheer exhaustion.

# FIFTEEN

*Why don't you just kill yourself? someone at school asked me once.*

*I think it was the kind of question intended to be cruel, but it was the first time I'd ever contemplated the possibility. I didn't know what to say. Maybe I was crazy to consider it, but I'd always hoped that if I were a good enough girl, if I did everything right, if I said the right things or said nothing at all—I thought my parents would change their minds. I thought they would finally listen when I tried to talk. I thought they would give me a chance. I thought they might finally love me.*

*I always had that ~~stupid~~ hope.*

"Good morning."

My eyes snap open with a start. I've never been a heavy sleeper.

Warner is staring at me, sitting at the foot of his own bed in a fresh suit and perfectly polished boots. Everything about him is meticulous. Pristine. His breath is cool and fresh in the crisp morning air. I can feel it on my face.

It takes me a moment to realize I'm tangled in the same sheets Warner himself has slept in. My face is suddenly on fire and I'm fumbling to free myself. I nearly fall off the bed.

I don't acknowledge him.

"Did you sleep well?" he asks.

I look up. His eyes are such a strange shade of green: bright, crystal clear, piercing in the most alarming way. His hair is thick, the richest slice of gold; his frame is lean and unassuming, but his grip is effortlessly strong. I notice for the first time that he wears a jade ring on his left pinkie finger.

He catches me staring and stands up. Slips his gloves on and clasps his hands behind his back.

"It's time for you to go back to your room."

I blink. Nod. Stand up and nearly fall down. I catch myself on the side of the bed and try to steady my dizzying head. I hear Warner sigh.

"You didn't eat the food I left for you last night."

I grab the water with trembling hands and force myself to eat some of the bread. My body has gotten so used to hunger I don't know how to recognize it anymore.

Warner leads me out the door once I find my footing. I'm still clutching a piece of cheese in my hand.

I nearly drop it when I step outside.

There are even more soldiers here than there are on my floor. Each is equipped with at least 4 different kinds of guns, some slung around their necks, some strapped to their belts. All of them betray a look of terror when they see my face. It flashes in and out of their features so quickly I might've missed it, but it's obvious enough: everyone grips their weapons a little tighter as I walk by.

Warner seems pleased.

"Their fear will work in your favor," he whispers in my ear.

My humanity is lying in a million pieces on this carpeted floor. "I never wanted them to be afraid of me."

"You should." He stops. His eyes are calling me an idiot. "If they don't fear you, they will hunt you."

"People hunt things they fear all the time."

"At least now they know what they're up against." He resumes walking down the hall, but my feet are stitched into the ground. Realization is ice-cold water and it's dripping down my back.

"You made me do that—what I did—to Jenkins? On *purpose*?"

Warner is already 3 steps ahead but I can see the smile on his face. "Everything I do is done on purpose."

"You wanted to make a spectacle out of me." My heart is racing in my wrist, pulsing in my fingers.

"I was trying to protect you."

"From your own soldiers?" I'm running to catch up to him now, burning with indignation. "At the expense of a man's *life*—"

"Get inside." Warner has reached the elevator. He's holding the doors open for me.

I follow him in.

He presses the right buttons.

The doors close.

I turn to speak.

He corners me.

I'm backed into the far edge of this glass receptacle and I'm suddenly nervous. His hands are holding my arms and his lips are dangerously close to my face. His gaze is locked into mine, his eyes flashing; dangerous. He says one word: "Yes."

It takes me a moment to find my voice. "Yes, what?"

"Yes, from my own soldiers. Yes, at the expense of one man's life." He tenses his jaw. Speaks through his teeth. "There is very little you understand about my world, Juliette."

"I'm trying to understand—"

"No you're not," he snaps. His eyelashes are like individual threads of spun gold lit on fire. I almost want to touch them. "You don't understand that power and control can slip from your grasp at any moment and even when you think you're most prepared. These two things are not easy to earn. They are even harder to retain." I try to speak and he cuts me off. "You think I don't know how many of my own soldiers hate me? You think I don't know that they'd like to see me fall? You think there aren't others who would love to have the position I work so hard to have—"

"Don't *flatter* yourself—"

He closes the last few inches between us and my words fall to the floor. I can't breathe. The tension in his entire body is so intense it's nearly palpable and I think my muscles have begun to freeze. "You are naive," he says to me, his voice harsh, low, a grating whisper against my skin. "You don't realize that you're a threat to everyone in this building.

They have every reason to harm you. You don't see that I am trying to help you—"

"By hurting me!" I explode. "By hurting others!"

His laugh is cold, mirthless. He backs away from me, suddenly disgusted. The elevator slides open but he doesn't step outside. I can see my door from here. "Go back to your room. Wash up. Change. There are dresses in your armoire."

"I don't like dresses."

"I don't think you like seeing *that,* either," he says with a tilt of his head. I follow his gaze to see a hulking shadow across from my door. I turn to him for an explanation but he says nothing. He's suddenly composed, his features wiped clean of emotion. He takes my hand, squeezes my fingers, says, "I'll be back for you in exactly one hour," and closes the elevator doors before I have a chance to protest. I begin to wonder if it's coincidence that the one person most unafraid to touch me is a monster himself.

I step forward and dare to peer closer at the soldier standing in the dark.

*Adam.*

Oh Adam.

Adam who now knows exactly what I'm capable of.

My heart is a water balloon exploding in my chest. My lungs are swinging from my rib cage. I feel as though every fist in the world has decided to punch me in the stomach. I shouldn't care so much, but I do.

He'll hate me forever now. He won't even look at me.

I wait for him to open my door but he doesn't move.

"Adam?" I venture, tentative. "I need your key card."

I watch him swallow hard and take a tiny breath and immediately I sense something is wrong. I move closer and a quick, stiff shake of his head tells me not to. ~~I do not touch people I do not get close to people I am a monster.~~ He doesn't want me near him. Of course he doesn't. I should never forget my place.

He opens my door with immense difficulty and I realize someone's hurt him where I can't see it. Warner's words come back to me and I recognize his airy good-bye as a warning. A warning that severs every nerve ending in my body.

Adam will be punished for my mistakes. For my disobedience.

I want to bury my tears in a bucket of regret.

I step through the door and glance back at Adam one last time, unable to feel any kind of triumph in his pain. Despite everything he's done I don't know if I'm capable of hating him. Not Adam. Not the boy I used to know.

"The purple dress," he says, his voice broken and a little breathy like it hurts to inhale. I have to wring my hands to keep from running to him. "Wear the purple dress." He coughs. "Juliette."

I will be the perfect mannequin.

# SIXTEEN

As soon as I'm in the room I open the armoire and yank the purple dress off the hanger before I remember I'm being watched. *The cameras.* I wonder if Adam was punished for telling me about the cameras, too. I wonder if he's taken any other risks with me. I wonder why he would.

I touch the stiff, modern material of the plum dress and my fingers find their way to the hem, just as Adam's did yesterday. I can't help but wonder why he likes this dress so much. Why it has to be this one. Why I even have to wear a dress.

I am not a doll.

My hand comes to rest on the small wooden shelf beneath the hanging clothes and an unfamiliar texture brushes my skin. It's rough and foreign but familiar at the same time. I step closer to the armoire and hide between the doors. My fingers feel their way around the surface and a surge of sunshine rushes through my stomach until I'm certain I'm bursting with hope and feeling and a force of stupid happiness so strong I'm surprised there aren't tears streaming down my face.

My notebook.

He saved my notebook. ~~Adam saved the only thing I own.~~

I grab the purple dress and tuck the paper pad into its folds before stealing away to the bathroom.

~~The bathroom where there are no cameras.~~

~~The bathroom where there are no cameras.~~

~~The bathroom where there are no cameras.~~

He was trying to tell me, I realize. Before, in the bathroom. He was trying to tell me something and I was so scared I scared him away.

*I scared him away.*

I close the door behind me and my hands are shaking as I unfurl the familiar papers bound together by old glue. I flip through the pages to make sure they're all there and my eyes land on my most recent entry. At the very bottom there is a shift. A new sentence not written in my handwriting.

A new sentence that must've come from him.

*It's not what you think.*

I stand perfectly still.

Every inch of my skin is taut with tension, fraught with feeling and the pressure is building in my chest, pounding louder and faster and harder, overcompensating for my stillness. I do not tremble when I'm frozen in time. I train my breaths to come slower, I count things that do not exist, I make up numbers I do not have, I pretend time is a broken hourglass bleeding seconds through sand. I dare to believe.

I dare to hope Adam is trying to reach out to me. I'm crazy enough to consider the possibility.

I rip the page out of the small notebook and clutch it close, actively swallowing the hysteria tickling every broken moment in my mind.

I hide the notebook in a pocket of the purple dress. The pocket Adam must've slipped it into. The pocket it must've fallen out of. ~~The pocket of the purple dress. The pocket of the purple dress.~~

Hope is a pocket of possibility.

I'm holding it in my hand.

Warner is not late.

He doesn't knock, either.

I'm slipping on my shoes when he walks in without a single word, without even an effort to make his presence known. His eyes are falling all over my frame. My jaw tightens on its own.

"You hurt him," I find myself saying.

"You shouldn't care," he says with a tilt of his head, gesturing to my dress. "But it's obvious you do."

I zip my lips and pray my hands aren't shaking too much. I don't know where Adam is. I don't know how badly he's hurt. I don't know what Warner will do, how far he'll go in the pursuit of what he wants but the prospect of Adam in pain is like a cold hand clutching my esophagus. I can't catch my breath. I feel like I'm struggling to swallow a toothpick. If Adam is trying to help me it could cost him his life.

I touch the piece of paper tucked into my pocket.

Breathe.

Warner's eyes are on my window.

Breathe.

"It's time to go," he says.

Breathe.

"Where are we going?"

He doesn't answer.

We step out the door. I look around. The hallway is abandoned; empty. "Where is ~~Adam~~ everyone . . . ?"

"I really like that dress," Warner says as he slips an arm around my waist. I jerk away but he pulls me along, guiding me toward the elevator. "The fit is spectacular. It helps distract me from all your questions."

"Your poor mother."

Warner almost trips over his own feet. His eyes are wide; alarmed. He stops a few feet short of our goal. Spins around. "What do you mean?"

My stomach falls over.

The look on his face: the unguarded strain, the flinching terror, the sudden apprehension in his features.

I was trying to make a joke, is what I don't say to him. I feel sorry for your poor mother, is what I was going to say to him, that she has to deal with such a miserable, pathetic son. But I don't say any of it.

He grabs my hands, focuses my eyes. Urgency is pulsing at his temples. "What do you mean?" he insists.

"N-nothing," I stammer. My voice breaks in half. "I didn't—it was just a joke—"

Warner drops my hands like they've burned him. He looks away. Charges toward the elevator and doesn't wait for me to catch up.

I wonder what he's not telling me.

Only once we've gone down several floors and are making our way down an unfamiliar hall toward an unfamiliar exit does he finally look at me. He offers me 4 words.

"Welcome to your future."

# SEVENTEEN

I'm swimming in sunlight.

Warner is holding open a door that leads directly outside and I'm so unprepared for the experience I can hardly see straight. He grips my elbow to steady my path and I glance back at him.

"We're going outside." I say it because I have to say it out loud. Because the outside world is a treat I'm so seldom offered. Because I don't know if Warner is trying to be nice again. I look from him to what looks like a concrete courtyard and back to him again. "What are we doing outside?"

"We have some business to take care of." He tugs me toward the center of this new universe and I'm breaking away from him, reaching out to touch the sky like I'm hoping it will remember me. The clouds are gray like they've always been, but they're sparse and unassuming. The sun is high high high, lounging against a backdrop propping up its rays and redirecting its warmth in our general direction. I stand on tiptoe and try to touch it. The wind folds itself into my arms and smiles against my skin. Cool, silky-smooth air braids a soft breeze through my hair. This square courtyard could be my ballroom.

I want to dance with the elements.

Warner grabs my hand. I turn around.

He's smiling.

"This," he says, gesturing to the cold gray world under our feet, "this makes you happy?"

I look around. I realize the courtyard is not quite a roof, but somewhere between two buildings. I edge toward the ledge and can see dead land and naked trees and scattered compounds stretching on for miles. "Cold air smells so clean," I tell him. "Fresh. Brand-new. It's the most wonderful smell in the world."

His eyes look amused, troubled, interested, and confused all at once. He shakes his head. Pats down his jacket and reaches for an inside pocket. He pulls out a gun with a gold hilt that glints in the sunlight.

I pull in a sharp breath.

He inspects the gun in a way I wouldn't understand, presumably to check whether or not it's ready to fire. He slips it into his hand, his finger poised directly over the trigger. He turns and finally reads the expression on my face.

He almost laughs. "Don't worry. It's not for you."

"Why do you have a gun?" I swallow, hard, gripping my arms tight across my chest. "What are we doing up here?"

Warner slips the gun back into his pocket and walks to the opposite end of the ledge. He motions for me to follow him. I creep closer. Follow his eyes. Peer over the barrier.

Every soldier in the building is standing not 15 feet below.

I distinguish almost 50 lines, each perfectly straight,

perfectly spaced, so many soldiers standing single file I lose count. ~~I wonder if Adam is in the crowd. I wonder if he can see me.~~

~~I wonder what he thinks of me now.~~

The soldiers are standing in a square space almost identical to the one Warner and I occupy, but they're one organized mass of black: black pants, black shirts, shin-high black boots; not a single gun in sight. Each is standing with his left fist pressed to his heart. Frozen in place.

Black and gray

and

black and gray

and

black and gray

and

bleak.

Suddenly I'm acutely aware of my impractical outfit. Suddenly the wind is too callous, too cold, too painful as it slices its way through the crowd. I shiver and it has nothing to do with the temperature. I look for Warner but he has already taken his place at the edge of the courtyard; it's obvious he's done this many times before. He pulls a small square of perforated metal out of his pocket and presses it to his lips; when he speaks, his voice carries over the crowd like it's been amplified.

"Sector 45."

One word. One number.

The entire group shifts: left fists released, dropped to

103

their sides; right fists planted in place on their chests. They are an oiled machine, working in perfect collaboration with one another. If I weren't so apprehensive I think I'd be impressed.

"We have two matters to deal with this morning." Warner's voice penetrates the atmosphere: crisp, clear, unbearably confident. "The first is standing by my side."

Thousands of eyes snap up in my direction. I feel myself flinch.

"Juliette, come here, please." 2 fingers bend in 2 places to beckon me forward.

I inch into view.

Warner slips his arm around me. I cringe. The crowd starts. My heart careens out of control. I'm too scared to back away from him. His gun is too close to my body.

The soldiers seem stunned that Warner is willing to touch me.

"Jenkins, would you step forward, please?"

My fingers are running a marathon down my thigh. I can't stand still. I can't calm the palpitations crashing my nervous system. Jenkins steps out of line; I spot him immediately.

He's okay.

*Dear God.*

He's okay.

"Jenkins had the pleasure of meeting Juliette just last night," he continues. The tension among the men is very nearly tangible. No one, it seems, knows where this speech is headed. And no one, it seems, hasn't already heard Jenkins' story. My story. "I hope you'll all greet her with the same sort of kindness," Warner adds, his lips laughing without a sound. "She will be with us for some time, and will be a very valuable asset to our efforts. The Reestablishment welcomes her. I welcome her. You should welcome her."

The soldiers drop their fists all at once, all at exactly the same time.

They shift as one, 5 steps backward, 5 steps forward, 5 steps standing in place. They raise their left arms high and curl their fingers into a fist.

And fall on one knee.

I run to the edge, desperate to get a closer look at such a strangely choreographed routine. I've never seen anything like it.

Warner makes them stay like that, bent like that, fists raised in the air like that. He doesn't speak for at least 30 seconds. And then he does.

"Good."

The soldiers rise and rest their right fists on their chests again.

"The second matter at hand is even more pleasant than the first," Warner continues, though he seems to take no pleasure in saying it. His eyes are sharpening over the soldiers below, shards of emerald flickering like green flames over their bodies. "Delalieu has a report for us."

He spends an eternity simply staring at the soldiers,

letting his few words marinate in their minds. Letting their own imaginations drive them insane. Letting the guilty among them tremble in anguish.

Warner says nothing for so long.

No one moves for so long.

I begin to fear for my life despite his earlier reassurances. I begin to wonder if perhaps I am the guilty one. If perhaps the gun in his pocket is destined for me. I finally dare to turn in his direction. He glances at me for the first time and I have no idea how to read him.

His face is 10,000 possibilities staring straight through me.

"Delalieu," he says, still looking at me. "You may step forward."

A thin, balding sort of man in a slightly more decorated outfit steps out from the very front of the fifth line. He doesn't look entirely stable. He ducks his head an inch. His voice warbles when he speaks. "Sir."

Warner finally unshackles my eyes and nods, almost imperceptibly, in the balding man's direction.

Delalieu recites: "We have a charge against Private 45B-76423. Fletcher, Seamus."

The soldiers are all frozen in line, frozen in relief, frozen in fear, frozen in anxiety. Nothing moves. Nothing breathes. Even the wind is afraid to make a sound.

"Fletcher." One word from Warner and several hundred necks snap in the same direction.

Fletcher steps out of line.

He looks like a gingerbread man. Ginger hair. Ginger

freckles. Lips almost artificially red. His face is blank of every possible emotion.

I've never been more afraid for a stranger in my life.

Delalieu speaks again. "Private Fletcher was found on unregulated grounds, fraternizing with civilians believed to be rebel party members. He had stolen food and supplies from storage units dedicated to Sector 45 citizens. It is not known whether he betrayed sensitive information."

Warner levels his gaze at the gingerbread man. "Do you deny these accusations, soldier?"

Fletcher's nostrils flare. His jaw tenses. His voice cracks when he speaks. "No, sir."

Warner nods. Takes a short breath. Licks his lips.

And shoots him in the forehead.

# EIGHTEEN

No one moves.

Fletcher's face is etched in permanent horror as he crumbles to the ground. I'm so struck by the impossibility of it all that I can't decide whether or not I'm dreaming, I can't determine whether or not I'm dying, I can't figure out whether or not fainting is a good idea.

Fletcher's limbs are bent at odd angles on the cold, concrete floor. Blood is pooling around him and still no one moves. No one says a single word. No one betrays a single look of fear.

I keep touching my lips to see if my screams have escaped.

Warner tucks his gun back into his jacket pocket. "Sector 45, you are dismissed."

Every soldier falls on one knee.

Warner slips the metal amplification device back into his suit and has to yank me free from the spot where I'm glued to the ground. I'm tripping over myself, my limbs weak and aching through the bone. I feel nauseous, delirious, incapable of holding myself upright. I keep trying to speak but the words are sticking to my tongue. I'm suddenly sweating and suddenly freezing and suddenly so sick

I see spots clouding my vision.

Warner is trying to get me through the door. "You really must eat more," he says to me.

I am gaping with my eyes, gaping with my mouth, gaping wide open because I feel holes everywhere, punched into the terrain of my body.

My heart must be bleeding out of my chest.

I look down and can't understand why there's no blood on my dress, why this pain in my heart feels so real.

"You killed him," I manage to whisper. "You just killed him—"

"You're very astute."

"Why did you *kill him* why would you *kill him* how could you *do* something like that—"

"Keep your eyes open, Juliette. Now's not the time to fall asleep."

I grab his shirt. I stop him before he gets inside. A gust of wind slaps me across the face and I'm suddenly in control of my senses. I push him hard, slamming his back up against the door. "You disgust me." I stare hard into his crystal-cold eyes. "You *disgust* me—"

He twists me around, pinning me against the door where I just held him. He cups my face in his gloved hands, holding my eyes in place. The same hands he just used to kill a man.

I'm trapped.

Transfixed.

Slightly terrified.

His thumb brushes my cheek.

"Life is a bleak place," he whispers. "Sometimes you have to learn how to shoot first."

Warner follows me into my room.

"You should probably sleep," he says to me. It's the first time he's spoken since we left the rooftop. "I'll have food sent up to your room, but other than that I'll make sure you're not disturbed."

"Where is Adam? ~~Is he safe? Is he healthy? Are you going to hurt him?~~"

Warner flinches before finding his composure. "Why do you care?"

~~I've cared about Adam Kent since I was in third grade.~~ "Isn't he supposed to be watching me? Because he's not here. Does that mean you're going to kill him, too?" I'm feeling stupid. I'm feeling brave because I'm feeling stupid. My words wear no parachutes as they fall out of my mouth.

"I only kill people if I need to."

"Generous."

"More than most."

I laugh a sad laugh, sharing it with only myself.

"You can have the rest of the day to yourself. Our real work will begin tomorrow. Adam will bring you to me." He holds my eyes. Suppresses a smile. "In the meantime, try not to kill anyone."

"You and I," I tell him, anger coursing through my veins, "you and I are not the same—"

110

"You don't really believe that."

"You think you can compare my—my *disease*—with your insanity—"

"*Disease?*" He rushes forward, abruptly impassioned, and I struggle to hold my ground. "You think you have a *disease?*" he shouts. "You have a gift! You have an extraordinary ability that you don't care to understand! Your *potential*—"

"I have no potential!"

"You're wrong." He's glaring at me. There's no other way to describe it. I could almost say he hates me in this moment. Hates me for hating myself.

"Well you're the murderer," I tell him. "So you must be right."

His smile is laced with dynamite. "Go to sleep."

"Go to hell."

He works his jaw. Walks to the door. "I'm working on it."

# NINETEEN

The darkness is choking me.

My dreams are bloody and bleeding and blood is bleeding all over my mind and I can't sleep anymore. The only dreams that ever used to give me peace are gone and I don't know how to get them back. I don't know how to find the white bird. I don't know if it will ever fly by. All I know is that now when I close my eyes I see nothing but devastation. Fletcher is being shot over and over and over again and Jenkins is dying in my arms and Warner is shooting Adam in the head and the wind is singing outside my window but it's high-pitched and off-key and I don't have the heart to tell it to stop.

I'm freezing through my clothes.

The bed under my back is filled with broken clouds and freshly fallen snow; it's too soft, too comfortable. It reminds me too much of sleeping in Warner's room and I can't stand it. I'm afraid to slip under these covers.

I can't help but wonder if Adam is okay, if he'll ever come back, if Warner is going to keep hurting him whenever I disobey. I really shouldn't care so much.

Adam's message in my notebook might just be a part of Warner's plan to drive me insane.

I crawl onto the hard floor and check my fist for the crumpled piece of paper I've been clutching for 2 days. It's the only hope I have left and I don't even know if it's real.

I'm running out of options.

"What are you doing here?"

I bite down on a scream and stumble up, over, and sideways, nearly slamming into Adam where he's lying on the floor next to me. I didn't even see him.

"Juliette?" He doesn't move an inch. His gaze is fixed on me: calm, unflappable; 2 buckets of river water at midnight. I'd like to cry into his eyes.

I don't know why I tell him the truth. "I couldn't sleep up there."

He doesn't ask me why. He pulls himself up and coughs back a grunt and I remember how he's been hurt. I wonder what kind of pain he's in. I don't ask questions as he grabs a pillow and the blanket off my bed. He puts the pillow on the floor. "Lie down," is all he says to me. Quietly, is how he says it to me.

~~All day every day forever is when I want him to say it to me.~~

They're just 2 words and I don't know why I'm blushing. I lie down despite the sirens spinning in my blood and rest my head on the pillow. He drapes the blanket over my body. I let him do it. I watch as his arms curve and flex in the shadow of night, the glint of the moon peeking in through the window, illuminating his figure in its glow. He lies down on the floor leaving only a few feet of space between us. He requires no blanket. He uses no pillow. He still sleeps without a shirt on and I've discovered I don't know how to breathe. I've realized I'll probably never exhale in his presence.

"You don't need to scream anymore," he whispers.

Every breath in my body escapes me.

I curl my fingers around the possibility of Adam in my hand and sleep more soundly than I have in my life.

My eyes are 2 windows cracked open by the chaos in this world.

A cool breeze startles my skin and I sit up, rub the sleep from my eyes, and realize Adam is no longer beside me. I blink and crawl back up to the bed, where I replace the pillow and the blanket.

I glance at the door and wonder what's waiting for me on the other side.

I glance at the window and wonder if I'll ever see a bird fly by.

I glance at the clock on the wall and wonder what it means to be living according to numbers again. I wonder what 6:30 in the morning means in this building.

I decide to wash my face. The idea exhilarates me and I'm a little ashamed.

I open the bathroom door and catch Adam's reflection in the mirror. His fast hands pull his shirt down before I have a chance to latch on to details but I saw enough to see what I couldn't see in the darkness.

He's covered in bruises.

My legs feel broken. I don't know how to help him. I wish I could help him.

"I'm sorry," he says quickly. "I didn't know you were awake." He tugs on the bottom of his shirt like it's not long enough to pretend I'm blind.

I nod at nothing at all. I look at the tile under my feet. I don't know what to say.

"Juliette." His voice hugs the letters in my name so softly I die 5 times in that second. His face is a forest of emotion. He shakes his head. "I'm sorry," he says, so quietly I'm certain I imagined it. "It's not . . ." He clenches his jaw and runs a nervous hand through his hair. "All of this—it's not—"

I open my palm to him. The paper is a crumpled wad of possibility. "I know."

Relief washes over every feature on his face and suddenly his eyes are the only reassurance I'll ever need. Adam did not betray me. I don't know why or how or what or anything at all except that he is still my friend.

He is still standing right in front of me and he doesn't want me to die.

I step forward and close the door.

I open my mouth to speak.

"No!"

My jaw falls off.

"Wait," he says with one hand. His lips move but make no sound. I realize in the absence of cameras there might still be microphones in the bathroom. Adam looks around and back and forth and everywhere.

He stops looking.

The shower is 4 walls of marbled glass and he's sliding the glass open before I have any idea what's happening. He flips the spray on at full power and the sound of water is rushing through, rumbling through the room, muffling everything as it thunders into the emptiness around us. The mirror is already fogging up on account of the steam and just as I think I'm beginning to understand his plan he pulls me into his arms and lifts me into the shower.

My screams are vapor, wisps of gasps I can't grasp.

Hot water is puddling in my clothes. It's pelting my hair and pouring down my neck but all I feel are his hands around my waist. I want to cry out for all the wrong reasons.

His eyes pin me in place. His urgency ignites my bones. Rivulets of water snake their way down the polished planes of his face and his fingers press me up against the wall.

His lips his lips his lips his lips his lips

My eyes are fighting not to flutter

My legs have won the right to tremble

My skin is scorched everywhere he's not touching me.

His lips are so close to my ear I'm water and nothing and everything and melting into a wanting so desperate it burns as I swallow it down.

"I can touch you," he says, and I wonder why there are hummingbirds in my heart. "I didn't understand until the other night," he murmurs, and I'm too drunk to digest the weight of anything but his body hovering so close to mine.

"Juliette—" His body presses closer and I realize I'm paying attention to nothing but the dandelions blowing wishes in my lungs. My eyes snap open and he licks his bottom lip for the smallest second and something in my brain bursts to life.

I gasp. I gasp. I gasp. "What are you *doing*—"

"Juliette, *please*—" His voice is anxious and he glances behind him like he's not sure we're alone. "The other night—" He presses his lips together. He closes his eyes for half of a second and I marvel at the drop drop drops of hot water caught in his eyelashes like pearls forged from pain. His fingers inch up the sides of my body like he's struggling to keep them in one place, like he's struggling not to touch me everywhere everywhere everywhere and his eyes are drinking in the 63 inches of my frame and I'm so I'm so I'm so

caught.

"I finally get it now," he says into my ear. "I know— I know why Warner wants you." His fingertips are 10 points of electricity killing me with something I've never known before. ~~Something I've always wanted to feel.~~

"Then why are you here?" I whisper, broken, dying in his arms. "Why . . ." 1, 2 attempts at inhalation. "Why are you touching me?"

"Because I *can*." He almost cracks a smile and I almost sprout a pair of wings. "I already have."

"What?" I blink, suddenly sobered. "What do you mean?"

"That first night in the cell," he sighs. He looks down. "You were screaming in your sleep."

I wait.

I wait.

I wait forever.

"I touched your face." He speaks into the shape of my ear. "Your hand. I brushed the length of your arm. . . ." He pulls back and his eyes rest at my shoulder, trail down to my elbow, land on my wrist. I'm suspended in disbelief. "I didn't know how to wake you up. You wouldn't wake up. So I sat back and watched you. I waited for you to stop screaming."

"That's. Not. Possible." 3 words are all I manage.

But his hands become arms around my waist his lips become a cheek pressed against my cheek and his body is flush against mine, his skin touching me touching me touching me and he's not screaming he's not dying he's not running away from me and I'm crying

I'm choking

I'm shaking shuddering splintering into teardrops

and he's holding me the way no one has ever held me before.

Like he wants me.

"I'm going to get you out of here," he says, and his mouth is moving against my hair and his hands are traveling to my

118

arms and I'm leaning back and he's looking into my eyes and I must be dreaming.

"Why—why do you—I don't—" I'm shaking my head and shaking because this can't be happening and shaking off the tears glued to my face. This can't be real.

His eyes gentle, his smile unhinges my joints and I wish I knew the taste of his lips. I wish I had the courage to touch him. "I have to go," he says. "You have to be dressed and downstairs by eight o'clock."

I'm drowning in his eyes and I don't know what to say.

He peels off his shirt and I don't know where to look.

I catch myself on the glass panel and press my eyes shut and blink when something flutters too close. His fingers are a moment from my face and I'm dripping burning melting in anticipation.

"You don't have to look away," he says. He says it with a small smile the size of Jupiter.

I peek up at his features, at the crooked grin I want to savor, at the color in his eyes I'd use to paint a million pictures. I follow the line of his jaw down his neck to the peak of his collarbone; I memorize the sculpted hills and valleys of his arms, the perfection of his torso. The bird on his chest.

The bird on his chest.

*A tattoo.*

A white bird with streaks of gold like a crown atop its head. It's flying.

"Adam," I try to tell him. "Adam," I try to choke out. "Adam," I try to say so many times and fail.

I try to find his eyes only to realize he's been watching me study him. The pieces of his face are pressed into lines of emotion so deep I wonder what I must look like to him. He touches 2 fingers to my chin, tilts my face up just enough and I'm a live wire in water. "I'll find a way to talk to you," he says, and his hands are reeling me in and my face is pressed against his chest and the world is suddenly brighter, bigger, beautiful. The world suddenly means something to me, the possibility of humanity means something to me, the entire universe stops in place and spins in the other direction and I'm the bird.

I'm the bird and I'm flying away.

# TWENTY

It's 8:00 in the morning and I'm wearing a dress the color of dead forests and old tin cans.

The fit is tighter than anything I've worn in my life, the cut modern and angular, almost haphazard; the material is stiff and thick but somehow breathable. I stare at my legs and wonder that I own a pair.

I feel more exposed than I ever have in my life.

For 17 years I've trained myself to cover every inch of exposed skin and Warner is forcing me to peel the layers away. I can only assume he's doing it on purpose. My body is a carnivorous flower, a poisonous houseplant, a loaded gun with a million triggers and he's more than ready to fire.

Touch me and suffer the consequences. There have never been exceptions to this rule.

Never but Adam.

He left me standing sopping wet in the shower, soaking up a torrential downpour of hot tears. I watched through the blurred glass as he dried himself off and slipped into his standard uniform.

I watched as he slipped away, wondering every moment why why why

Why can he touch me?

Why would he help me?

~~Does he remember me?~~

My skin is still steaming.

My bones are bandaged in the tight folds of this strange dress, the zipper the only thing holding me together. That, and the prospect of something I've ~~always~~ never dared to dream of.

My lips will stay stitched shut with the secrets of this morning forever but my heart is so full of confidence and wonder and peace and possibility that it's about to burst and I wonder if it will rip the dress.

Hope is hugging me, holding me in its arms, wiping away my tears and telling me that today and tomorrow and two days from now I will be just fine and I'm so delirious I actually dare to believe it.

I am sitting in a blue room.

The walls are wallpapered in cloth the color of a perfect summer sky, the floor tucked into a carpet 2 inches thick, the entire room empty but for 2 velvet chairs punched out of a constellation. Every varying hue is like a bruise, like a beautiful mistake, like a reminder of what they did to Adam ~~because of me.~~

I am sitting all alone in a velvet chair in a blue room wearing a dress made of olives. The weight of the notebook in my pocket feels like I'm balancing a bowling ball on my knee.

"You look lovely."

Warner whisks into the room like he treads air for a living. He's accompanied by no one.

My eyes involuntarily peek down at my tennis shoes and I wonder if I've broken any rules by avoiding the stilts in my closet I'm sure are not for feet. I look up and he's standing right in front of me.

"Green is a great color on you," he says with a stupid smile. "It really brings out the color of your eyes."

"What color are my eyes?" I ask the wall.

He laughs. "You're not serious."

"How old are you?"

He stops laughing. "You care to know?"

"I'm curious."

He takes the seat beside me. "I won't answer your questions if you won't look at me when I speak to you."

"You want me to torture people against my will. You want me to be a weapon in your war. You want me to become a monster for you." I pause. "Looking at you makes me sick."

"You're far more stubborn than I thought you'd be."

"I'm wearing your dress. I ate your food. I'm here." I lift my eyes to look at him and he's already staring straight at me. I'm momentarily caught off guard by the power in his gaze.

"You did none of that for me," he says quietly.

I nearly laugh out loud. "Why would I?"

His eyes are fighting his lips for the right to speak. I look away.

"What are we doing in this room?"

"Ah." He takes a deep breath. "Breakfast. Then I give you your schedule."

He presses a button on the arm of his chair and almost instantly, carts and trays are wheeled into the room by men and women who are clearly not soldiers. Their faces are hard and cracked and too thin to be healthy.

It breaks my heart right in half.

"I usually eat alone," Warner continues, his voice like an icicle piercing the flesh of my memories. "But I figured you and I should be more thoroughly acquainted. Especially since we'll be spending so much time together."

The ~~servants~~ ~~maids~~ people-who-are-not-soldiers leave and Warner offers me something on a dish.

"I'm not hungry."

"This is not an option."

I look up and realize he's very, very serious.

"You are not allowed to starve yourself to death. You don't eat enough and I need you to be healthy. You are not allowed to commit suicide. You are not allowed to harm yourself. You are too valuable to me."

"I am not your *toy*," I nearly spit.

He drops his plate onto the rolling cart and I'm surprised it doesn't shatter into pieces. He clears his throat and I might actually be scared. "This process would be so much easier if you would just cooperate," he says, enunciating every word.

Five Five Five Five Five heartbeats.

"The world is disgusted by you," he says, his lips twitching with humor. "Everyone you've ever known has hated you. Run from you. Abandoned you. Your own parents gave

124

up on you and *volunteered* your existence to be given up to the authorities. They were so desperate to get rid of you, to make you someone else's problem, to convince themselves the abomination they raised was not, in fact, their child."

My face has been slapped by a hundred hands.

"And yet—" He laughs openly now. "You insist on making *me* the bad guy." He meets my eyes. "I am trying to *help* you. I'm giving you an opportunity no one would ever offer you. I'm willing to treat you as an equal. I'm willing to give you everything you could ever want, and above all else, I can put power in your hands. I can make them suffer for what they did to you." He leans in just enough. "I can change your world."

He's wrong he's so wrong he's more wrong than an upside-down rainbow.

But everything he said is right.

"Don't dare to hate me so quickly," he continues. "You might find yourself enjoying this situation a lot more than you anticipated. Lucky for you, I'm willing to be patient." He grins. Leans back. "Though it certainly doesn't hurt that you're so alarmingly beautiful."

I'm dripping red paint on the carpet.

He's a liar and a horrible, horrible, horrible human being and I don't know if I care because he's right, or because it's so wrong, or because I'm so desperate for some semblance of recognition in this world. No one has ever said anything like that to me before.

It makes me want to look in the mirror.

"You and I are not as different as you might hope." His grin is so cocky I want to twist it with my fist.

"You and I are not as similar as you might hope."

He smiles so wide I'm not sure how to react. "I'm nineteen, by the way."

"Excuse me?"

"I'm nineteen years old," he clarifies. "I'm a fairly impressive specimen for my age, I know."

I pick up my spoon and poke at the edible matter on my plate. I don't know what food really is anymore. "I have no respect for you."

"You will change your mind," he says easily. "Now hurry up and eat. We have a lot of work to do."

# TWENTY-ONE

Killing time isn't as difficult as it sounds.

I can shoot a hundred numbers through the chest and watch them bleed decimal points in the palm of my hand. I can rip the numbers off a clock and watch the hour hand tick tick tick its final tock just before I fall asleep. I can suffocate seconds just by holding my breath. I've been murdering minutes for hours and no one seems to mind.

It's been one week since I've spoken a word to Adam.

I turned to him once. Opened my mouth just once but never had a chance to say anything before Warner intercepted me. "You are not allowed to speak to the soldiers," he said. "If you have questions, you can find *me*. I am the only person you need to concern yourself with while you're here."

*Possessive* is not a strong enough word for Warner.

He escorts me everywhere. Talks to me too much. My schedule consists of meetings with Warner and eating with Warner and listening to Warner. If he is busy, I am sent to my room. If he is free, he finds me. He tells me about the books they've destroyed. The artifacts they're preparing to burn. The ideas he has for a new world and how I'll be a great help to him just as soon as I'm ready. Just as soon as I realize how much I want *this*, how much I want *him*, how much I want this new, glorious, powerful life. He is waiting for me to harness my *potential*. He tells me how grateful I should be for his patience. His kindness. His willingness to understand that this transition must be difficult.

I cannot look at Adam. I cannot speak to him. He sleeps in my room but I never see him. He breathes so close to my body but does not part his lips in my direction. He does not follow me into the bathroom. He does not leave secret messages in my notebook.

I'm beginning to wonder if I imagined everything he said to me.

I need to know if something has changed. I need to know if I'm crazy for holding on to this hope blossoming in my heart and I need to know what Adam's message meant but every day that he treats me like a stranger is another day I begin to doubt myself.

I need to talk to him but I can't.

Because now Warner is watching me.

The cameras are watching everything.

"I want you to take the cameras out of my room."

Warner stops chewing the food/garbage/breakfast/nonsense in his mouth. He swallows carefully before leaning back and looking me in the eye. "Absolutely not."

"If you treat me like a prisoner," I tell him, "I'm going to act like one. I don't like to be watched."

"You can't be trusted on your own." He picks up his spoon again.

"Every breath I take is monitored. There are guards stationed in five-foot intervals in all the hallways. I don't even have access to my own room," I protest. "Cameras aren't going to make a difference."

A strange kind of amusement dances on his lips. "You're not exactly stable, you know. You're liable to kill someone."

"No." I grip my fingers. "No—I wouldn't—I didn't kill Jenkins—"

"I'm not talking about Jenkins." His smile is a vat of acid seeping into my skin.

He won't stop looking at me. Smiling at me. Torturing me with his eyes.

This is me, screaming silently into my fist.

"That was an accident." The words tumble out of my mouth so quietly, so quickly I don't even know if I've actually spoken or if I'm actually still sitting here or if I'm actually 14 years old all over again all over again all over again and I'm screaming and dying and diving into a pool of memories I never ever ever ever ever

I can't seem to forget.

I saw her at the grocery store. Her legs were standing crossed at the ankles, her child was on a leash she thought he thought was a backpack. She thought he was too dumb/too young/too immature to understand that the rope tying him to her wrist was a device designed to trap him in her uninterested circle of self-sympathy. She's too young to have a kid, to have these responsibilities, to be buried by a child who has needs that don't accommodate her own. Her life is so incredibly unbearable so immensely multifaceted too glamorous for the leashed legacy of her loins to understand.

Children are not stupid, was what I wanted to tell her.

I wanted to tell her that his seventh scream didn't mean he was trying to be obnoxious, that her fourteenth admonishment in the form of brat/you're such a brat/you're embarrassing me you little brat/don't make me tell Daddy you were being a brat was uncalled for. I didn't mean to watch but I couldn't help myself. His 3-year-old face puckered in pain, his little hands tried to undo the chains she'd strapped across his chest and she tugged so hard he fell down and cried and she told him he deserved it.

I wanted to ask her why she would do that.

I wanted to ask her so many questions but I didn't because we don't talk to people anymore because saying something would be stranger than saying nothing to a stranger. He fell to the floor and writhed around until I'd dropped everything in my hands and every feature on my face.

I'm so sorry, is what I never said to her son.

I thought my hands were helping

I thought my heart was helping

I thought so many things

I never

never

never

never

never thought

"You killed a little boy."

I'm nailed into my velvet chair by a million memories and I'm haunted by a horror my bare hands created and I'm reminded in every moment that I am unwanted for good reason. My hands can kill people. My hands can destroy everything.

I should not be allowed to live.

"I want," I gasp, struggling to swallow the fist lodged in my throat, "I want you to get rid of the cameras. Get rid of them or I will die fighting you for the right."

"Finally!" Warner stands up and clasps his hands together as if to congratulate himself. "I was wondering when you'd wake up. I've been waiting for the fire I know must be eating away at you every single day. You're buried in hatred, aren't you? Anger? Frustration? Itching to do *something*? To be *someone*?"

"No."

"Of course you are. You're just like me."

"I hate you more than you will ever understand."

"We're going to make an excellent team."

"We are *nothing*. You are *nothing* to me—"

"I know what you want." He leans in, drops his voice. "I know what your little heart has always longed for. I can give you the acceptance you seek. I can be your *friend*."

I freeze. Falter. Fail to speak.

"I know *everything* about you, love." He grins. "I've wanted you for a very long time. I've waited forever for you to be ready. I'm not going to let you go so easily."

"I don't want to be a monster," I say, perhaps more for my sake than his.

"Don't fight what you're born to be." He grasps my shoulders. "Stop letting everyone else tell you what's wrong and right. Stake a claim! You cower when you could conquer. You have so much more power than you're aware of and quite frankly I'm"—he shakes his head—"fascinated."

"I am not your *freak*," I snap. "I will not *perform* for you."

He tightens his hold around my arms and I can't squirm away from him. He leans in dangerously close to my face and I don't know why but I can't breathe. "I'm not afraid of you, my dear," he says softly. "I'm absolutely enchanted."

"Either you get rid of the cameras or I will find and break every single one of them." I'm a liar. I'm lying through my teeth but I'm angry and desperate and horrified. Warner wants to morph me into an animal who preys on the weak. On the innocent.

If he wants me to fight for him, he's going to have to fight me first.

A slow smile spreads across his face. He touches gloved fingers to my cheek and tilts my head up, catching my chin in his grip when I flinch away. "You're absolutely delicious when you're angry."

"Too bad my taste is poisonous for your palate." I'm vibrating in disgust from head to toe.

"That detail makes this game so much more appealing."

"You're sick, you're so *sick*—"

He laughs and releases my chin only to take inventory of my body parts. His eyes draw a lazy trail down the length of my frame and I feel the sudden urge to rupture his spleen.

"If I get rid of your cameras, what will you do for me?" His eyes are wicked.

"Nothing."

He shakes his head. "That won't do. I might agree to your proposition if you agree to a condition."

I clench my jaw. "What do you want?"

The smile is bigger than before. "That is a dangerous question."

"What is your *condition?*" I clarify, impatient.

"Touch me."

"What?" My gasp is so loud it catches in my throat only to race around the room.

"I want to know exactly what you're capable of." His voice is steady, his eyebrows taut, tense.

"I won't do it again!" I explode. "You saw what you made me do to Jenkins—"

"Screw Jenkins," he spits. "I want you to touch *me*— I want to feel it *myself*—"

"No—" I'm shaking my head so hard it makes me dizzy. "No. Never. You're crazy—I won't—"

"You will, actually."

"I will NOT—"

"You will have to . . . *work* . . . at one point or another," he says, making an effort to moderate his voice. "Even if you were to forgo my condition, you are here for a reason, Juliette. I convinced my father that you would be an asset to The Reestablishment. That you'd be able to restrain any rebels we—"

"You mean *torture*—"

"Yes." He smiles. "Forgive me, I mean torture. You will be able to help us torture anyone we capture." A pause. "Inflicting pain, you see, is an incredibly efficient method of getting information out of anyone. And with you?" He glances at my hands. "Well, it's cheap. Fast. Effective." He smiles wider. "And as long as we keep you alive, you'll be good for at least a few decades. It's very fortunate that you're not battery-operated."

"You—*you*—" I sputter.

"You should be thanking me. I saved you from that sick hole of an asylum—I brought you into a position of power. I've given you everything you could possibly need to be comfortable." He levels his gaze at me. "Now I need you to focus. I need you to relinquish your hopes of living like everyone else. You are *not* normal. You never have been, and you never will be. Embrace who you *are*."

"I"—I swallow—"I am not—I'm not—I'm—"

"A murderer?"

"NO—"

"An instrument of torture?"

"STOP—"

"You're lying to yourself."

I'm ready to destroy him.

He cocks his head and presses back a smile. "You've been on the edge of insanity your entire life, haven't you? So many people called you crazy you actually started to believe it. You wondered if they were right. You wondered if you could fix it. You thought if you could just try a little harder, be a little better, smarter, nicer—you thought the world would change its mind about you. You blamed yourself for everything."

I gasp.

My bottom lip trembles without my permission. I can hardly control the tension in my jaw.

~~I don't want to tell him he's right.~~

"You've suppressed all your rage and resentment because you wanted to be loved," he says, no longer smiling. "Maybe I understand you, Juliette. Maybe you should trust me. Maybe you should accept the fact that you've tried to be someone you're not for so long and that no matter what you did, those bastards were never happy. They were never satisfied. They never gave a damn, did they?" He looks at me and for a moment he seems almost human. For a moment I want to believe him. For a moment I want to sit on the floor and cry out the ocean lodged in my throat.

"It's time you stopped pretending," he says, so softly. "Juliette—" He takes my face in his gloved hands, so unexpectedly gentle. "You don't have to be nice anymore. You can destroy all of them. You can take them down and own this whole world and—"

A steam engine hits me in the face.

"I don't want to destroy anyone," I tell him. "I don't want to *hurt* people—"

"But they *deserve* it!" He pushes away from me, frustrated. "How could you not want to retaliate? How could you not want to *fight back*—"

I stand up slowly, shaking with anger, hoping my legs

won't collapse beneath me. "You think that because I am unwanted, because I am neglected and—and *discarded*—" My voice inches higher with every word, the unrestrained emotions suddenly screaming through my lungs. "You think I don't have a heart? You think I don't *feel*? You think that because I *can* inflict pain, that I should? You're just like everyone else. You think I'm a monster just like everyone else. You don't understand me at all—"

"Juliette—"

"No."

I don't want this. I don't want his life.

I don't want to be anything for anyone but myself. I want to make my own choices and I've never wanted to be a monster. My words are slow and steady when I speak. "I value human life a lot more than you do, Warner."

He opens his mouth to speak before he stops. Laughs out loud and shakes his head.

Smiles at me.

"What?" I ask before I can stop myself.

"You just said my name." He grins even wider. "You've never addressed me directly before. That must mean I'm making progress with you."

"I just told you I don't—"

He cuts me off. "I'm not worried about your moral dilemmas. You're just stalling for time because you're in denial. Don't worry," he says. "You'll get over it. I can wait a little longer."

"I'm not in *denial*—"

"Of course you are. You don't know it yet, Juliette, but you are a very bad girl," he says, clutching his heart. "Just my type."

This conversation is impossible.

"There is a soldier *living* in my room." I'm breathing hard. "If you want me to be here, you need to get rid of the cameras."

Warner's eyes darken for just an instant. "Where *is* your soldier, anyway?"

"I wouldn't know." I hope to God I'm not blushing. "You assigned him to me."

"Yes." He looks thoughtful. "I like watching you squirm. He makes you uncomfortable, doesn't he?"

I think about Adam's hands on my body and his lips so close to mine and the scent of his skin drenched in a steaming downpour soaking the two of us together and suddenly my heart is two fists pounding on my ribs demanding escape. "Yes." *God.* "Yes. He makes me very . . . uncomfortable."

"Do you know why I chose him?" Warner asks, and I'm run over by a tractor trailer.

Adam was *chosen.*

Of course he was. He wasn't just any soldier sent to my cell. Warner does nothing without reason. He must know Adam and I have a history. He is more cruel and calculative than I gave him credit for.

"No." Inhale. "I don't know why." Exhale. I can't forget to breathe.

"He volunteered," Warner says simply, and I'm momentarily dumbstruck. "He said he'd gone to school with you so many years ago. He said you probably wouldn't remember him, that he looks a lot different now than he did back then. He put together a very convincing case." A beat of breath. "He said he was thrilled to hear you'd been locked up." Warner finally looks at me.

My bones are like cubes of ice clinking together, chilling me to my core.

"I'm curious," he continues, tilting his head as he speaks. "Do you remember him?"

"No," I lie, and I'm not sure I'm alive. I'm trying to untangle the truth from the false from assumptions from the postulations but run-on sentences are twisting around my throat.

Adam knew me when he walked into that cell.

He knew exactly who I was.

He already knew my name.

*Oh*

*Oh*

*Oh*

This was all a trap.

"Does this information make you . . . angry?" he asks, and I want to sew his smiling lips into a permanent scowl.

I say nothing and somehow it's worse.

Warner is beaming. "I never told him, of course, why it was that you'd been locked up—I thought the experiment in the asylum should remain untainted by extra information—but he said you were always a threat to the students. That everyone was always warned to stay away from you, though the authorities never explained why. He said he wanted to get a closer look at the freak you've become."

My heart cracks. My eyes flash. I'm so hurt so angry so horrified so humiliated and burning with indignation so raw that it's like a fire raging within me, a wildfire of decimated hopes. I want to crush Warner's spine in my hand. I want him to know what it's like to wound, to inflict such unbearable agony on others. I want him to know my pain and Jenkins' pain and Fletcher's pain and I want him to *hurt*. Because maybe Warner is right.

Maybe some people do deserve it.

"Take off your shirt."

For all his posturing, Warner looks genuinely surprised, but he wastes no time unbuttoning his jacket, slipping off his gloves, and peeling away the thin cotton shirt clinging closest to his skin.

His eyes are bright, sickeningly eager; he doesn't mask his curiosity.

Warner drops his clothes to the floor and looks at me almost intimately. I have to swallow back the revulsion bubbling in my mouth. His perfect face. His perfect body. His eyes as hard and beautiful as frozen gemstones. He repulses me. I want his exterior to match his broken black interior. I want to cripple his cockiness with the palm of my hand.

He walks up to me until there's less than a foot of space

139

between us. His height and build make me feel like a fallen twig. "Are you ready?" he asks, arrogant and foolish.

I contemplate breaking his neck.

"If I do this you'll get rid of all the cameras in my room. All the bugs. Everything."

He steps closer. Dips his head. He's staring at my lips, studying me in an entirely new way. "My promises aren't worth much, love," he whispers. "Or have you forgotten?" 3 inches forward. His hand on my waist. His breath sweet and warm on my neck. "I'm an exceptional liar."

Realization slams into me like 200 pounds of common sense. I shouldn't be doing this. I shouldn't be making deals with him. I shouldn't be contemplating torture dear God I have lost my mind. My fists are balled at my sides and I'm shaking everywhere. I can hardly find the strength to speak. "You can go to hell."

I'm limp.

I trip backward against the wall and slump into a heap of uselessness; desperation. I think of Adam and my heart deflates.

I can't be here anymore.

I fly to the double doors facing the room and yank them open before Warner can stop me. But Adam stops me instead. He's standing just outside. Waiting. Guarding me wherever I go.

I wonder if he heard everything and my eyes fall to the floor, the color flushed from my face, my heart in pieces in my hand. Of course he heard everything. Of course he now knows I'm a murderer. A monster. A worthless soul stuffed into a poisonous body.

Warner did this on purpose.

And I'm standing between them. Warner with no shirt on. Adam looking at his gun.

"Soldier." Warner speaks. "Take her back up to her room and disable all the cameras. She can have lunch alone if she wants, but I'll expect her for dinner."

Adam blinks for a moment too long. "Yes, sir."

"Juliette?"

I freeze. My back is to Warner and I don't turn around.

"I do expect you to hold up your end of the bargain."

# TWENTY-TWO

It takes 5 years to walk to the elevator. 15 more to ride it up. I'm a million years old by the time I walk into my room. Adam is still, silent, perfectly put together and mechanical in his movements. There's nothing in his eyes, in his limbs, in the motions of his body that indicate he even knows my name.

I watch him move quickly, swiftly, carefully around the room, finding the little devices meant to monitor my behavior and disabling them one by one. If anyone asks why my cameras aren't working, Adam won't get in trouble. This order came from Warner. This makes it official.

This makes it possible for me to have some privacy.

I thought I would need privacy.

I'm such a fool.

Adam is not the boy I remember.

I was in third grade.

I'd just moved into town after being ~~thrown out of~~ asked to leave my old school. My parents were always moving, always running away from the messes I made, from the playdates I'd ruined, from the friendships I never had. No one ever wanted to talk about my "problem," but the mystery surrounding my existence somehow made things worse. The human imagination is often disastrous when left to its own devices. I only heard bits and pieces of their whispers.

"Freak!"

"Did you hear what she *did*—?"

"What a loser."

"—got kicked out of her old school—"

"Psycho!"

"She's got some kind of disease—"

No one talked to me. Everyone stared. I was young enough that I still cried. I ate lunch alone by a chain-link fence and never looked in the mirror. I never wanted to see the face everyone hated so much. Girls used to kick me and run away. Boys used to throw rocks at me. I still have scars somewhere.

I watched the world pass by through those chain-link fences. I stared out at the cars and the parents dropping off their kids and the moments I'd never be a part of. This was before the diseases became so common that death was a natural part of conversation. This was before we realized the clouds were the wrong color, before we realized all the animals were dying or infected, before we realized everyone was going to starve to death, and fast. This was back when we still thought our problems had solutions. Back then, Adam was the boy who used to walk to school. Adam was the boy who sat 3 rows in front of me. His clothes were worse than mine, his lunch nonexistent. I never saw him eat.

One morning he came to school in a car.

I know because I saw him being pushed out of it. His father was drunk and driving, yelling and flailing his fists for some reason. Adam stood very still and stared at the ground like he was waiting for something, steeling himself for the inevitable. I watched a father slap his 8-year-old son in the face. I watched Adam fall to the floor and I stood there, motionless as he was kicked repeatedly in the ribs.

"It's all your fault! It's *your* fault, you worthless piece of shit," his father screamed over and over and over again until I threw up right there, all over a patch of dandelions.

Adam didn't cry. He stayed curled up on the ground until his father gave up, until he drove away. Only once he was sure everyone was gone did his body break into heaving sobs, his small face smeared into the dirt, his arms clutching at his bruised abdomen. I couldn't look away.

I could never get that sound out of my head, that scene out of my head.

That's when I started paying attention to Adam Kent.


"Juliette."

I suck in my breath and wish my hands weren't trembling. I wish I had no eyes.

"Juliette," he says again, this time even softer and my body is in a blender and I'm made of mush. My bones are aching aching aching for his warmth.

I won't turn around.

"You always knew who I was," I whisper.

144

He says nothing and I'm suddenly desperate to see his eyes. I suddenly need to see his eyes. I turn to face him despite everything only to see he's staring at his hands. "I'm sorry," is all he says.

I lean back against the wall and press my lids shut. Everything was a performance. Stealing my bed. Asking for my name. Asking me about my family. He was performing for Warner. For the guards. For whoever was watching. I don't even know what to believe anymore.

I need to say it. I need to get it out. I need to rip my wounds open and bleed fresh for him. "It's true," I tell him. "About the little boy." My voice is shaking so much more than I thought it would. "I did that."

He's quiet for so long. "I never understood before. When I first heard about it. I didn't realize until just now what must've happened."

"What?" I never knew I could blink so much.

"It never made sense to me," he says, and each word kicks me in the gut. He looks up and looks more agonized than I ever want him to be. "When I heard about it. We all heard about it. The whole school—"

"It was an accident," I choke out, failing not to fall apart. "He—h-he fell—and I was trying to help him—and I just— I didn't—I thought—"

"I know."

"What?" I gasp so loud I've swallowed the entire room in one breath.

"I believe you," he says to me.

"What . . . why?" My eyes are blinking back tears, my hands unsteady, my heart filled with nervous hope.

He bites his bottom lip. Looks away. Walks to the wall. Opens and closes his mouth several times before the words rush out. "Because I *knew* you, Juliette—I—God—I just—" He covers his mouth with his hand, drops his fingers to his neck. Rubs his forehead, closes his eyes, presses his lips together. Pries them open. "That was the day I was going to talk to you." A strange sort of smile. A strange sort of laugh. He runs a hand through his hair. Looks up at the ceiling. Turns his back to me. "I was finally going to talk to you. I was finally going to talk to you and I—" He shakes his head, hard, and attempts another painful laugh. "God, you don't remember me."

Hundreds of thousands of seconds pass and I can't stop dying.

I want to laugh and cry and scream and run and I can't choose which to do first.

I confess.

"Of course I remember you." My voice is a strangled whisper. I squeeze my eyes shut. ~~I remember you every day forever in every single broken moment of my life.~~ "You were the only one who ever looked at me like a human being."

He never talked to me. He never spoke a single word to me, but he was the only one who dared to sit close to my fence. He was the only one who stood up for me, the only person who fought for me, the only one who'd punch someone in the face for throwing a rock at my head. I didn't even know how to say thank you.

He was the closest thing to a friend I ever had.

I open my eyes and he's standing right in front of me. My heart is a field of lilies blooming under a pane of glass, pitter-pattering to life like a rush of raindrops. His jaw is as tight as his eyes as tight as his fists as tight as the strain in his arms.

"You've always known?" 3 whispered words and he's broken my dam, unlocked my lips and stolen my heart all over again. I can hardly feel the tears streaming down my face.

"Adam." I try to laugh and my lips trip on a stifled sob. "I'd recognize your eyes anywhere in the world."

And that's it.

This time there's no self-control.

This time I'm in his arms and against the wall and I'm trembling everywhere and he's so gentle, so careful, touching me like I'm made of porcelain and I want to shatter.

He's running his hands down my body running his eyes across my face running laps with his heart and I'm running marathons with my mind.

Everything is on fire. My cheeks my hands the pit of my stomach and I'm drowning in waves of emotion and a storm of fresh rain and all I feel is the strength of his silhouette against mine and I never ever ever ever want to forget this moment. I want to stamp him into my skin and save him forever.

He takes my hands and presses my palms to his face and I know I never knew the beauty of feeling human before this. I know I'm still crying when my eyes flutter closed.

I whisper his name.

And he's breathing harder than I am and suddenly his lips are on my neck and I'm gasping and dying and clutching at his arms and he's touching me touching me touching me and I'm thunder and lightning and wondering when the hell I'll be waking up.

Once, twice, a hundred times his lips taste the nape of my neck and I wonder if it's possible to die of euphoria. He meets my eyes only to cup my face in his hands and I'm blushing through these walls from pleasure and pain and impossibility.

"I've wanted to kiss you for so long." His voice is husky, uneven, deep in my ear.

I'm frozen in anticipation in expectation and I'm so worried he'll kiss me, so worried he won't. I'm staring at his lips and I don't realize how close we are until we're pulled apart.

3 distinct electronic screeches reverberate around the room and Adam looks past me like he can't understand where he is for a moment. He blinks. And runs toward an intercom to press the appropriate buttons. I notice he's still breathing hard.

I'm shaking in my skin.

"Name and number," the voice of the intercom demands.

"Kent, Adam. 45B-86659."

A pause.

"Soldier, are you aware the cameras in your room have been deactivated?"

"Yes, sir. I was given direct orders to dismantle the devices."

"Who cleared this order?"

"Warner, sir."

A longer pause.

"We'll verify and confirm. Unauthorized tampering with security devices may result in your immediate dishonorable discharge, soldier. I hope you're aware of that."

"Yes, sir."

The line goes quiet.

Adam slumps against the wall, his chest heaving. I'm not sure but I could've sworn his lips twitched into the tiniest smile. He closes his eyes and exhales.

I'm not sure what to do with the relief tumbling into my hands.

"Come here," he says, his eyes still shut.

I tiptoe forward and he pulls me into his arms. Breathes in the scent of my hair and kisses the side of my head and I've never felt anything so incredible in my life. I'm not even human anymore. I'm so much more. The sun and the moon have merged and the earth is upside down. I feel like I can be exactly who I want to be in his arms.

He makes me forget the terror I'm capable of.

"Juliette," he whispers in my ear. "We need to get the hell out of here."

# TWENTY-THREE

I'm 14 years old again and I'm staring at the back of his head in a small classroom. I'm 14 years old and I've been in love with Adam Kent for years. I made sure to be extra careful, to be extra quiet, to be extra cooperative because I didn't want to move away again. I didn't want to leave the school with the one friendly face I'd ever known. I watched him grow up a little more every day, grow a little taller every day, a little stronger, a little tougher, a little more quiet every day. He eventually got too big to get beat up by his dad, but no one really knows what happened to his mother. The students shunned him, harassed him until he started fighting back, until the pressure of the world finally cracked him.

But his eyes always stayed the same.

Always the same when he looked at me. Kind. Compassionate. Desperate to understand. But he never asked questions. He never pushed me to say a word. He just made sure he was close enough to scare away everyone else.

I thought maybe I wasn't so bad. Maybe.

I thought maybe he saw something in me. I thought maybe I wasn't as horrible as everyone said I was. I hadn't touched anyone in years. I didn't dare get close to people. I couldn't risk it.

Until one day I did, and I ruined everything.

I killed a little boy in a grocery store simply by helping him to his feet. By grabbing his little hands. I didn't understand why he was screaming. It was my first experience ever touching someone for such a long period of time and I didn't understand what was happening to me. The few times I'd ever accidentally put my hands on someone I'd always pulled away. I'd pull away as soon as I remembered I wasn't supposed to be touching anyone. As soon as I heard the first scream escape their lips.

The little boy was different.

I wanted to help him. I felt such a surge of sudden anger toward his mother for neglecting his cries. Her lack of compassion as a parent devastated me ~~and it reminded me too much of my own mother.~~ I just wanted to help him. I wanted him to know that someone else was listening— that someone else cared. I didn't understand why it felt so strange and exhilarating to touch him. I didn't know that I was draining his life and I couldn't comprehend why he'd grown limp and quiet in my arms. I thought maybe the rush of power and positive feeling meant that I'd been cured of my horrible disease. I thought so many stupid things and I ruined everything.

I thought I was helping.

I spent the next 3 years of my life in hospitals, law offices, juvenile detention centers, and suffered through pills and electroshock therapy. Nothing worked. Nothing helped. Outside of killing me, locking me up in an institution was the only solution. The only way to protect the public from the terror of Juliette.

Until he stepped into my cell, I hadn't seen Adam Kent in 3 years.

And he does look different. Tougher, taller, harder, sharper, tattooed. He's muscle, mature, quiet and quick. It's almost like he can't afford to be soft or slow or relaxed. He can't afford to be anything but muscle, anything but strength and efficiency. The lines of his face are smooth, precise, carved into shape by years of hard living and training and trying to survive.

He's not a little boy anymore. He's not afraid. He's in the army.

But he's not so different, either. He still has the most unusually blue eyes I've ever seen. Dark and deep and drenched in passion. I always wondered what it'd be like to see the world through such a beautiful lens. I wondered if your eye color meant you saw the world differently. If the world saw you differently as a result.

I should have known it was him when he showed up in my cell.

A part of me did. But I'd tried so hard to repress the memories of my past that I refused to believe it could be possible. Because a part of me didn't want to remember. A part of me was too scared to hope. A part of me didn't know if it would make any difference to know that it was him, after all.

I often wonder what I must look like.

I wonder if I'm just a punctured shadow of the person I was before. I haven't looked in the mirror in 3 years. I'm so scared of what I'll see.

Someone knocks on the door.

I'm catapulted across the room by my own fear. Adam locks eyes with me before opening the door and I decide to retreat into a far corner of the room.

I sharpen my ears only to hear muted voices, hushed tones, and someone clearing his throat. I'm not sure what to do.

"I'll be down in a minute," Adam says a little loudly. I realize he's trying to end the conversation.

"C'mon, man, I just wanna see her—"

"She's not a goddamn spectacle, Kenji. Get the hell out of here."

"Wait—just tell me: Does she light shit on fire with her eyes?" Kenji laughs and I cringe, slumping to the floor behind the bed. I curl into myself and try not to hear the rest of the conversation.

I fail.

Adam sighs. I can picture him rubbing his forehead. "Just get out."

Kenji struggles to muffle his laughter. "Damn you're sensitive all of a sudden, huh? Hangin' out with a girl is changin' you, man—"

Adam says something I can't hear.

The door slams shut.

I peek up from my hiding place. Adam looks embarrassed.

My cheeks go pink. I study the intricate threads of the finely woven carpet under my feet. I touch the cloth wallpaper and wait for him to speak. I stand up to stare out the small square of a window only to be met by the bleak backdrop of a broken city. I lean my forehead against the glass.

Metal cubes are clustered together off in the distance: compounds housing civilians wrapped in multiple layers, trying to find refuge from the cold. A mother holding the hand of a small child. Soldiers standing over them, still like statues, rifles poised and ready to fire. Heaps and heaps and heaps of trash, dangerous scraps of iron and steel glinting on the ground. Lonely trees waving at the wind.

Adam's hands slip around my waist.

His lips are at my ear and he says nothing at all, but I melt until I'm a handful of hot butter dripping down his body. I want to eat every minute of this moment.

I allow my eyes to shut against the truth outside my window. Just for a little while.

Adam takes a deep breath and pulls me even closer. I'm molded to the shape of his silhouette; his hands are circling my waist and his cheek is pressed against my head. "You feel incredible."

I try to laugh but seem to have forgotten how. "Those are words I never thought I'd hear."

Adam spins me around so I'm facing him and suddenly I'm looking and not looking at his face, I'm licked by a million flames and swallowing a million more. He's staring at me like he's never seen me before. I want to wash my soul in the bottomless blue of his eyes.

He leans in until his forehead rests against mine and our lips still aren't close enough. He whispers, "How are you?" and I want to kiss every beautiful beat of his heart.

*How are you?* 3 words no one ever asks me.

"I want to get out of here," is all I can think of.

He squeezes me against his chest and I marvel at the power, the glory, the wonder in such a simple movement. He feels like 1 block of strength, 6 feet tall.

Every butterfly in the world has migrated to my stomach.

"Juliette."

I lean back to see his face.

"Are you serious about leaving?" he asks me. His fingers brush the side of my cheek. He tucks a stray strand of hair behind my ear. "Do you understand the risks?"

I take a deep breath. I know that the only real risk is death. "Yes."

He nods. Drops his eyes, his voice. "The troops are mobilizing for some kind of attack. There have been a lot of protests from groups who were silent before, and our job is to obliterate the resistance. I think they want this attack to be their last one," he adds quietly. "There's something huge going on, and I'm not sure what, not yet. But whatever it is, we have to be ready to go when they are."

I freeze. "What do you mean?"

"When the troops are ready to deploy, you and I should

be ready to run. It's the only way out that will give us time to disappear. Everyone will be too focused on the attack—it'll buy us some time before they notice we're missing or can get enough people together to search for us."

"But—you mean—you'll come with me . . . ? You'd be willing to do that for me?"

He smiles a small smile. His lips twitch like he's trying not to laugh. His eyes soften as they study my own. "There's very little I wouldn't do for you."

I take a deep breath and close my eyes, touching my fingers to his chest, imagining the bird soaring across his skin, and I ask him the one question that scares me the most. "Why?"

"What do you mean?" He steps back.

"Why, Adam? Why do you care? Why do you want to help me? I don't understand—I don't know why you'd be willing to risk your life—"

But then his arms are around my waist and he's pulling me so close and his lips are at my ear and he says my name, once, twice and I had no idea I could catch on fire so quickly. His mouth is smiling against my skin. "You don't?"

I don't know anything, is what I would tell him if I had any idea how to speak.

He laughs a little and pulls back. Takes my hand and studies it. "Do you remember in fourth grade," he says, "when Molly Carter signed up for the school field trip too late? All the spots were filled, and she stood outside the bus, crying because she wanted to go?"

He doesn't wait for me to answer.

"I remember you got off the bus. You offered her your seat and she didn't even say thank you. I watched you standing on the sidewalk as we pulled away."

I'm no longer breathing.

"Do you remember in fifth grade? That week Dana's parents nearly got divorced? She came to school every day without her lunch. And you offered to give her yours." He pauses. "As soon as that week was over she went back to pretending you didn't exist."

I'm still not breathing.

"In seventh grade Shelly Morrison got caught cheating off your math test. She kept screaming that if she failed, her father would kill her. You told the teacher that you were the one cheating off of *her* test. You got a zero on the exam, and detention for a week." He lifts his head but doesn't look at me. "You had bruises on your arms for at least a month after that. I always wondered where they came from."

My heart is beating too fast. Dangerously fast. I clench my fingers to keep them from shaking. I lock my jaw in place and wipe my face clean of emotion but I can't slow the thrumming in my chest no matter how hard I try.

"A million times," he says, his voice so quiet now. "I saw you do things like that a million times. But you never said a word unless it was forced out of you." He laughs again, this time a hard, heavy sort of laugh. He's staring at a point directly past my shoulder. "You never asked for anything

157

from anyone." He finally meets my eyes. "But no one ever gave you a chance."

I swallow hard, try to look away but he catches my face.

He whispers, "You have no idea how much I've thought about you. How many times I've dreamt"—he takes a tight breath—"how many times I've dreamt about being this close to you." He moves to run a hand through his hair before he changes his mind. Looks down. Looks up. "God, Juliette, I'd follow you anywhere. You're the only good thing left in this world."

I'm begging myself not to burst into tears and I don't know if it's working. I'm everything broken and glued back together and blushing everywhere and I can hardly find the strength to meet his gaze.

His fingers find my chin. Tip me up.

"We have three weeks at the most," he says. "I don't think they can control the mobs for much longer."

I nod. I blink. I rest my face against his chest and pretend I'm not crying.

3 weeks.

# TWENTY-FOUR

2 weeks pass.

2 weeks of dresses and showers and food I want to throw across the room. 2 weeks of Warner smiling and touching my waist, laughing and guiding the small of my back, making sure I look my best as I walk beside him. He thinks I'm his trophy. His secret weapon.

I have to stifle the urge to crack his knuckles into concrete.

But I offer him 2 weeks of cooperation because in 1 week we'll be gone.

Hopefully.

But then, more than anything else, I've found I don't hate Warner as much as I thought I did.

I feel sorry for him.

He finds a strange sort of solace in my company; he thinks I can relate to him and his twisted notions, his cruel upbringing, his absent and simultaneously demanding father.

But he never says a word about his mother.

Adam says that no one knows anything about Warner's mother—that she's never been discussed and no one has any idea who she is. He says that Warner is only known to be the consequence of ruthless parenting, and a cold, calculated desire for power. He hates happy children and happy parents and their happy lives.

I think Warner thinks that I understand. That I understand him.

And I do. And I don't.

Because we're not the same.

I want to be better.

Adam and I have little time together but nighttime. And even then, not so much. Warner watches me more closely every day; disabling the cameras only made him more suspicious. He's always walking into my room unexpectedly, taking me on unnecessary tours around the building, talking about nothing but his plans and his plans to make more plans and how together we'll conquer the world. I don't pretend to care.

Maybe it's me who's making this worse.

"I can't believe Warner actually agreed to get rid of your cameras," Adam said to me one night.

"He's insane. He's not rational. He's sick in a way I'll never understand."

Adam sighed. "He's obsessed with you."

"What?" I nearly snapped my neck in surprise.

"You're all he ever talks about." Adam was silent a moment, his jaw too tight. "I heard stories about you before you even got here. That's why I got involved—it's why I volunteered to go get you. Warner spent months collecting information about you: addresses, medical records, personal histories, family relations, birth certificates, blood tests. The entire army was talking about his new project; everyone knew he was looking for a girl who'd killed a little boy in a grocery store. A girl named Juliette."

I held my breath.

Adam shook his head. "I knew it was you. It had to be. I asked Warner if I could help with the project—I told him I'd gone to school with you, that I'd heard about the little boy, that I'd seen you in person." He laughed a hard laugh. "Warner was thrilled. He thought it would make the experiment more interesting," he added, disgusted. "And I knew that if he wanted to claim you as some kind of sick project—" He hesitated. Looked away. Ran a hand through his hair. "I just knew I had to do something. I thought I could try to help. But now it's gotten worse. Warner won't stop talking about what you're capable of or how valuable you are to his efforts and how excited he is to have you here. Everyone is beginning to notice. Warner is ruthless—he has no mercy for anyone. He loves the power, the thrill of destroying people. But he's starting to crack, Juliette. He's so desperate to have you . . . *join* him. And for all his threats, he doesn't want to force you. He wants you to want it. To choose *him*, in a way." He looked down, took a tight breath. "He's losing his edge. And whenever I see his face I'm always about two inches away from doing something stupid. I'd love to break his jaw."

Yes. Warner is losing his edge.

He's paranoid, though with good reason. But then he's

patient and impatient with me. Excited and nervous all the time. He's a walking oxymoron.

He disables my cameras, but some nights he orders Adam to sleep outside my door to make sure I don't escape. He says I can eat lunch alone, but always ends up summoning me to his side. The few hours Adam and I would've had together are stolen from us, but the fewer nights Adam is allowed to sleep inside my room I manage to spend huddled in his arms.

We both sleep on the floor now, wrapped up in each other for warmth even with the blanket covering our bodies. Every time he touches me it's like a burst of fire and electricity that ignites my bones in the most amazing way. It's the kind of feeling I wish I could hold in my hand.

Adam tells me about new developments, whispers he's heard around the other soldiers. He tells me how there are multiple headquarters across what's left of the country. How Warner's dad is at the capital, how he's left his son in charge of this entire sector. He says Warner hates his father but loves the power. The destruction. The devastation. He strokes my hair and tells me stories and tucks me close like he's afraid I'll disappear. He paints pictures of people and places until I fall asleep, until I'm drowning in a drug of dreams to escape a world with no refuge, no relief, no release but his reassurances in my ear. Sleep is the only thing I look forward to these days. I can hardly remember why I used to scream.

Things are getting too comfortable and I'm beginning to panic.

"Put these on," Warner says to me.

Breakfast in the blue room has become routine. I eat and don't ask where the food comes from, whether or not the workers are being paid for what they do, how this building manages to sustain so many lives, pump so much water, or use so much electricity. I bide my time now. I cooperate.

Warner hasn't asked me to touch him again, and I don't offer.

"What are they for?" I eye the small pieces of fabric in his hands and feel a nervous twinge in my gut.

He smiles a slow, sneaky smile. "An aptitude test." He grabs my wrist and places the bundle in my hand. "I'll turn around, just this once."

I'm almost too nervous to be disgusted by him.

My hands shake as I change into the outfit that turns out to be a tiny tank top and tinier shorts. I'm practically naked. I'm practically convulsing in fear of what this might mean. I clear my throat just the tiniest bit and Warner spins around.

He takes too long to speak; his eyes are busy traveling the road map of my body. I want to rip up the carpet and sew it to my skin. He smiles and offers me his hand.

I'm granite and limestone and marbled glass. I don't move.

He drops his hand. He cocks his head. "Follow me."

Warner opens the door. Adam is standing outside. He's gotten so good at masking his emotions that I hardly register the look of shock that shifts in and out of his features.

Nothing but the strain in his forehead, the tension in his temples, gives him away. He knows something's not right. He actually turns his neck to take in my appearance. He blinks. "Sir?"

"Remain where you are, soldier. I'll take it from here."

Adam doesn't answer doesn't answer doesn't answer— "Yes, sir," he says, his voice suddenly hoarse.

I feel his eyes on me as I turn down the hall.

Warner takes me somewhere new. We're walking through corridors I've never seen, blacker and bleaker and more narrow as we go. I realize we're heading downward.

Into a basement.

We pass through 1, 2, 4 metal doors. Soldiers everywhere, their eyes everywhere, appraising me with both fear and something else I'd rather not consider. I've realized there are very few females in this building.

If there were ever a place to be grateful for being untouchable, it'd be here.

It's the only reason I have asylum from the preying eyes of hundreds of lonely men. It's the only reason Adam is staying with me—because Warner thinks Adam is a cardboard cutout of vanilla regurgitations. He thinks Adam is a machine oiled by orders and demands. He thinks Adam is a reminder of my past, and he uses it to make me uncomfortable. He'd never imagine Adam could lay a finger on me.

No one would. Everyone I meet is absolutely petrified.

The darkness is like a black canvas punctured by a blunt knife, with beams of light peeking through. It reminds me too much of my old cell. My skin ripples with uncontrollable dread.

I'm surrounded by guns.

"In you go," Warner says. I'm pushed into an empty room smelling faintly of mold. Someone hits a switch and fluorescent lights flicker on to reveal pasty yellow walls and carpet the color of dead grass. The door slams shut behind me.

There's nothing but cobwebs and a huge mirror in this room. The mirror is half the size of the wall. Instinctively I know Warner and his accomplices must be watching me. I just don't know why.

There are secrets everywhere.

There are answers nowhere.

Mechanical clinks/cracks/creaks and shifts shake the space I'm standing in. The ground rumbles to life. The ceiling trembles with the promise of chaos. Metal spikes are suddenly everywhere, scattered across the room, puncturing every surface at all different heights. Every few seconds they disappear only to reappear with a sudden jolt of terror, slicing through the air like needles.

I realize I'm standing in a torture chamber.

Static and feedback from speakers older than my dying heart crackle to life. I'm a racehorse galloping toward a false finish line, breathing hard for someone else's gain.

"Are you ready?" Warner's amplified voice echoes around the room.

"What am I supposed to be ready for?" I yell into the

empty space, certain that someone can hear me. ~~I'm calm. I'm calm. I'm calm.~~ I'm petrified.

"We had a deal, remember?" the room responds.

"Wha—"

"I disabled your cameras. Now it's your turn to hold up your end of the bargain."

"I won't touch you!" I shout, spinning in place, terrified, horrified, worried I might faint at any moment.

"That's all right," he says. "I'm sending in my replacement."

The door squeals open and a toddler waddles in wearing nothing but a diaper. He's blindfolded and hiccupping sobs, shuddering in fear.

One pin pops my entire existence into nothing.

"If you don't save him," Warner's words crackle through the room, "we won't, either."

This child.

He must have a mother a father someone who loves him this child this child this child stumbling forward in terror. He could be speared through by a metal stalagmite at any second.

Saving him is simple: I need to pick him up, find a safe spot of ground, and hold him in my arms until the experiment is over.

There's only one problem.

If I touch him, he might die.

# TWENTY-FIVE

Warner knows I don't have a choice. He wants to force me into another situation where he can see the impact of my abilities, and he has no problem torturing an innocent child to get exactly what he wants.

Right now I have no options.

I have to take a chance before this little boy steps forward in the wrong direction.

I quickly memorize as much as I can of the traps and dodge/hop/narrowly avoid the spikes until I'm as close as possible.

I take a deep, shaky breath and focus on the shivering limbs of the boy in front of me and pray to God I'm making the right decision. I'm about to pull off my shirt to use as a barrier between us when I notice the slight vibration in the ground. The tremble that precedes the terror. I know I have half of a second before the spikes slice up through the air and even less time to react.

I yank him up and into my arms.

His screams pierce through me like I'm being shot to death, one bullet for every second. He's clawing at my arms, my chest, kicking my body as hard as he can, crying out in agony until the pain paralyzes him. He goes weak in my grip and I'm being ripped to pieces, my eyes, my bones, my veins all tumbling out of place, all turning on me to torture me forever with memories of the horrors I'm responsible for.

Pain and power are bleeding through his body into mine, jolting through his limbs and crashing into me until I nearly drop him. ~~It's like reliving a nightmare I've spent 3 years trying to forget.~~

"Absolutely amazing," Warner sighs through the speakers, and I realize I was right. He must be watching through a 2-way mirror. "Brilliant, love. I'm thoroughly impressed."

I'm too desperate to be able to focus on Warner right now. I have no idea how long this sick game is going to last, and I need to lessen the amount of skin I'm exposing to this little boy's body.

My skimpy outfit makes so much sense now.

I rearrange him in my arms and manage to grab hold of his diaper. I'm holding him up with the palm of my hand. I'm desperate to believe I couldn't have touched him long enough to cause serious damage.

He hiccups once; his body quivers back to life.

I could cry from happiness.

But then the screams start back up again, no longer cries of torture but of fear. He's desperate to get away from me and I'm losing my grip, my wrist nearly breaking from the effort. I don't dare remove his blindfold. I'd rather die than allow him to see this space, to see my face.

I clench my jaw so fast I'm afraid I'm going to break

my teeth. If I put him down, he'll start running. And if he starts running, he's finished. I have to keep holding on.

The roar of an old mechanical wheeze revives my heart. The spikes slip back into the ground, one by one until they've all disappeared. The room is harmless again so swiftly I fear I may have imagined the danger. I drop the boy back onto the floor and bite down on my lip to swallow the pain welling in my wrist.

The child starts running and accidentally bumps my bare legs.

He screams and shudders and falls to the floor, curled up into himself, sobbing until I consider destroying myself, ridding myself of this world. Tears are streaming fast down my face and I want nothing more than to reach out to him and help him, hug him close, kiss his beautiful cheeks and tell him I'll take care of him forever, that we'll run away together, that I'll play games with him and read him stories at night and I know I can't. I know I never will. I know it will never be possible.

And suddenly the world shifts out of focus.

I'm overcome by a rage, an intensity, an anger so potent I'm almost elevated off the ground. I'm boiling with blind hatred and disgust. I don't even understand how my feet move in the next instant. I don't understand my hands and what they're doing or how they decided to fly forward, fingers splayed, charging toward the window. I only know I want to feel Warner's neck snap between my own two hands. I want him to experience the same terror he just inflicted upon a child. I want to watch him die. I want to watch him beg for mercy.

I catapult through the concrete walls.

I crush the glass with 10 fingers.

I'm clutching a fistful of gravel and a fistful of fabric at Warner's neck and there are 50 different guns pointed at my head. The air is heavy with cement and sulfur, the glass falling in an agonized symphony of shattered hearts.

I slam Warner into the corroded stone.

"Don't you *dare* shoot her," Warner wheezes at the guards. I haven't touched his skin yet, but I have the strangest suspicion that I could smash his rib cage into his heart if I just pressed a little harder.

"I should kill you." My voice is one deep breath, one uncontrolled exhalation.

"You—" He tries to swallow. "You just—you just broke through concrete with your bare hands."

I blink. I don't dare look behind me. But I know without looking backward that he can't be lying. I must have. My mind is a maze of impossibility.

I lose focus for one instant.

The guns

*click*

*click*

*click*

Every moment is loaded.

"If any of you hurt her I will shoot you myself," Warner barks.

"But sir—"

"STAND DOWN, SOLDIER—"

The rage is gone. The sudden uncontrollable anger is gone. My mind has already surrendered to disbelief. Confusion. I don't know what I've done. I obviously don't know what I'm capable of because I had no idea I could destroy anything at all and I'm suddenly so terrified so terrified so terrified of my own two hands. I stumble backward, stunned, and catch Warner watching me hungrily, eagerly, his emerald eyes bright with boyish fascination. He's practically trembling in excitement.

There's a snake in my throat and I can't swallow it down. I meet Warner's gaze. "If you ever put me in a position like that again, I *will* kill you. And I will enjoy it."

I don't even know if I'm lying.

# TWENTY-SIX

Adam finds me curled into a ball on the shower floor.

I've been crying for so long I'm certain the hot water is made of nothing but my tears. My clothes are stuck to my skin, wet and useless. I want to wash them away. I want to drown in ignorance. I want to be stupid, dumb, mute, completely devoid of a brain. I want to cut off my own limbs. I want to be rid of this skin that can kill and these hands that destroy and this body I don't even know how to understand.

Everything is falling apart.

"Juliette . . ." He presses his hand against the glass. I can hardly hear him.

When I don't respond he opens the shower door. He's pelted with rebel raindrops and kicks his boots off before falling to his knees on the tile floor. He reaches in to touch my arms and the feeling only makes me more desperate to die. He sighs and pulls me up, just enough to lift my head. His hands trap my face and his eyes search me, search through me until I look away.

"I know what happened," he says softly.

My throat is a reptile, covered in scales. "Someone should just kill me," I croak, cracking with every word.

Adam's arms wrap around me until he's tugged me up and I'm wobbling on my legs and we're both standing upright. He steps into the shower and slides the door shut behind him.

I gasp.

He holds me up against the wall and I see nothing but his white T-shirt soaked through, nothing but the water dancing down his face, nothing but his eyes full of a world I'm dying to be a part of.

"It wasn't your fault," he whispers.

"It's what I *am*," I choke.

"No. Warner's wrong about you," Adam says. "He wants you to be someone you're not, and you can't let him break you. Don't let him get into your head. He *wants* you to think you're a monster. He wants you to think you have no choice but to join him. He wants you to think you'll never be able to live a normal life—"

"But I won't live a normal life." I swallow a hiccup. "Not ever—I'll n-never—"

Adam is shaking his head. "You will. We're going to get out of here. I won't let this happen to you."

"H-how could you possibly care about someone . . . like *me*?" I'm barely breathing, nervous and petrified but somehow staring at his lips, studying the shape, counting the drops of water tumbling over the hills and valleys of his mouth.

"Because I'm in love with you."

I swallow my stomach. My eyes snap up to read his face but I'm a mess of electricity, humming with life and lightning, hot and cold and my heart is erratic. I'm shaking in his arms and my lips have parted for no reason at all.

His mouth softens into a smile. My bones have disappeared.

I'm spinning with delirium.

His nose is touching my nose, his lips one breath away, his eyes devouring me already and I'm a puddle with no arms and no legs. I can smell him everywhere; I feel every point of his figure pressed against mine. His hands at my waist, gripping my hips, his legs flush against my own, his chest overpowering me with strength, his frame built by bricks of desire. The taste of his words lingers on my lips.

"Really . . . ?" I have one whisper of incredulity, one conscious effort to believe what's never been done. I'm flushed through my feet, filled with unspoken everything.

He looks at me with so much emotion I nearly crack in half.

"God, Juliette—"

And he's kissing me.

Once, twice, until I've had a taste and realize I'll never have enough. He's everywhere up my back and over my arms and suddenly he's kissing me harder, deeper, with a fervent urgent need I've never known before. He breaks for air only to bury his lips in my neck, along my collarbone, up my chin and cheeks and I'm gasping for oxygen and he's destroying me with his hands and we're drenched in water and beauty and the exhilaration of a moment I never knew was possible.

He pulls back with a low groan and I want him to take his shirt off.

I need to see the bird. I need to tell him about the bird.

My fingers are tugging at the hem of his wet clothes and his eyes widen for only a second before he rips the material off himself. He grabs my hands and lifts my arms above my head and pins me against the wall, kissing me until I'm sure I'm dreaming, drinking in my lips with his lips and he tastes like rain and sweet musk and I'm about to explode.

My knees are knocking together and my heart is beating so fast I don't understand why it's still working. He's kissing away the pain, the hurt, the years of self-loathing, the insecurities, the dashed hopes for a future I always pictured as obsolete. He's lighting me on fire, burning away the torture of Warner's games, the anguish that poisons me every single day. The intensity of our bodies could shatter these glass walls.

It nearly does.

For a moment we're just staring at each other, breathing hard until I'm blushing, until he closes his eyes and takes one ragged, steadying breath and I place my hand on his chest. I dare to trace the outline of the bird soaring across his skin, I dare to trail my fingers down the length of his abdomen.

"You're my bird," I tell him. "You're my bird and you're going to help me fly away."

Adam is gone by the time I get out of the shower.

He wrung his clothes out and dried himself off and

granted me privacy to change. Privacy I'm not sure I care about anymore. I touch 2 fingers to my lips and taste him everywhere.

But when I step into the room he's not anywhere. He had to report downstairs.

I stare at the clothes in my closet.

I always choose a dress with pockets because I don't know where else to store my notebook. It doesn't carry any incriminating information, and the one piece of paper that bore Adam's handwriting has since been destroyed and flushed down the toilet, but I like to keep it close to me. It represents so much more than a few words scribbled on paper. It's a small token of my resistance.

I tuck the notebook into a pocket and decide I'm finally ready to face myself. I take a deep breath, push the wet strands of hair away from my eyes, and pad into the bathroom. The steam from the shower has clouded the mirror. I reach out a tentative hand to wipe away a small circle. Just big enough.

A scared face stares back at me.

I touch my cheeks and study the reflective surface, study the image of a girl who's simultaneously strange and familiar to me. My face is thinner, paler, my cheekbones higher than I remember them, my eyebrows perched above 2 wide eyes not blue not green but somewhere in between. My skin is flushed with heat and something named Adam. My lips are too pink. My teeth are unusually straight. My finger is trailing down the length of my nose, tracing the shape of my chin when I see a movement in the corner of my eye.

"You're so beautiful," he says to me.

I'm pink and red and maroon all at once. I duck my head and trip away from the mirror only to have him catch me in his arms. "I'd forgotten my own face," I whisper.

"Just don't forget who you *are*," he says.

"I don't even know."

"Yes you do." He tilts my face up. "I do."

I stare at the strength in his jaw, in his eyes, in his body. I try to understand the confidence he has in who he thinks I am and realize his reassurance is the only thing stopping me from diving into a pool of my own insanity. He's always believed in me. Even soundlessly, silently, he fought for me. Always.

He's my only friend.

I take his hand and hold it to my lips. "I've loved you forever," I tell him.

The sun rises, rests, shines in his face and he almost smiles, almost can't meet my eyes. His muscles relax, his shoulders find relief in the weight of a new kind of wonder and he exhales. He touches my cheek, touches my lips, touches the tip of my chin and I blink and he's kissing me, he's pulling me into his arms and into the air and somehow we're on the bed and tangled in each other and I'm drugged with emotion, drugged by each tender moment. His fingers skim my shoulder, trail down my silhouette, rest at my hips. He pulls me closer, whispers my name, drops kisses down my throat and struggles with the stiff fabric of my dress. His hands are shaking so slightly, his eyes brimming with feeling, his heart thrumming with pain and affection and I want to live here, in his arms, in his eyes for the rest of my life.

I slip my hands under his shirt and he chokes on a moan that turns into a kiss that needs me and wants me and has to have me so desperately it's like the most acute form of torture. His weight is pressed into mine, on top of mine, infinite points of feeling for every nerve ending in my body and his right hand is behind my neck and his left hand is reeling me in and his lips are falling down my shirt and I don't understand why I need to wear clothes anymore and I'm a cumulonimbus existence of thunder and lightning and the possibility of exploding into tears at any inopportune moment. Bliss Bliss Bliss is beating through my chest.

I don't remember what it means to breathe.

I never

ever

ever

knew

what it meant to *feel*.


An alarm is hammering through the walls.


The room beeps and blares to life and Adam stiffens, pulls back; his face collapses.

"This is a CODE SEVEN. All soldiers must report to the Quadrant immediately. This is a CODE SEVEN. All soldiers must report to the Quadrant immediately. This is a

CODE SEVEN. All soldiers must report to the Quadra—"

Adam is on his feet and pulling me up and the voice is still shouting orders through a speaker system wired into the building. "There's been a breach," he says, his voice broken and breathy, his eyes darting between me and the door. "Jesus. I can't just leave you here—"

"Go," I tell him. "You have to go—I'll be fine—"

Footsteps are thundering through the halls and soldiers are barking at each other so loudly I can hear it through the walls. Adam is still on duty. He has to perform. He has to keep up appearances until we can leave. I know this.

He pulls me close. "This isn't a joke, Juliette—I don't know what's happening—it could be anything—"

A metal click. A mechanical switch. The door slides open and Adam and I jump 10 feet apart.

Adam rushes to exit just as Warner is walking in. They both freeze.

"I'm pretty sure that alarm has been going off for at least a minute, soldier."

"Yes sir. I wasn't sure what to do about her." He's suddenly composed, a perfect statue. He nods at me like I'm an afterthought but I know he's just slightly too stiff in the shoulders. Breathing just a beat too fast.

"Lucky for you, I'm here to take care of that. You may report to your commanding officer."

"Sir." Adam nods, pivots on one heel, and darts out the door. I hope Warner didn't notice his hesitation.

Warner turns to face me with a smile so calm and casual I begin to question whether the building is actually in chaos.

He studies my face. My hair. Glances at the rumpled sheets behind me and I feel like I've swallowed a spider. "You took a nap?"

"I couldn't sleep last night."

"You've ripped your dress."

"What are you doing here?" I need him to stop staring at me, I need him to stop drinking in the details of my existence.

"If you don't like the dress, you can always choose a different one, you know. I picked them out for you myself."

"That's okay. The dress is fine." I glance at the clock for no real reason. It's already 4:30 in the afternoon. "Why won't you tell me what's going on?"

He's too close. He's standing too close and he's looking at me and my lungs are failing to expand. "You should really change."

"I don't want to change." I don't know why I'm so nervous. Why he's making me so nervous. Why the space between us is closing too quickly.

He hooks a finger in the rip close to the drop-waist of my dress and I bite back a scream. "This just won't do."

"It's fine—"

He tugs so hard on the rip that it splits open the fabric and creates a slit up the side of my leg. "That's a bit better."

"What are you *doing*—"

His hands snake up my waist and clamp my arms in place and I know I need to defend myself but I'm frozen and I want to scream but my voice is broken broken broken. I'm a ragged breath of desperation.

"I have a question," he says, and I try to kick him in this worthless dress and he just squeezes me up against the wall, the weight of his body pressing me into place, every inch of him covered in clothing, a protective layer between us. "I said I have a question, Juliette."

His hand slips into my pocket so quickly it takes me a moment to realize what he's done. I'm panting up against the wall, shaking and trying to find my head.

"I'm curious," he says. "What is *this*?"

He's holding my notebook between 2 fingers.

Oh God.

This dress is too tight to hide the outline of the notebook and I was too busy looking at my face to check the dress in the mirror. ~~This is all my fault all my fault all my fault all my fault~~ I can't believe it. This is all my fault. I should've known better.

I say nothing.

He cocks his head. "I don't recall giving you a notebook. I certainly don't remember granting you allowance for any possessions, either."

"I brought it with me." My voice catches.

"Now you're lying." "What do you want from me?" I panic.

"That's a stupid question, Juliette."

The soft sound of smooth metal slipping out of place. Someone has opened my door.

*Click.*

"Get your hands off of her before I bury a bullet in your head."

181

# TWENTY-SEVEN

Warner's eyes close very slowly. He steps away very slowly. His lips twitch into a dangerous smile. "Kent."

Adam's hands are steady, the barrel of his gun pressed into the back of Warner's skull. "You're going to clear our exit out of here."

Warner actually laughs. He opens his eyes and whips a gun out of his inside pocket only to point it directly at my forehead. "I will kill her right now."

"You're not that stupid," Adam says.

"If she moves even a millimeter, I will shoot her. And then I will rip you to pieces."

Adam shifts quickly, slamming the butt of his gun into Warner's head. Warner's gun misfires and Adam catches his arm and twists his wrist until his grip on the weapon wavers. I grab the gun from Warner's limp hand and slam the butt of it into his face. I'm stunned by my own reflexes. I've never held a gun before but I guess there's a first time for everything.

I point it at Warner's eyes. "Don't underestimate me."

"Holy *shit*." Adam doesn't bother hiding his surprise.

Warner coughs through a laugh, steadies himself, and tries to smile as he wipes the blood from his nose. "I never underestimate you," he says to me. "I never have."

Adam shakes his head for less than a second before his face splits into an enormous grin. He's beaming at me as he presses the gun harder into Warner's skull. "Let's get out of here."

I grab the two duffel bags stowed away in the armoire and toss one to Adam. We've been packed for a week already. If he wants to make a break for it earlier than expected, I have no complaints.

Warner's lucky we're showing him mercy.

But we're lucky the entire building has been evacuated. He has no one to rely on.

Warner clears his throat. He's staring straight at me when he speaks. "I can assure you, soldier, your triumph will be short-lived. You may as well kill me now, because when I find you, I will thoroughly enjoy destroying every bone in your body. You're a fool if you think you can get away with this."

"I am not your soldier." Adam's face is stone. "I never have been. You've been so caught up in the details of your own fantasies you failed to notice the dangers right in front of your face."

"We can't kill you yet," I add. "You have to get us out of here."

"You're making a huge mistake, Juliette," he says to me. His voice actually softens. "You're throwing away an entire future." He sighs. "How do you know you can trust him?"

I glance at Adam. Adam, the boy who's always defended me, even when he had nothing to gain. I shake my head to

clear it. I remind myself that Warner is a liar. A crazed luna-
tic. A psychotic murderer. He would never try to help me.

I think.

"Let's go before it's too late," I say to Adam. "He's just
trying to stall us until the soldiers get back."

"He doesn't even care about you!" Warner explodes.
I flinch at the sudden, uncontrolled intensity in his voice.
"He just wants a way out of here and he's *using* you!"
He steps forward. "I could love you, Juliette—I would treat
you like a *queen*—"

Adam puts him in a swift headlock and points the gun
at his temple. "You obviously don't understand what's happening here," he says very carefully.

"Then educate me, soldier," Warner wheezes out.
His eyes are dancing flames; dangerous. "Tell me what I'm
failing to understand."

"Adam." I'm shaking my head.

He meets my eyes. Nods. Turns to Warner. "Make the
call," he says, squeezing his neck a little tighter. "Get us out
of here *now*."

"Only my dead body would allow her to walk out that
door." Warner exercises his jaw and spits blood on the
floor. "You I would kill for pleasure," he says to Adam. "But
Juliette is the one I want forever."

"I'm not yours to *want*." I'm breathing too hard. I'm
anxious to get out of here. I'm angry he won't stop talking
but as much as I'd love to break his face, he's no good to
us unconscious.

"You could love me, you know." He's smiling a strange sort of smile. "We would be unstoppable. We would change the world. I could make you happy," he says to me.

Adam looks like he might snap Warner's neck. His face is so taut, so tense, so angry. I've never seen him like this before. "You have nothing to offer her, you sick bastard."

Warner presses his eyes shut for one second. "Juliette. Don't be hasty. Don't make a rash decision. Stay with me. I'll be patient with you. I'll give you time to adjust. I'll take care of you—"

"You're insane." My hands are shaking but I hold the gun up to his face again. I need to get him out of my head. I need to remember what he's done to me. "You want me to be a *monster* for you—"

"I want you to live up to your *potential*!"

"Let me go," I say quietly. "I don't want to be your creature. I don't want to hurt people."

"The world has already hurt *you*," he counters. "The world *put* you here. You're here because of them! You think if you leave they're going to accept you? You think you can run away and live a normal life? No one will care for you. No one will come near you—you'll be an outcast like you've always been! Nothing has changed! You belong with me!"

"She belongs with *me*." Adam's voice could cut through steel.

Warner flinches. For the first time he seems to be understanding what I thought was obvious. His eyes are wide, horrified, unbelieving, staring at me with a new kind of anguish. "No." A short, crazed laugh. "Juliette. Please. Please. Don't tell me he's filled your head with romantic notions. Please don't tell me you fell for his false proclamations—"

Adam slams his knee into Warner's spine. Warner falls to the floor with a muffled crack and a sharp intake of breath. Adam has thoroughly overpowered him. I feel like I should be cheering.

But I'm too anxious. I'm too suspended in disbelief. I'm too insecure to be confident in my own decisions. I need to pull myself together.

"Adam—"

"I *love* you," he says to me, his eyes just as earnest as I remember them, his words just as urgent as they should be. "Don't let him confuse you—"

"You *love* her?" Warner practically spits. "You don't even—"

"Adam." The room shifts in and out of focus. I'm staring at the window. I glance back at him.

His eyes touch his eyebrows. "You want to *jump* out?"

I nod.

"But we're fifteen stories up—"

"What choice do we have if he won't cooperate?" I look at Warner. Cock my head. "There is no Code Seven, is there?"

Warner's lips twitch. He says nothing.

"Why would you do that?" I ask him. "Why would you pull a false alarm?"

186

"Why don't you ask the soldier you're so suddenly fond of?" Warner snaps, disgusted. "Why don't you ask yourself why you're trusting your life to someone who can't even differentiate between a real and an imaginary threat?"

Adam swears under his breath.

I lock eyes with him and he tosses me his gun.

He shakes his head. Swears again. Clenches and unclenches his fist. "It was just a drill."

Warner actually laughs.

Adam glances at the door, the clock, my face. "We don't have much time."

I'm holding Warner's gun in my left hand and Adam's gun in my right and pointing them both at Warner's forehead, doing my best to ignore the eyes he's drilling in my direction. Adam uses his free hand to dig in his pockets for something. He pulls out a pair of plastic zip ties and kicks Warner onto his back just before binding his limbs together. Warner's boots and gloves have been discarded on the floor. Adam keeps one boot pressed on his stomach.

"A million alarms are going to go off the minute we jump through that window," he tells me. "We'll have to run, so we can't risk breaking our legs. We can't jump."

"So what do we do?"

He runs a hand through his hair and bites down on his bottom lip and for one delirious moment all I want to do is taste him. I force myself back into focus.

"I have rope," he says. "We'll have to climb down. And fast."

He sets to work pulling out a coil of cord attached to a small clawlike anchor. I'd asked him a million times what on earth he would need it for, why he would pack it in his escape bag. He told me a person could never have too much rope. Now, I almost want to laugh.

He turns to me. "I'm going to go down first so I can catch you on the other side—"

Warner laughs loud, too loud. "You can't *catch* her, you fool." He squirms in his plastic shackles. "She's wearing next to nothing. She'll kill you and kill herself from the fall!"

My eyes dart between Warner and Adam. I don't have time to entertain Warner's charades any longer. I make a hasty decision. "Do it. I'll be right behind you."

Warner looks crazed, confused. "What are you doing?"

I ignore him.

"Wait—"

I ignore him.

"Juliette."

I ignore him.

"Juliette!" His voice is tighter, higher, laced with anger and terror and denial and betrayal. Realization is a new piece in his puzzled mind. "He can *touch* you?"

Adam is wrapping his fist in the bedsheet.

"Goddamn it, Juliette, answer me!" Warner is writhing on the floor, unhinged in a way I never thought possible. He looks wild, his eyes disbelieving, horrified. "Has he *touched* you?"

I can't understand why the walls are suddenly on the ceiling. Everything is stumbling sideways.

"Juliette—"

Adam breaks through the glass with one swift crack, one solid punch, and instantly the entire room is ringing with the sound of hysteria like no alarm I've heard before. The room is rumbling under my feet, footsteps are thundering down the halls, and I know we're about one minute from being discovered.

Adam throws the cord through the window and slings his pack over his back. "Throw me your bag!" he shouts and I can barely hear him. I toss my duffel and he catches it right before slipping through the window. I run to join him.

Warner tries to grab my leg.

His failed attempt nearly trips me but I manage to stumble my way to the window without losing much time. I glance back at the door and feel my heart racing through my bones. The sound of soldiers running and yelling is getting louder, closer, clearer by the second.

"Hurry!" Adam is calling to me.

"Juliette, *please*—"

Warner swipes for my leg again and I gasp so loud I almost hear it through the sirens shattering my eardrums. I won't look at him. I won't look at him. I won't look at him.

I swing one leg through the window and latch on to the cord. My bare legs are going to make this an excruciating ordeal. Both legs are through. My hands are in place. Adam is calling to me from below, and I don't know how far down he is. Warner is screaming my name and I look up despite my best efforts.

His eyes are two shots of green punched through a pane of glass. Cutting through me.

I take a deep breath and hope I won't die.

I take a deep breath and inch my way down the rope.

I take a deep breath and hope Warner doesn't realize what just happened.

I hope he doesn't know he just touched my leg.

And nothing happened.

# TWENTY-EIGHT

I'm burning.

The cord is chafing my legs into a fiery mass so painful I'm surprised there's no smoke. I bite back the pain because I have no choice. The mass hysteria of the building is bulldozing my senses, raining down danger all around us. Adam is shouting to me from below, telling me to jump, promising he'll catch me. I'm too ashamed to admit I'm afraid of the fall.

I never have a chance to make my own decision.

Soldiers are already pouring into what used to be my room, shouting and confused, probably shocked to find Warner in such a feeble position. It was really too easy to overpower him. It worries me.

It makes me think we did something wrong.

A few soldiers pop their heads out of the shattered window and I'm frantic to shimmy down the rope but they're already moving to unlatch the anchor. I prepare myself for the nauseating sensation of free fall only to realize they're not trying to drop me. They're trying to reel me back inside.

Warner must be telling them what to do.

I glance down at Adam below me and finally give in to his calls. I squeeze my eyes shut and let go.

And fall right into his open arms.

We collapse onto the ground, but the breath is knocked out of us for only a moment. Adam grabs my hand and then we're running.

There's nothing but empty, barren space stretching out ahead of us. Broken asphalt, uneven pavement, dirt roads, naked trees, dying plants, a yellowed city abandoned to the elements drowning in dead leaves that crunch under our feet. The civilian compounds are short and squat, grouped together in no particular order, and Adam makes sure to stay as far away from them as possible. The loudspeakers are already working against us. The sound of a young, smoothly mechanical female voice drowns out the sirens.

*"Curfew is now in effect. Everyone return to their homes immediately. There are rebels on the loose. They are armed and ready to fire. Curfew is now in effect. Everyone return to their homes immediately. There are rebels on the loose. They are armed and ready to fi—"*

My sides are cramping, my skin is tight, my throat dry, desperate for water. I don't know how far we've run. All I know is the sound of boots pounding the pavement, the screech of tires peeling out of underground storage units, alarms wailing in our wake.

I look back to see people screaming and running for shelter, ducking away from the soldiers rushing through their homes, pounding down doors to see if we've found refuge somewhere inside. Adam pulls me away from civilization and heads toward the abandoned streets of an earlier decade: old shops and restaurants, narrow side streets and abandoned playgrounds. The unregulated land of our past lives has been strictly off-limits. It's forbidden territory. Everything closed down. Everything broken, rusted shut, lifeless. No one is allowed to trespass here. Not even soldiers.

And we're charging through these streets, trying to stay out of sight.

The sun is slipping through the sky and tripping toward the edge of the earth. Night will be coming quickly, and I have no idea where we are. I never expected so much to happen so quickly and I never expected it all to happen on the same day. I just have to hope to survive but I haven't the faintest idea where we might be headed. It never occurred to me to ask Adam where we might go.

We're darting in a million directions. Turning abruptly, going forward a few feet only to head back in an opposite path. My best guess is that Adam is trying to confuse and/or distract our followers as much as possible. I can do nothing but attempt to keep up.

And I fail.

Adam is a trained soldier. He's built for exactly these kinds of situations. He understands how to flee, how to stay inconspicuous, how to move soundlessly in any space. I, on the other hand, am a broken girl who's known no exercise for too long. My lungs are burning with the effort to inhale oxygen, wheezing with the effort to exhale carbon dioxide.

I'm suddenly gasping so desperately Adam is forced

to pull me into a side street. He's breathing a little harder than usual, but I've acquired a full-time job choking on the weakness of my limp body.

Adam takes my face in his hands and tries to focus my eyes. "I want you to breathe like I am, okay?"

I wheeze a bit more.

"Focus, Juliette." His eyes are so determined. Infinitely patient. He looks fearless and I envy him his composure. "Calm your heart," he says. "Breathe exactly as I do."

He takes 3 small breaths in, holds it for a few seconds, and releases it in one long exhalation. I try to copy him. I'm not very good at it.

"Okay. I want you to keep breathing like—" He stops. His eyes dart up and around the abandoned street for a split second. I know we have to move.

Gunshots shatter the atmosphere. I'd never realized just how loud they are or just how much that sound fractures every functioning bone in my body. An icy chill seeps through my blood and I know immediately that they're not trying to kill me. They're trying to kill Adam.

I'm suddenly asphyxiated by a new kind of anxiety. I can't let them hurt him.

Not for me.

But Adam doesn't have time for me to catch my breath and find my head. He flips me up and into his arms and takes off in a diagonal dash across another alleyway.

And we're running.

And I'm breathing.

And he shouts, "Wrap your arms around my neck!" and I release the choke hold I have on his T-shirt and I'm stupid enough to feel shy as I slip my arms around him. He readjusts me against him so I'm higher, closer to his chest. He carries me like I weigh less than nothing.

I close my eyes and press my cheek against his neck.

The gunshots are somewhere behind us, but even I can tell from the sound that they're too far away and too far in the wrong direction. We seem to have momentarily out-maneuvered them. Their cars can't even find us, because Adam has avoided all main streets. He seems to have his own map of this city. He seems to know exactly what he's doing—like he's been planning this for a very long time.

After inhaling exactly 594 times Adam drops me to my feet in front of a stretch of chain-link fence. I realize he's struggling to swallow oxygen, but he doesn't pant like I do. He knows how to regulate his breathing. He knows how to steady his pulse, calm his heart, maintain control over his organs. He knows how to survive. I hope he'll teach me, too.

"Juliette," he says after a breathless moment. "Can you jump this fence?"

I'm so eager to be more than a useless lump that I nearly sprint up and over the metal barrier. But I'm reckless. And too hasty. I practically rip my dress off and scratch my legs in the process. I wince against the stinging pain, and in the moment it takes me to reopen my eyes, Adam is already standing next to me.

He looks down at my legs and sighs. He almost laughs.

I wonder what I must look like, tattered and wild in this shredded dress. The slit Warner created now stops at my hip bone. I must look like a crazed animal.

Adam doesn't seem to mind.

He's slowed down, too. We're moving at a brisk walk now, no longer barreling through the streets. I realize we must be closer to some semblance of safety, but I'm not sure if I should ask questions now, or save them for later. Adam answers my silent thoughts.

"They won't be able to track me out here," he says, and it dawns on me that all soldiers must have some kind of tracking device on their person. I wonder why I never got one.

It shouldn't be this easy to escape.

"Our trackers aren't tangible," he explains. We make a left into another alleyway. The sun is just dipping below the horizon. I wonder where we are. How far away from Reestablished settlements we must be that there are no people here. "It's a special serum injected into our bloodstream," he continues, "and it's designed to work with our bodies' natural processes. It would know, for example, if I died. It's an excellent way to keep track of soldiers lost in combat." He glances at me out of the corner of his eye. He smiles a crooked smile I want to kiss.

"So how did you confuse the tracker?"

His grin grows bigger. He waves one hand around us. "This space we're standing in? It was used for a nuclear power plant. One day the whole thing exploded."

My eyes are as big as my face. "When did that happen?"

"About five years ago. They cleaned it up pretty quickly.

Hid it from the media, from the people. No one really knows what happened here. But the radiation alone is enough to kill." He pauses. "It already has."

He stops walking. "I've been through this area a million times already, and I haven't been affected by it. Warner used to send me up here to collect samples of the soil. He wanted to study the effects." He runs a hand through his hair. "I think he was hoping to manipulate the toxicity into a poison of some kind.

"The first time I came up here, Warner thought I'd died. The tracker is linked to all of our main processing systems—an alert goes off whenever a soldier is lost. He knew there was a risk in sending me, so I don't think he was too surprised to hear I'd died. He was more surprised to see me return." He shrugs, as though his death would've been an insignificant detail. "There's something about the chemicals here that counteracts the molecular composition of the tracking device. So basically—right now everyone thinks I'm dead."

"Won't Warner suspect you might be here?"

"Maybe." He squints up at the fading sunlight. Our shadows are long and unmoving. "Or I could've been shot. In any case, it buys us some time."

He takes my hand and grins at me before something slams into my consciousness.

"What about *me*?" I ask. "Can't this radiation kill me?" I hope I don't sound as nervous as I feel. I've never wanted to be alive so much in my life. I don't want to lose everything so soon.

"Oh—no." He shakes his head. "Sorry, I forgot to tell you—one of the reasons why Warner wanted me collecting these samples? Is because you're immune to it, too. He was studying you. He said he found the information in your hospital records. That you'd been tested—"

"But no one ever—"

"—probably without your knowledge, and despite testing positive for the radiation, you were entirely whole, biologically. There was nothing inherently wrong with you."

*Nothing inherently wrong with you.*

The observation is so blatantly false I actually start laughing. I try to stifle my incredulity. "There's nothing wrong with me? You're kidding, right?"

Adam stares at me so long I begin to blush. He tips my chin up so I meet his eyes. Blue blue blue boring into me. His voice is deep, steady. "I don't think I've ever heard you laugh."

He's so excruciatingly correct I don't know how to respond except with the truth. My smile is tucked into a straight line. "Laughter comes from living." I shrug, try to sound indifferent. "I've never really been alive before."

His eyes haven't wavered in their focus. He's holding me in place with the strength of one powerful pull coming from deep within him. I can almost feel his heart beating against my skin. I can almost feel his lips breathing against my lungs. I can almost taste him on my tongue.

He takes a shaky breath and pulls me close. Kisses the top of my head.

"Let's go home," he whispers.

# TWENTY-NINE

Home.

*Home.*

What does he mean?

I part my lips to ask the question and his sneaky smile is the only answer I receive. I'm embarrassed and excited and anxious and eager. My stomach is filled with beating drums pounded into synchronicity by my heart. I'm practically humming with electric nerves.

Every step is a step away from the asylum, away from Warner, away from the futility of the existence I've always known. Every step is one I take because I *want* to. For the first time in my life, I walk forward because I *want* to, because I feel hope and love and the exhilaration of beauty, because I want to know what it's like to *live*. I could jump up to catch a breeze and live in its windblown ways forever.

I feel like I've been fitted for wings.

Adam leads me into an abandoned shed on the outskirts of this wild field, overgrown by rogue vegetation and crazed bushlike tentacles, scratchy and hideous, likely poisonous to ingest. I wonder if this is where Adam meant for us to stay. I step into the dark space and squint. An outline comes into focus.

There's a car inside.

I blink.

Not just a car. A tank.

Adam almost can't control his own eagerness. He looks at my face for a reaction and seems pleased with my astonishment. His words tumble out. "I convinced Warner I'd managed to break one of the tanks I brought up here. These things are designed to run on electricity—so I told him the main unit fried on contact with the chemical traces. That it was corrupted by something in the atmosphere. He arranged for a car to deliver and collect me after that, and said we should leave the tank where it is." He almost smiles. "Warner was sending me up here against his father's wishes, and didn't want anyone to find out he'd broken a 500-thousand-dollar tank. The official report says it was hijacked by rebels."

"Couldn't someone else have come up and seen the tank sitting here?"

Adam opens the passenger door. "The civilians stay far, far away from this place, and no other soldier has been up here. No one else wanted to risk the radiation." He cocks his head. "It's one of the reasons why Warner trusted me with you. He liked that I was willing to die for my *duty*."

"He never thought you'd step out of line," I murmur, comprehending.

Adam shakes his head. "Nope. And after what happened with the tracking serum, he had no reason to doubt that crazy things were possible up here. I deactivated the tank's electrical unit myself, just in case he wanted to check." He nods back to the monstrous vehicle. "I had a feeling it would come in handy one day. It's always good to be prepared."

*Prepared.* He was always prepared. To run. To escape.

I wonder why.

"Come here," he says, his voice noticeably gentler. He reaches for me in the dim light and I pretend it's a happy coincidence that his hands brush my bare thighs. I pretend it doesn't feel incredible to have him struggle with the rips in my dress as he helps me into the tank. I pretend I can't see the way he's looking at me as the last of the sun falls below the horizon.

"I need to take care of your legs," he says, a whisper against my skin, electric in my blood. For a moment I don't even understand what he means. I don't even care. My thoughts are so impractical I surprise myself. I've never had the freedom to touch anyone before. Certainly no one has ever *wanted* my hands on them. Adam is an entirely new experience.

Touching him is all I want to think about.

"The cuts aren't too bad," he continues, the tips of his fingers running across my calves. I suck in my breath. "But we'll have to clean them up, just in case. Sometimes it's safer being cut by a butcher knife than being scratched by a random scrap of metal. You don't want it to get infected."

He looks up. His hand is now on my knee.

I'm nodding and I don't know why. I wonder if I'm

trembling on the outside as much as I am on the inside. I hope it's too dark for him to see just how flushed my face is, just how embarrassing it is that he can't touch my knee without making me crazy. I need to say something. "We should probably get going, right?"

"Yeah." He takes a deep breath and seems to return to himself. "Yeah. We have to go." He peers through the evening light. "We have some time before they realize I'm still alive. And we have to use it to our advantage."

"But once we leave this place—won't the tracker start back up again? Won't they know you're not dead?"

"No." He jumps into the driver's side and fumbles for the ignition. There's no key, just a button. I wonder if it recognizes Adam's thumbprint as authorization. A small sputter and the machine roars to life. "Warner had to renew my tracker serum every time I got back. Once it's gone? It's gone." He grins. "So now we can really get the hell out of here."

"But where are we going?" I finally ask.

He shifts into gear before he responds.

"My house."

# THIRTY

"You have a *house?*" I'm too shocked for manners.

Adam laughs and pulls out of the field. The tank is surprisingly fast, surprisingly swift and stealthy. The engine has quieted to a soothing hum, and I wonder if that's why they switched their tanks from gas to electric. It's certainly less conspicuous this way. "Not exactly," he answers. "But a home of sorts. Yeah."

I want to ask and don't want to ask and need to ask and never want to ask. I have to ask. I steel myself. "Your fathe—"

"He's been dead for a while now." Adam's not smiling anymore. His voice is tight with something only I would know how to place. Pain. Bitterness. Anger.

"Oh."

We drive in silence, each of us absorbed in our own thoughts. I don't dare ask what became of his mother. I only wonder how he turned out so well despite having such a despicable father. And I wonder why he ever joined the army if he hates it so much. Right now, I'm too shy to ask. I don't want to infringe on his emotional boundaries.

God knows I have a million of my own.

I peer out the window and strain my eyes to see what

we're passing through, but I can't make out much more than the sad stretches of deserted land I've grown accustomed to. There are no civilians where we are: we're too far from Reestablished settlements and civilian compounds. I notice another tank patrolling the area not 100 feet away, but I don't think it sees us. Adam is driving without headlights, presumably to draw as little attention to us as possible. I wonder how he's even able to navigate. The moon is the only lamp to light our way.

It's eerily quiet.

For a moment I allow my thoughts to drift back to Warner, wondering what must be going on right now, wondering how many people must be searching for me, wondering what lengths he'll go to until he has me back. He wants Adam dead. He wants me alive. He won't stop until I'm trapped beside him.

He can never never never know that I can touch him.

I can only imagine what he'd do if he had access to my body.

I breathe in one quick, sharp, shaky breath and contemplate telling Adam what happened. No. No. No. No. I squeeze my eyes shut and consider I may have misjudged the situation. It was chaotic. My brain was distracted. Maybe I imagined it. Yes.

*Maybe I imagined it.*

It's strange enough that Adam can touch me. The likelihood of there being 2 people in this world who are immune to my touch doesn't seem possible. In fact, the more I think about it, the more I'm determined I must have made a mistake. It could've been anything brushing my leg. Maybe a piece of the sheet Adam abandoned after using it to punch through the window. Maybe a pillow that'd fallen from the bed. Maybe Warner's gloves lying, discarded, on the floor. Yes.

There's no way he could've touched me, because if he had, he would've cried out in agony.

Just like everyone else.

Adam's hand slips silently into mine and I grip his fingers in both my hands, suddenly desperate to reassure myself that he has immunity from me. I'm suddenly desperate to drink in every drop of his being, desperate to savor every moment I've never known before. I suddenly worry that there's an expiration date on this phenomenon. A clock striking midnight. A pumpkin carriage.

The possibility of losing him

The possibility of losing him

The possibility of losing him is 100 years of solitude I don't want to imagine. I don't want my arms to be devoid of his warmth. His touch. His lips, God his lips, his mouth on my neck, his body wrapped around mine, holding me together as if to affirm that my existence on this earth is not for nothing.

Realization is a pendulum the size of the moon. It won't stop slamming into me.

"Juliette?"

I swallow back the bullet in my throat. "Yes?"

"Why are you crying . . . ?" His voice is almost as gentle as his hand as it breaks free from my grip. He touches the tears rolling down my face and I'm so humiliated I almost don't know what to say.

"You can *touch* me," I say for the first time, recognize out loud for the first time. My words fade to a whisper. "You can touch me. You care and I don't know why. You're kind to me and you don't have to be. My own mother didn't care enough to—t-to—" My voice catches and I press my lips together. Glue them shut. Force myself to be still.

I am a rock. A statue. A movement frozen in time. Ice feels nothing at all.

Adam doesn't answer, doesn't say a single word until he pulls off the road and into an old underground parking garage. I realize we've reached some semblance of civilization, but it's pitch-black belowground. I can see next to nothing and once again wonder at how Adam is managing. My eyes fall on the screen illuminated on his dashboard only to realize the tank has night vision. *Of course.*

Adam shuts off the engine. I hear him sigh. I can hardly distinguish his silhouette before I feel his hand on my thigh, his other hand tripping its way up my body to find my face. Warmth spreads through my limbs like molten lava. The tips of my fingers and toes are tingling to life and I have to bite back the shiver aching to rock my frame.

"Juliette," he whispers, and I realize just how close he is. I'm not sure why I haven't evaporated into nothingness. "It's been me and you against the world forever," he says.

"It's always been that way. It's my fault I took so long to do something about it."

"No." I'm shaking my head. "It's not your fault—"

"It is. I fell in love with you a long time ago. I just never had the guts to act on it."

"Because I could've killed you."

He laughs a quiet laugh. "Because I didn't think I deserved you."

I'm one piece of astonishment forged into being. "What?"

He touches his nose to mine. Leans into my neck. Wraps a piece of my hair around his fingers and I can't I can't I can't breathe. "You're so . . . *good*," he whispers.

"But my hands—"

"Have never done anything to hurt anyone."

I'm about to protest when he corrects himself. "Not on purpose." He leans back. I can just barely see him rubbing the side of his neck. "You never fought back," he says after a moment. "I always wondered why. You never yelled or got angry or tried to say anything to anyone," he says, and I know we're both back in third fourth fifth sixth seventh eighth ninth grade all over again. "But damn, you must've read a million books." I know he's smiling when he says it. A pause. "You bothered no one, but you were a moving target every day. You could've fought back. You could've hurt everyone if you wanted to."

"I don't want to hurt anyone." My voice is less than a whisper. I can't get the image of 8-year-old Adam out of my head. Lying on the floor. Broken. Abandoned. Crying into the dirt.

The things people will do for power.

"That's why you'll never be what Warner wants you to be."

I'm staring at a point in the blackness, my mind tortured by possibilities. "How can you be sure?"

His lips are so close to mine. "Because you still give a damn about the world."

I gasp and he's kissing me, deep and powerful and unrestrained. His arms wrap around my back, dipping my body until I'm practically horizontal and I don't care. My head is on the seat, his frame hovering over me, his hands gripping my hips from under my tattered dress and I'm licked by a million flames of wanting so desperate I can hardly inhale. He's a hot bath, a short breath, 5 days of summer pressed into 5 fingers writing stories on my body. I'm an embarrassing mess of nerves crashing into him, controlled by one current of electricity coursing through my core. His scent is assaulting my senses.

His eyes

His hands

His chest

His lips

are at my ear when he speaks. "We're here, by the way." He's breathing harder now than when he was running for his life. I feel his heart pounding against my ribs. His words are a broken whisper. "Maybe we should go inside. It's safer." But he doesn't move.

I almost don't understand what he's talking about. I just nod, my head bobbing on my neck, until I remember he can't see me. I try to remember how to speak, but I'm too focused on the fingers he's running down my thighs to form sentences. There's something about the absolute darkness, about not being able to see what's happening that makes me drunk with a delicious dizziness. "Yes," is all I manage.

He helps me back up to a seated position, leans his forehead against mine. "I'm sorry," he says. "It's so hard for me to stop myself." His voice is dangerously husky; his words tingle on my skin.

I allow my hands to slip up under his shirt and feel him stiffen, swallow. I trace the perfectly sculpted lines of his body. He's nothing but lean muscle. "You don't have to," I tell him.

His heart is racing so fast I can't distinguish it from my own. It's 5,000 degrees in the air between us. His fingers are at the dip right below my hip bone, teasing the small piece of fabric keeping me halfway decent. "Juliette . . ."

"Adam?"

My neck snaps up in surprise. Fear. Anxiety. Adam stops moving, frozen in front of me. I'm not sure he's breathing. I look around but can't find a face to match the voice that called his name and begin to panic before Adam is slamming open the door, flying out before I hear it again.

"Adam . . . is that you?"

It's a boy.

"James!"

The muffled sound of impact, 2 bodies colliding, 2 voices too happy to be dangerous.

"I can't believe it's really you! I mean, well, I thought it was you because I thought I heard something and at first I figured it was nothing but then I decided I should probably check just to be sure because what if it *was* you and—" He pauses. "Wait—what are you doing here?"

"I'm home." Adam laughs a little.

"Really?" James squeaks. "Are you home for good?"

"Yeah." He sighs. "Damn it's good to see you."

"I missed you," James says, suddenly quiet.

One deep breath. "Me too, kid. Me too."

"Hey, so, have you eaten anything? Benny just delivered my dinner package, and I could share some with y—"

"James?"

He pauses. "Yeah?"

"There's someone I want you to meet."

My palms are sweaty. My heart is in my throat. I hear Adam walk back toward the tank and don't realize he's popped his head inside until he hits a switch. A faint emergency light illuminates the cabin. I blink a few times and see a young boy standing about 5 feet away, dirty-blond hair framing a round face with blue eyes that look too familiar. He's pressed his lips together in concentration. He's staring at me.

Adam is opening my door. He helps me to my feet, barely able to control the smile on his face and I'm stunned by the level of my own nervousness. I don't know why I'm so nervous but God I'm nervous. This boy is obviously important to Adam. I don't know why but I feel like this *moment* is important, too. I'm so worried I'm going to ruin everything. I try to fix the ripped folds of my dress, try to soften the wrinkles ironed into the fabric. I run haphazard fingers through my hair. It's useless.

The poor kid will be petrified.

Adam leads me forward. James is a handful of inches short of my height, but it's obvious in his face that he's young, unblemished, untouched by most of the world's harsh realities. I want to revel in the beauty of his innocence.

"James? This is Juliette." Adam glances at me.

"Juliette, this is my brother, James."

# THIRTY-ONE

His brother.

I try to shake off the nerves. I try to smile at the boy studying my face, studying the pathetic pieces of fabric barely covering my body. How did I not know Adam had a brother? How could I have never known?

James turns to Adam. "*This* is Juliette?"

I'm standing here like a lump of nonsense. I don't remember my manners. "You know who I am?"

James spins back in my direction. "Oh yeah. Adam talks about you *a lot*."

I flush and can't help but glance at Adam. He's staring at a point on the floor. He clears his throat.

"It's really nice to meet you," I manage.

James cocks his head. "So do you always dress like that?"

I'd like to die a little.

"Hey, kid," Adam interrupts. "Juliette is going to be staying with us for a little while. Why don't you go make sure you don't have any underwear lying on the floor, huh?"

James looks horrified. He darts into the darkness without another word.

It's quiet for so many seconds I lose count. I hear some kind of drip in the distance.

I take a deep breath. Bite my bottom lip. Try to find the right words. Fail. "I didn't know you had a brother."

Adam hesitates. "Is it okay . . . that I do? We'll all be sharing the same space and I—"

My stomach drops onto my knees. "Of *course* it's okay! I just—I mean—are you sure it's okay—for *him*? If I'm here?"

"There's no underwear *anywhere*," James announces, marching forward into the light. I wonder where he disappeared to, where the house is. He looks at me. "So you're going to be staying with us?"

Adam intervenes. "Yeah. She's going to crash with us for a bit."

James looks from me to Adam back to me again. He sticks out his hand. "Well, it's nice to finally meet you."

All the color drains from my face. My heart is pounding in my ears. My knees are about to break. I can't stop staring at his small hand outstretched, offered to me.

"*James*," Adam says a little curtly.

James starts laughing. "I was only kidding." He drops his hand.

"What?" I can barely breathe. My head is spinning, confused.

"Don't *worry*," James says, still chuckling. "I won't touch you. Adam told me all about your magical powers." He rolls his eyes.

"Adam—told—he—*what*?"

"Hey, maybe we should go inside." Adam clears his throat a little too loudly. "I'll just grab our bags real quick—"

And he jogs off toward the tank. I'm left staring at James. He doesn't conceal his curiosity.

"How old are you?" he asks me.

"Seventeen."

He nods. "That's what Adam said."

I bristle. "What else did Adam tell you about me?"

"He said you don't have parents, either. He said you're like us."

My heart is a stick of butter, melting recklessly on a hot summer day. My voice softens. "How old are *you*?"

"I'll be eleven next year."

I grin. "So you're ten years old?"

He crosses his arms. Frowns. "I'll be twelve in two years."

I think I already love this kid.

The cabin light shuts off and for a moment we're immersed in absolute darkness. A soft *click* and a faint circular glow illuminates the view. Adam has a flashlight.

"Hey, James? Why don't you lead the way for us?"

"Yes, sir!" He skids to a halt in front of Adam's feet, offers us an exaggerated salute, and runs off so quickly there's no possible way to follow him. I can't help the smile spreading across my face.

Adam's hand slips into mine as we move forward. "You okay?"

I squeeze his fingers. "You told your ten-year-old brother about my magical powers?"

He laughs. "I tell him a lot of things."

"Adam?"

"Yeah?"

"Isn't your *house* the first place Warner will go looking for you? Isn't this dangerous?"

"It would be. But according to public records, I don't have a home."

"And your brother?"

"Would be Warner's first target. It's safer for him where I can watch over him. Warner knows I have a brother, he just doesn't know where. And until he figures it out—which he will—we have to prepare."

"To fight?"

"To fight back. Yeah." Even in the dim light of this foreign space I can see the determination holding him together. It makes me want to sing.

I close my eyes. "Good."

"What's taking you so long?" James shouts in the distance.

And we're off.

The parking garage is located underneath an old abandoned office building buried in the shadows. A fire exit leads directly up to the main floor.

James is so excited he's jumping up and down the stairs, running forward a few steps only to run back to complain we're not coming fast enough. Adam catches him from behind and lifts him off the floor. He laughs. "You're going to break your neck."

James protests but only halfheartedly. He's all too happy to have his brother back.

A sharp pang of some distant kind of emotion hits me

in the heart. It hurts in a bittersweet way I can't place. I feel oddly warm and numb at the same time.

Adam punches a pass code into a keypad by a massive steel door. There's a soft *click*, a short *beep*, and he turns the handle.

I'm stunned by what I see inside.

# THIRTY-TWO

It's a full living room, open and plush. A thick rug, soft chairs, one sofa stretched across the wall. Green and red and orange hues, warm lamps softly lit in the large space. It feels more like a home than anything I've ever seen. The cold, lonely memories of my childhood can't even compare. I feel so safe so suddenly it scares me.

"You like it?" Adam is grinning at me, amused no doubt by the look on my face. I manage to pick my jaw up off the floor.

"I love it," I say, out loud or in my head I'm unsure.

"Adam did it," James says, proud, puffing his chest out a little more than necessary. "He made it for me."

"I didn't *make* it," Adam protests, chuckling. "I just . . . cleaned it up a bit."

"You live here by yourself?" I ask James.

He shoves his hands into his pockets and nods. "Benny stays with me a lot, but mostly I'm here alone. I'm lucky, though."

Adam is dropping our bags onto the couch. He runs a hand through his hair and I watch as the muscles in his back flex, tight, pulled together. I watch as he exhales the tension from his body.

I know why, but I ask anyway. "Why are you lucky?"

"Because I have a visitor. None of the other kids have visitors."

"There are other kids here?" I hope I don't look as horrified as I feel.

James is nodding so quickly his head is wobbling on his neck. "Oh yeah. This whole street. All the kids are here. I'm the only one with my own room, though." He gestures around the space. "This is all mine because Adam got it for me. But everyone else has to share. We have school, sort of. And Benny brings me my food packages. Adam says I can play with the other kids but I can't bring them inside." He shrugs. "It's okay."

The reality of what he's saying spreads like poison in the pit of my stomach.

*A street dedicated to orphaned children.*

I wonder how their parents died. I don't wonder for long.

I take inventory of the room and notice a tiny refrigerator and a tiny microwave perched on top, both nestled into a corner, see some cabinets set aside for storage. Adam brought as much stuff as he could—all sorts of canned food and nonperishable items. We both brought our toiletries and multiple sets of clothes. We packed enough to survive for at least a little while.

James pulls a tinfoil package out of the fridge and sticks it in the microwave.

"Wait—James—don't—" I try to stop him.

His eyes are wide, frozen. "What?"

218

"The tinfoil—you can't—you can't put metal in the microwave—"

"What's a microwave?"

I blink so many times the room spins. "What . . . ?"

He pulls the lid off the tinfoil container to reveal a small square. It looks like a bouillon cube. He points to the cube and then nods at the microwave. "It's okay. I always put this in the Automat. Nothing happens."

"It takes the molecular composition of the food and multiplies it." Adam is standing beside me. "It doesn't add any extra nutritional value, but it makes you feel fuller, longer."

"And it's cheap!" James says, grinning as he sticks it back in the contraption.

It astounds me how much has changed. People have become so desperate they're faking *food*.

I have so many questions I'm liable to burst. Adam squeezes my shoulder, gently. He whispers, "We'll talk later, I promise." But I'm an encyclopedia with too many blank pages.

James falls asleep with his head in Adam's lap.

He talked nonstop once he finished his food, telling me all about his sort-of school, and his sort-of friends, and Benny, the elderly lady who takes care of him because "I think she likes Adam better than me but she sneaks me sugar sometimes so it's okay." Everyone has a curfew. No one but soldiers are allowed outside after sunset, each soldier armed and instructed to fire at their own discretion.

"Some people get more food and stuff than other people," James said, but that's because the people are sorted based on what they can provide to The Reestablishment, and not because they're human beings with the right not to starve to death.

My heart cracked a little more with every word he shared with me.

"You don't mind that I talk a lot, huh?" He bit down on his bottom lip and studied me.

"I don't mind at all."

"Everyone says I talk a lot." He shrugged. "But what am I supposed to do when I have so much to say?"

"Hey—about that—" Adam interrupted. "You can't tell anyone we're here, okay?"

James' mouth stopped midmovement. He blinked a few times. He stared hard at his brother. "Not even Benny?"

"No one," Adam said.

For one infinitesimal moment I saw something that looked like raw understanding flash in his eyes. A 10-year-old who can be trusted absolutely. He nodded again and again. "Okay. You were never here."

Adam brushes back wayward strands of hair from James' forehead. He's looking at his brother's sleeping face as if trying to memorize each brushstroke of an oil painting. I'm staring at him staring at James.

I wonder if he knows he's holding my heart in his hand. I take a shaky breath.

Adam looks up and I look down and we're both embarrassed for different reasons.

He whispers, "I should probably put him in bed," but doesn't make an effort to move. James is sound sound sound asleep.

"When was the last time you saw him?" I ask, careful to keep my voice down.

"About six months ago." A pause. "But I talked to him on the phone a lot." Smiles a little. "Told him a lot about you."

I flush. Count my fingers to make sure they're all there. "Didn't Warner monitor your calls?"

"Yeah. But Benny has an untraceable line, and I was always careful to keep it to official reporting, only. In any case, James has known about you for a long time."

"Really . . . ?" I hate that I have to know, but I can hardly help myself. I'm a tangle of butterflies.

He looks up, looks away. Locks eyes with me. Sighs. "Juliette, I've been searching for you since the day you left."

My eyelashes trip into my eyebrows; my jaw drops into my lap.

"I was worried about you," he says quietly. "I didn't know what they were going to do to you."

"Why," I gasp, I swallow, I stumble on words. "Why would you possibly care?"

He leans back against the couch. Runs a free hand over his face. Seasons change. Stars explode. Someone is walking on the moon. "You know I still remember the first day you showed up at school?" He laughs a soft, sad laugh. "Maybe I was too young, and maybe I didn't know much about the world, but there was something about you I was immediately drawn to. It's like I just wanted to be near you, like you had this—this *goodness* I never found in my life. This sweetness that I never found at home. I just wanted to hear you talk. I wanted you to see me, to smile at me. Every single day I promised myself I would talk to you. I wanted to *know* you. But every day I was a coward. And one day you just disappeared.

"I'd heard the rumors, but I knew better. I knew you'd never hurt anyone." He looks down. The earth cracks open and I'm falling into the fissure. "It sounds crazy," he says finally, so quietly. "To think that I cared so much without ever talking to you." He hesitates. "But I couldn't stop thinking about you. I couldn't stop wondering where you went. What would happen to you. I was afraid you'd never fight back."

He's silent for so long I want to bite through my tongue.

"I had to find you," he whispers. "I asked around everywhere and no one had answers. The world kept falling apart. Things were getting worse and I didn't know what to do. I had to take care of James and I had to find a way to live and I didn't know if joining the army would help but I never forgot about you. I always hoped," he falters, "that one day I would see you again."

I've run out of words. My pockets are full of letters I can't string together and I'm so desperate to say something that I say nothing and my heart is about to burst through my chest.

"Juliette . . . ?"

"You found me." 3 syllables. 1 whisper of astonishment.

"Are you . . . upset?"

I look up and for the first time I realize he's nervous. Worried. Uncertain how I'll react to this revelation. I don't know whether to laugh or cry or kiss every inch of his body. I want to fall asleep to the sound of his heart beating in the atmosphere. I want to know he's alive and well, breathing in and out, strong and sane and healthy forever. "You're the only one who ever cared." My eyes are filling with tears and I'm blinking them back and feeling the burn in my throat and everything everything everything hurts. The weight of the entire day crashes into me, threatens to break my bones. I want to cry out in happiness, in agony, in joy and the absence of justice. I want to touch the heart of the only person who ever gave a damn.

"I love you," I whisper. "So much more than you will ever know."

His eyes are a midnight moment filled with memories, the only windows into my world. His jaw is tight. His mouth is tight. He looks up and tries to clear his throat and I know he needs a moment to pull himself together. I tell him he should probably put James in bed. He nods. Cradles his brother to his chest. Gets to his feet and carries James to the storage closet that's become his bedroom.

I watch him walk away with the only family he has left and I know why Adam joined the army.

I know why he suffered through being Warner's whipping boy. I know why he dealt with the horrifying reality of war, why he was so desperate to run away, so ready to run away as soon as possible. Why he's so determined to fight back.

He's fighting for so much more than himself.

# THIRTY-THREE

"Why don't I take a look at those cuts?"

Adam is standing in front of James' door, his hands tucked into his pockets. He's wearing a dark red T-shirt that hugs his torso. His arms are expertly chiseled, professionally painted with tattoos I now know how to recognize. He catches me staring.

"I didn't really have a choice," he says, now examining the consecutive black bands of ink etched into his forearms. "We had to survive. It was the only job I could get."

I meet him across the room, touch the designs on his skin. Nod. "I understand."

He almost laughs, nearly smiles. Shakes his head just a millimeter.

"What?" I jerk my hand away.

"Nothing." He grins. Slips his arms around my waist. "It just keeps hitting me. You're really here. In my house."

Heat rushes up my neck and I fall off a ladder holding a paintbrush dipped in red. Compliments are not things I know how to process. I bite my lip. "Where'd you get your tattoo from?"

"These?" He looks at his arms again.

"No." I reach for his shirt, tugging it up so unsuccessfully he nearly loses his balance. He stumbles back against the wall. I push the material up toward his collar. Fight back a blush. Touch his chest. Touch the bird. "Where'd you get *this* from?"

"Oh." He's looking at me but I'm suddenly distracted by the beauty of his body and the cargo pants set a little too low on his hips. I realize he must've taken his belt off. I force my eyes upward. Allow my fingers to fumble down his abs. He takes a tight breath. "I don't know," he says. "I just—I kept dreaming about this white bird. Birds used to fly, you know."

"You used to dream about it?"

"Yeah. All the time." He smiles a little, exhales a little, remembering. "It was nice. It felt good—hopeful. I wanted to hold on to that memory because I wasn't sure it would last. So I made it permanent."

I cover the tattoo with the palm of my hand. "I used to dream about this bird all the time."

"*This* bird?" His eyebrows could touch the sky.

I nod. "This exact one." Something like realization slides into place. "Until the day you showed up in my cell. I haven't dreamt of it ever since." I peek up at him.

"You're kidding." But he knows I'm not.

I drop his shirt and lean my forehead on his chest. Breathe in the scent of him. He wastes no time pulling me closer. Rests his chin on my head, his hands on my back.

And we stand like that until I'm too old to remember a world without his warmth.

Adam cleans my cuts in a bathroom set a little off to the side of the space. It's a miniature room with a toilet, a sink, a small mirror, and a tiny shower. I love all of it. By the time I get out of the bathroom, finally changed and washed up for bed, Adam is waiting for me in the dark. There are blankets and pillows laid out on the floor and it looks like heaven. I'm so exhausted I could sleep through a few centuries.

I slip in beside him and he scoops me into his arms. The temperature is significantly lower in this place, and Adam is the perfect furnace. I bury my face in his chest and he pulls me tight. I trail my fingers down his naked back, feel the muscles tense under my touch. I rest my hand on the waist of his pants. Hook my finger into a belt loop. Test the taste of the words on my tongue. "I meant it, you know."

His breath is a beat too late. His heart just a beat too fast. "Meant what . . . ?" Though he knows exactly what I mean.

I feel so shy so suddenly. So blind, so unnecessarily bold. I know nothing about what I'm venturing into. All I know is I don't want anyone's hands on me but his. Forever.

Adam leans back and I can just make out the outline of his face, his eyes always shining in the darkness. I stare at his lips when I speak. "I've never asked you to stop." My fingers rest on the button holding his pants together. "Not once."

He's staring at me, his chest rising and falling a few times a second. He seems almost numb with disbelief.

I lean into his ear. "Touch me."

And he's nearly undone.

My face is in his hands and my lips are at his lips and he's kissing me and I'm oxygen and he's dying to breathe. His body is almost on top of mine, one hand in my hair, the other feeling its way down my silhouette, slipping behind my knee to pull me closer, higher, tighter. He drops kisses down my throat like ecstasy, electric energy searing into me, setting me on fire. I'm on the verge of combusting from the sheer thrill of every moment. I want to dive into his being, experience him with all 5 senses, drown in the waves of wonder enveloping my existence.

I want to taste the landscape of his body.

He takes my hands and presses them against his chest, guides my fingers as they trail down the length of his torso before his lips meet mine again and again and again drugging me into a delirium I never want to escape. But it's not enough. It's still not enough. I want to melt into him, trace the form of his figure with my lips alone. My heart is racing through my blood, destroying my self-control, spinning everything into a cyclone of intensity. He breaks for air and I pull him back, aching, desperate, dying for his touch. His hands slip up under my shirt, skirting my sides, touching me like he's never dared to before, and my top is nearly over my head when a door squeaks open. We both freeze.

"Adam . . . ?"

He can hardly breathe. He tries to lower himself onto the pillow beside me but I can still feel his heat, his figure, his heart pounding in my ears. I'm swallowing back a million screams. Adam leans his head up, just a little. Tries to sound normal. "James?"

"Can I come sleep out here with you?"

Adam sits up. He's breathing hard but he's suddenly alert. "Of course you can." A pause. His voice slows, softens. "You have bad dreams?"

James doesn't answer.

Adam is on his feet.

I hear the muffled hiccup of 10-year-old tears, but can barely distinguish the outline of Adam's body holding James together. "I thought you said it was getting better," I hear him whisper, but his words are kind, not accusing.

James says something I can't hear.

Adam picks him up, and I realize how tiny James seems in comparison. They disappear into the bedroom only to return with bedding. Only once James is tucked securely in place a few feet from Adam does he finally give in to exhaustion. His heavy breathing is the only sound in the room.

Adam turns to me. I've been a slice of silence, struck, shocked, cut deep by this reminder. I have no idea what James has witnessed at such a tender age. I have no idea what Adam has had to endure in leaving him behind. I have no idea how people live anymore. How they survive.

~~I don't know what's become of my parents.~~

Adam brushes my cheek. Slips me into his arms. Says, "I'm sorry," and I kiss the apology away.

"When the time is right," I tell him.

He swallows. Leans into my neck. Inhales. His hands are under my shirt. Up my back.

I bite back a gasp. "Soon."

# THIRTY-FOUR

Adam and I forced ourselves 5 feet apart last night, but somehow I wake up in his arms. He's breathing softly, evenly, steadily, a warm hum in the morning air. I blink, peering into the daylight only to be met by a set of big blue eyes on a 10-year-old's face.

"How come you can touch *him*?" James is standing over us with his arms crossed, back to the stubborn boy I remember. There's no trace of fear, no hint of tears threatening to spill down his face. It's like last night never happened. *"Well?"* His impatience startles me.

I jump away from Adam's uncovered upper half so quickly it jolts him awake. A little.

He reaches for me. "Juliette . . . ?"

"You're touching a *girl*!"

Adam sits up so quickly he tangles in the sheets and falls back on his elbows. "Jesus, James—"

"You were sleeping next to a *girl*!"

Adam opens and closes his mouth several times. He glances at me. Glances at his brother. Shuts his eyes and finally sighs. Runs a hand through his morning hair. "I don't know what you want me to say."

"I thought you said she couldn't touch anyone." James is staring at me now, suspicious.

"She can't."

"Except for you?"

"Right. Except for me."

~~And Warner.~~

"She can't touch anyone except for you."

~~And Warner.~~

"Right."

"That seems awfully *convenient*." James narrows his eyes.

Adam laughs out loud. "Where'd you learn to talk like that?"

James frowns. "Benny says that a lot. She says my excuses are 'awfully convenient.'" He makes air quotes with two fingers. "She says it means I don't believe you. And I don't believe you."

Adam gets to his feet. The early morning light filters through the small windows at the perfect angle, the perfect moment. He's bathed in gold, his muscles taut, his pants still a little low on his hips and I have to force myself to think straight. I'm shocked by my own lack of self-control, but I'm not sure I know how to contain these feelings. Adam makes me hungry for things I never knew I could have.

I watch as he drapes an arm over his brother's shoulders before squatting down to meet his gaze. "Can I talk to you about something?" he says. "Privately?"

"Just me and you?" James glances at me out of the corner of his eye.

"Yeah. Just me and you."

"Okay."

I watch the two of them disappear into James' room and wonder what Adam is going to tell him. It takes me a moment to realize James must feel threatened by my sudden appearance. He finally sees his brother after nearly 6 months only to have him come home with a strange girl with crazy magical powers. I nearly laugh at the idea. If only it were magic that made me this way.

I don't want James to think I'm taking Adam away from him.

I slip back under the covers and wait. The morning is cool and brisk and my thoughts begin to wander to Warner. I need to remember that we're not safe. Not yet, maybe not ever. I need to remember never to get too comfortable. I sit up. Pull my knees to my chest and wrap my arms around my ankles.

I wonder if Adam has a plan.

James' door squeaks open. The two brothers step out, the younger before the older. James looks a little pink and he can hardly meet my eyes. He looks embarrassed and I wonder if Adam punished him.

My heart fails for a moment.

Adam claps James on the shoulder. Squeezes. "You okay?"

"I know what a *girlfriend* is—"

"I never said you didn't—"

"So you're his *girlfriend*?" James crosses his arms, looks at me.

233

There are 400 cotton balls caught in my windpipe. I look at Adam because I don't know what else to do.

"Hey, maybe you should be getting ready for school, huh?" Adam opens the refrigerator and hands James a new foil package. I assume it's his breakfast.

"I don't *have* to go," James protests. "It's not like a *real* school, no one *has* to—"

"I want you to," Adam cuts him off. He turns back to his brother with a small smile. "Don't worry. I'll be here when you get back."

James hesitates. "You promise?"

"Yeah." Another grin. Nods him over. "Come here."

James runs forward and clings to Adam like he's afraid he'll disappear. Adam pops the foil food into the Automat and presses a button. He musses James' hair. "You need to get a haircut, kid."

James wrinkles his nose. "I like it."

"It's a little long, don't you think?"

James lowers his voice. "I think *her* hair is really long."

James and Adam glance back at me and I melt into pink Play-Doh. I touch my hair without intending to, suddenly self-conscious. I look down. I've never had a reason to cut my hair. I've never even had the tools. No one offers me sharp objects.

I chance a peek and see Adam is still staring at me. James is staring at the Automat.

"I like her hair," Adam says, and I'm not sure who he's talking to.

I watch the two of them as Adam helps his brother get ready for school. James is so full of life, so full of energy, so excited to have his brother around. It makes me wonder what it must be like for a 10-year-old to live on his own. What it must be like for all the kids who live on this street.

I'm itching to get up and change, but I'm not sure what I should do. I don't want to take up the bathroom in case James needs it, or if Adam needs it. I don't want to take up any more space than I already have. It feels so private, so personal, this relationship between Adam and James. It's the kind of bond I've never had, will never have. But being around so much love has managed to thaw my frozen parts into something human. I *feel* human. Like maybe I could be a part of this world. Like maybe I don't have to be a monster. Maybe I'm not a monster.

Maybe things can change.

# THIRTY-FIVE

James is at school, Adam is in the shower, and I'm staring at a bowl of granola Adam left for me to eat. It feels so wrong to be eating this food when James has to eat the unidentifiable substance in the foil container. But Adam says James is allocated a certain portion for every meal, and he's required to eat it by law. If he's found wasting it or discarding it, he could be punished. All the orphans are expected to eat the foil food that goes in their Automat. James claims it "doesn't taste too bad."

I shiver slightly in the cool morning air and smooth a hand over my hair, still damp from the shower. The water here isn't hot. It isn't even warm. It's freezing. Warm water is a luxury.

Someone is pounding on the door.

I'm up.
Spinning.
Scanning.
Scared.
*They found us* is the only thing I can think of. My stomach is a flimsy crepe, my heart a raging woodpecker, my blood a river of anxiety.
Adam is in the shower.

James is at school.

~~I'm absolutely defenseless.~~

I rummage through Adam's duffel bag until I find what I'm looking for. 2 guns, 1 for each hand. 2 hands, just in case the guns fail. I'm finally wearing the kind of clothes that would be comfortable to fight in. I take a deep breath and beg my hands not to shake.

The pounding gets harder.

I point the guns at the door.

"Juliette . . . ?"

I spin back to see Adam staring at me, the guns, the door. His hair is wet. His eyes are wide. He nods toward the extra gun in my hand and I toss it to him without a word.

"If it were Warner he wouldn't be knocking," he says, though he doesn't lower his weapon.

I know he's right. Warner would've shot down the door, used explosives, killed a hundred people to get to me. He certainly wouldn't wait for me to open the door. Something calms inside of me but I won't allow myself to get comfortable. "Who do you think—?"

"It might be Benny—she usually checks up on James—"

"But wouldn't she know he'd be at school right now?"

"No one else knows where I live—"

The pounding is getting weaker. Slower. There's a low, guttural sound of agony.

Adam and I lock eyes.

One more fist flailing into the door. A slump. Another moan. The thud of a body against the door.

I flinch.

Adam rakes a hand through his hair.

"Adam!" someone cries. Coughs. "Please, man, if you're in there—"

I freeze. The voice sounds familiar.

Adam's spine straightens in an instant. His lips are parted, his eyes astonished. He punches in the pass code and turns the latch. Points his gun toward the door as he eases it open.

*"Kenji?"*

A short wheeze. A muffled groan. "Shit, man, what took you so long?"

"What the hell are you *doing here*?" *Click.* I can hardly see through the small slit of the door, but it's clear Adam isn't happy to have company. "Who sent you here? Who are you with?"

Kenji swears a few more times under his breath. *"Look at me,"* he demands, though it sounds more like a plea. "You think I came up here to kill you?"

Adam pauses. Breathes. Doubts. "I have no problem putting a bullet in your back."

"Don't worry, bro. I already have a bullet in my back. Or my leg. Or some shit. I don't even know."

Adam opens the door. "Get up."

"It's all right, I don't mind if you drag my ass inside."

Adam works his jaw. "I don't want your blood on my carpet. It's not something my brother needs to see."

Kenji stumbles up and staggers into the room. I'd heard his voice once before, but never seen his face. Though this probably isn't the best time for first impressions. His eyes are puffy, swollen, purple; there's a huge gash in the side of his forehead. His lip is split, slightly bleeding, his body slumped and broken. He winces, takes short breaths as he moves. His clothes are ripped to shreds, his upper body covered by nothing but a tank top, his well-developed arms cut and bruised. I'm amazed he didn't freeze to death. He doesn't seem to notice me until he does.

He stops. Blinks. Breaks into a ridiculous smile dimmed only by a slight grimace from the pain. "Holy shit," he says, still drinking me in. "Holy *shit*." He tries to laugh. "Dude, you're *insane*—"

"The bathroom is over here." Adam is set in stone.

Kenji moves forward but keeps looking back. I point the gun at his face. He laughs harder, flinches, wheezes a bit. "Dude, you ran off with the crazy chick! You ran off with the psycho girl!" he's calling after Adam. "I thought they made that shit up. What the hell were you thinking? What are you going to do with the psycho chick? No *wonder* Warner wants you dead—OW, MAN, what the *hell*—"

"She's not crazy. And she's not *deaf*, asshole."

The door slams shut behind them and I can only make out their muffled argument. I have a feeling Adam doesn't want me to hear what he has to say to Kenji. Either that, or it's the screaming.

I have no idea what Adam is doing, but I assume it has something to do with dislodging a bullet from Kenji's body and generally repairing the rest of his wounds as best he can. Adam has a pretty extensive first aid supply and strong, steady hands. I wonder if he picked up these skills in the army. Maybe for taking care of himself. Or maybe his brother. It would make sense.

Health insurance was a dream we lost a long time ago.

I've been holding this gun in my hand for nearly an hour. I've been listening to Kenji scream for nearly an hour and I only know that because I like counting the seconds as they pass by. I have no idea what time it is. I think there's a clock in James' bedroom but I don't want to go into his room without permission.

I stare at the gun in my hand, at the smooth, heavy metal, and I'm surprised to find that I enjoy the way it feels in my grip. Like an extension of my body. It doesn't frighten me anymore.

It frightens me more that I might use it.

The bathroom door opens and Adam walks out. He has a small towel in his hands. I get to my feet. He offers me a small smile. He reaches into the tiny fridge for the even tinier freezer section. Grabs a couple of ice cubes and drops them into the towel. Disappears into the bathroom again.

I sit back on the couch.

It's raining today. The sky is weeping for us.

Adam comes out of the bathroom, this time empty-handed, still alone.

I stand back up.

He rubs his forehead, the back of his neck. Meets me on the couch. "I'm sorry," he says.

My eyes are wide. "For what?"

"Everything." He sighs. "Kenji was a sort of friend of mine back on base. Warner had him tortured after we left. For information."

I swallow a gasp.

"He says he didn't say anything—didn't have anything to say, really—but he got messed up pretty bad. I have no idea if his ribs are broken or just bruised, but I managed to get the bullet out of his leg."

I take his hand. Squeeze.

"He got shot running away," Adam says after a moment.

And something slams into my consciousness. I panic. "The tracker serum—"

Adam nods, his eyes heavy, distraught. "I think it might be dysfunctional, but I have no way of knowing for sure. I do know that if it were working as it should, Warner would be here by now. But we can't risk it. We have to get out, and we have to get rid of Kenji before we go."

I'm shaking my head, caught between colliding currents of disbelief. "How did he even *find* you?"

Adam's face hardens. "He started screaming before I could ask."

"And James?" I whisper, almost afraid to wonder.

Adam drops his head into his hands. "As soon as he gets home, we have to go. We can use this time to prepare." He meets my eyes. "I can't leave James behind. It's not safe for him here anymore."

I touch his cheek and he leans into my hand, holds my palm against his face. Closes his eyes.

*"Son of a motherless goat—"*

Adam and I break apart. I'm blushing past my hairline. Adam looks annoyed. Kenji is leaning against the wall in the bathroom hallway, holding the makeshift ice pack to his face. Staring at us.

"You can *touch* her? I mean—shit, I just *saw* you touch her but that's not even—"

"You have to go," Adam says to him. "You've already left a chemical trace leading right to my home. We need to leave, and you can't come with us."

"Oh hey—whoa—hold on." Kenji stumbles into the living room, wincing as he puts pressure on his leg. "I'm not trying to slow you down, man. I know a place. A safe place. Like, a legit, super-safe place. I can take you. I can show you how to get there. I know a guy."

"Bullshit." Adam is still angry. "How did you even find me? How did you manage to show up at my *door*, Kenji? I don't trust you—"

"I don't know, man. I swear I don't remember what happened. I don't know where I was running after a certain point. I was just jumping fences. I found a huge field with an old shed. Slept in there for a while. I think I blacked out at one point, either from the pain or from the cold—it is cold as *hell* out here—and the next thing I know, some dude is carrying me. Drops me off at your door. Tells me to shut up about Adam, because Adam lives right here." He grins. Tries to wink. "I guess I was dreaming about you in my sleep."

242

"Wait—what?" Adam leans forward. "What do you mean some guy was carrying you? What guy? What was his name? How did he know *my* name?"

"I don't know. He didn't tell me, and it's not like I had the presence of mind to ask. But dude was *huge*. I mean, he had to be if he was going to lug my ass around."

"You can't honestly expect me to believe you."

"You have no choice." Kenji shrugs.

"Of course I have a choice." Adam is on his feet. "I have no reason to trust you. No reason to believe a word that's coming out of your mouth."

"Then why am I here with a bullet in my leg? Why hasn't Warner found you yet? Why am I *unarmed*—"

"This could be a part of your plan!"

"And you helped me anyway!" Kenji dares to raise his voice. "Why didn't you just let me die? Why didn't you shoot me dead? Why did you *help* me?"

Adam falters. "I don't know."

"You *do* know. You *know* I'm not here to mess you up. I took a goddamn beating for you—"

"You weren't protecting any information of mine."

"Well, shit, man, what the hell do you want me to say? They were going to *kill* my ass. I had to run. It wasn't my fault some dude dropped me off at your door—"

"This isn't just about *me*, don't you understand? I've worked so hard to find a safe place for my brother and in one morning you ruined *years* of planning. What the hell am I supposed to do now? I have to run until I can find a

243

way to keep him safe. He's too young to have to deal with this—"

"We're *all* too young to have to deal with this shit." Kenji is breathing hard. "Don't fool yourself, bro. No one should have to see what we've seen. No one should have to wake up in the morning and find dead bodies in their living room, but shit happens. We deal with it, and we find a way to *survive*. You're not the only one with problems."

Adam sinks into the sofa. 80 pounds of worry weigh down his shoulders. He leans forward with his head in his hands.

Kenji stares at me. I stare back.

He grins and hobbles forward. "You know, you're pretty sexy for a psycho chick."

*Click.*

Kenji is backing up with his hands in the air. Adam is pressing a gun to his forehead. "Show some respect, or I will burn it into your skull."

"I was *kidding*—"

"Like hell you were."

"Damn, Adam, calm the hell down—"

"Where's the 'super-safe place' you can take us?" I'm up, gun still gripped in my hand. I move into position next to Adam. "Or are you making that up?"

Kenji lights up. "No, that's real. Very real. In fact, I may or may not have mentioned something about you. And the dude who runs the place may or may not be ridiculously interested in meeting you."

"You think I'm some kind of freak you can show off to your friends?" Locked. Loaded.

Kenji clears his throat. "Not a freak. Just . . . interesting."

I point my gun at his nose. "I'm so interesting I can kill you with my bare hands."

A barely perceptible flash of fear flickers in his eyes. He swallows a few gallons of humility. Tries to smile. "You sure you're not crazy?"

"No." I cock my head. "I'm not sure."

Kenji grins. Looks me up and down. "Well damn. But you make crazy sound so *good*."

"I'm about five inches from breaking your face," Adam warns him, his voice like steel, his body stiff with anger, his eyes narrowed, unflinching. There's no hint of humor in his expression. "I don't need another reason."

"What?" Kenji laughs, undeterred. "I haven't been this close to a chick in *way too long*, bro. And crazy or not—"

"I'm not interested."

Kenji turns to face me. "Well I'm not sure I blame you. I look like hell right now. But I clean up okay." He attempts a grin. "Give me a couple days. You might change your mind—"

Adam elbows him in the face and doesn't apologize.

# THIRTY-SIX

Kenji is swearing, bleeding, running out of expletives and tripping his way toward the bathroom, holding his nose together.

Adam pulls me into James' bedroom.

"Tell me something," he says. He stares up at the ceiling, takes a hard breath. "Tell me anything—"

I try to focus his eyes, grasp his hands, gentle gentle gentle. I wait until he's looking at me. "Nothing is going to happen to James. We'll keep him safe. I promise."

His eyes are full of pain like I've never seen them before. He parts his lips. Presses them together. Changes his mind a million times until his words tumble through the air between us. "He doesn't even know about our dad." It's the first time he's acknowledged the issue. It's the first time he's acknowledged that I know anything about it. "I never wanted him to know. I made up stories for him. I wanted him to have a chance to be *normal*." His lips are spelling secrets and my ears are spilling ink, staining my skin with his stories. "I don't want anyone to touch him. I don't want to screw him up. I can't—God I can't let it happen," he says to me. Hushed. Quiet.

I've searched the world for all the right words and my mouth is full of nothing.

"It's never enough," he whispers. "I can never do enough. He still wakes up screaming. He still cries himself to sleep. He sees things I can't control." He blinks a million times. "So many people, Juliette."

I hold my breath.

"Dead."

I touch the word on his lips and he kisses my fingers. His eyes are two pools of perfection, open, honest, humble. "I don't know what to do," he says, and it's like a confession that costs him so much more than I can understand. Control is slipping through his fingers and he's desperate to hold on. *"Tell me what to do."*

I can hear our heartbeats in the silence between us. I study the shape of his lips, the strong lines of his face, the eyelashes any girl would kill for, the deep dark blue of the eyes I've learned to swim in. I offer him the only possibility I have. "Kenji's plan might be worth considering."

"You trust him?" Adam leans back, surprised.

"I don't think he's lying about knowing a place we can go."

"I don't know if that's a good idea."

"Why not . . . ?"

Something that might not be a laugh. "I might kill him before we even get there."

My lips twist into a sad smile. "There isn't any other place for us to hide, is there?"

The sun is revolving around the moon when he responds. He shakes his head. Once. Fast. Tight.

I squeeze his hand. "Then we have to try."

"What the hell are you doing in there?" Kenji shouts through the door. Pounds it a couple times. "I mean, shit, man, I don't think there's *ever* a bad time to get naked, but now is probably not the best time for a nooner. So unless you want to get killed, I suggest you get your ass out here. We have to get ready to go."

"I might kill him right now," Adam changes his mind.

I take his face in my hands, tip up on my toes and kiss him. His lips are 2 pillows, so soft, so sweet. "I love you."

He's looking into my eyes and looking at my mouth and his voice is a husky whisper. "Yeah?"

"Absolutely."

The 3 of us are packed and ready to go before James comes home from school. Adam and I collected the most important basic necessities: food, clothes, money Adam saved up. He keeps looking around the small space like he can't believe he's lost it so easily. I can only imagine how much work he put into it, how hard he tried to make a home for his little brother. My heart is in pieces for him.

His friend is an entirely different species.

Kenji is nursing new bruises, but seems in reasonable spirits, excited for reasons I can't fathom. He's oddly resilient and upbeat. It seems impossible to discourage him and I can't help but admire his determination. But he won't stop staring at me.

"So how come you can touch Adam?" he says after a moment.

"I don't know."

He snorts. "Bull."

I shrug. I don't feel the need to convince him that I have absolutely no idea how I got so lucky.

"How'd you even know you could touch him? Some kind of sick experiment?"

I hope I'm not blushing. "Where's this place you're taking us?"

"Why are you changing the subject?" He's grinning. I'm sure he's grinning. I refuse to look at him, though. "Maybe you can touch *me*, too. Why don't you try?"

"You don't want me to touch you."

"Maybe I do." He's definitely grinning.

"Maybe you should leave her alone before I put that bullet back in your leg," Adam offers.

"I'm sorry—is a lonely man not allowed to make a move, Kent? Maybe I'm actually interested. Maybe you should back the hell off and let her speak for herself."

Adam runs a hand through his hair. Always the same hand. Always through his hair. He's flustered. Frustrated. Maybe even embarrassed.

"I'm still not interested," I remind him, an edge to my voice.

"Yes, but let's not forget that *this*"—he motions to his battered face—"is not permanent."

"Well, I'm permanently uninterested." I want so badly to tell him that I'm unavailable. I want to tell him that I'm in a serious relationship. I want to tell him that Adam's made me promises.

But I can't.

I have no idea what it means to be in a relationship. I don't know if saying "I love you" is code for "mutually exclusive," and I don't know if Adam was serious when he told James I was his girlfriend. Maybe it was an excuse, a cover, an easy answer to an otherwise complicated question. I wish he would say something to Kenji—I wish he would tell him that we're together officially, exclusively.

But he doesn't.

And I don't know why.

"I don't think you should decide until the swelling goes down," Kenji continues matter-of-factly. "It's only fair. I have a pretty spectacular face."

Adam chokes on a cough that I think was a laugh.

"You know, I could've sworn we used to be cool," Kenji says, leveling his gaze at Adam.

"I can't remember why."

Kenji bristles. "Is there something you want to say to me?"

"I don't trust you."

"Then why am I still here?"

"Because I trust *her*."

Kenji turns to look at me. He manages a goofy smile. "Aw, you trust me?"

"As long as I have a clear shot." I tighten my hold on the gun in my hand.

His grin is crooked. "I don't know why, but I kind of like it when you threaten me."

"That's because you're an idiot."

"Nah." He shakes his head. "You've got a sexy voice. Makes everything sound naughty."

Adam stands up so suddenly he nearly knocks over the coffee table.

Kenji bursts out laughing, wheezing against the pain of his injuries. "Calm down, Kent, *damn*. I'm just messing with you guys. I like seeing psycho chick get all intense." He glances at me, lowers his voice. "I mean that as a compliment—because, you know"—he waves a haphazard hand in my direction—"psycho kind of works for you."

"What the hell is wrong with you?" Adam turns on him.

"What the hell is wrong with *you*?" Kenji crosses his arms, annoyed. "Everyone is so uptight in here."

Adam squeezes the gun in his hand. Walks to the door. Walks back. He's pacing.

"And don't worry about your brother," Kenji adds. "I'm sure he'll be here soon."

Adam doesn't laugh. He doesn't stop pacing. His jaw twitches. "I'm not worried about my brother. I'm trying to decide whether to shoot you now or later."

"Later," Kenji says, collapsing onto the couch. "You still need me right now."

Adam tries to speak but he's out of time.

The door clicks, beeps, unlatches open.

James is home.

# THIRTY-SEVEN

"I'm really happy you're taking it so well—I am—but James, this really isn't something to be excited about. We're running for our lives."

"But we're doing it *together*," he says for the fifth time, a huge grin overcrowding his face. He took a liking to Kenji almost too quickly, and now the pair of them are conspiring to turn our predicament into some kind of elaborate mission. "And I can *help*!"

"No, it's not—"

"Of course you can—"

Adam and Kenji speak at the same time. Kenji recovers first. "Why can't he help? Ten years old is old enough to help."

"That's not your call," Adam says, careful to control his voice. I know he's staying calm for his brother's sake. "And it's none of your business."

"I'll finally get to come *with* you," James says, undeterred. "And I want to help."

James took the news in stride. He didn't even flinch when Adam explained the real reason why he was home, and why we were together. I thought seeing Kenji's bruised and battered face would scare him, unnerve him, instill a sense of fear in his heart, but James was eerily unmoved. It occurred to me he must've seen much worse.

Adam takes a few deep breaths before turning to Kenji. "How far?"

"By foot?" Kenji looks uncertain for the first time. "At least a few hours. If we don't do anything stupid, we should be there by nightfall."

"And if we take a car?"

Kenji blinks. His surprise dissolves into an enormous grin. "Well, shit, Kent, why didn't you say so sooner?"

"Watch your mouth around my brother."

James rolls his eyes. "I hear worse stuff than that *every day*. Even Benny uses bad words."

"*Benny?*" Adam's eyebrows stumble up his forehead.

"Yup."

"What does she—" He stops. Changes his mind. "That doesn't mean it's okay for you to keep hearing it."

"I'm almost eleven!"

"Hey, little man," Kenji interrupts. "It's okay. It's my fault. I should be more careful. Besides, there are ladies present." Kenji winks at me.

I look away. Look around.

It's difficult for *me* to leave this humble home, so I can only imagine what Adam must be experiencing right now. I think James is too excited about the dangerous road ahead of us to realize what's happening. To truly understand that he'll never be coming back here.

We're all fugitives running for our lives.

"So, what—you stole a car?" Kenji asks.

"A tank."

Kenji barks out a laugh. "NICE."

"It's a little conspicuous for daytime, though."

"What's *conspicuous* mean?" James asks.

"It's a little too . . . noticeable." Adam cringes.

"*SHIT*." Kenji stumbles up to his feet.

"I told you to watch your mouth—"

"Do you hear that?"

"Hear what—?"

Kenji's eyes are darting in every direction. "Is there another way out of here?"

Adam is up. "JAMES—"

James runs to his brother's side. Adam checks his gun. I'm slinging bags over my back, Adam is doing the same, his attention diverted by the front door.

"HURRY—"

"How close—?"

"THERE'S NO TIME—"

"What do you—"

"KENT, RUN—"

And we're running, following Adam into James' room. Adam rips a curtain off of one wall to reveal a hidden door just as 3 beeps sound from the living room.

Adam shoots the lock on the exit door.

Something explodes not 15 feet behind us. The sound shatters in my ears, vibrates through my body. I nearly collapse from the impact. Gunshots are everywhere. Footsteps are pounding into the house but we're already running through the exit. Adam hauls James up and into his arms and we're flying through the sudden burst of light blinding our way through the streets. The rain has stopped. The roads are slick and muddy. There are children everywhere, bright colors of small bodies suddenly screaming at our approach. There's no point being inconspicuous anymore.

They've already found us.

Kenji is lagging behind, stumbling his way through the last of his adrenaline rush. We turn into a narrow alleyway and he slumps against the wall. "I'm sorry," he pants, "I can't—you can leave me—"

"We can't leave you—," Adam shouts, looking everywhere, drinking in our surroundings.

"That's sweet, bro, but it's okay—"

"We need you to show us where to go!"

"Well, *shit*—"

"You said you would help us—"

"I thought you said you had a *tank*—"

"If you hadn't noticed, there's been an unexpected change of plans—"

"I can't keep up, Kent. I can barely walk—"

"You have to *try*—"

*"There are rebels on the loose. They are armed and ready to fire. Curfew is now in effect. Everyone return to their homes immediately. There are rebels on the loose. They are armed and ready to fi—"*

The loudspeakers sound around the streets, drawing

attention to our bodies huddled together in the narrow alley. A few people see us and scream. Boots are getting louder. Gunshots are getting wilder.

I take a moment to analyze the surrounding buildings and realize we're not in a settled compound. The street James lives on is unregulated turf: a series of abandoned office buildings crammed together, leftovers from our old lives. I don't understand why he's not living in a compound like the rest of the population. I don't have time to figure out why I only see two age groups represented, why the elderly and the orphaned are the only residents, why they've been dumped on illegal land with soldiers who are not supposed to be here. I'm afraid to consider the answers to my own questions and in a panicked moment I fear for James' life. I spin around as we run, glimpsing his small body bundled in Adam's arms.

His eyes are squeezed shut so tight I'm sure it hurts.

Adam swears under his breath. He kicks down the first door we can find of a deserted building and yells for us to follow him inside.

"I need you to stay here," he says to Kenji. "And I'm out of my mind, but I need to leave James with you. I need you to watch out for him. They're looking for Juliette, and they're looking for *me*. They won't even expect to find you two."

"What are you going to do?" Kenji asks.

"I need to steal a car. Then I'll come back for you." James doesn't even protest as Adam puts him down. His little lips are white. His eyes wide. His hands trembling. "I'll come back for you, James," Adam says again. "I promise."

James nods over and over and over again. Adam kisses his head, once, hard, fast. Drops our duffel bags on the floor. Turns to Kenji. "If you let anything happen to him, I will kill you."

Kenji doesn't laugh. He doesn't scowl. He takes a deep breath. "I'll take care of him."

"Juliette?"

He takes my hand, and we disappear into the streets.

# THIRTY-EIGHT

The roads are packed with pedestrians trying to escape. Adam and I hide our guns in the waistbands of our pants, but our wild eyes and jerky movements seem to give us away. Everyone stays away from us, darting in opposite directions, some squeaking, shouting, crying, dropping the things in their hands. But for all the people, I don't see a single car in sight. They must be hard to come by, especially in this area.

Adam pushes me to the ground just as a bullet flies past my head. He shoots down another door and we run through the ruins toward another exit, trapped in the maze of what used to be a clothing store. Gunshots and footsteps are close behind. There must be at least a hundred soldiers following us through these streets, clustered in different groups, dispersed in different areas of the city, ready to capture and kill.

But I know they won't kill me.

It's Adam I'm worried about.

I try to stay as close as possible to his body because I'm certain Warner has given them orders to bring me back alive. My efforts, however, are weak at best. Adam has enough height and muscle to dwarf me. Anyone with an excellent shot would be able to target him. They could shoot him right in the head.

Right in front of me.

He turns to fire two shots. One falls short. Another elicits a strangled cry. We're still running.

Adam doesn't say anything. He doesn't tell me to be brave. He doesn't ask me if I'm okay, if I'm scared. He doesn't offer me encouragement or assure me that we'll be just fine. He doesn't tell me to leave him behind and save myself. He doesn't tell me to watch his brother in case he dies.

He doesn't need to.

We both understand the reality of our situation. Adam could be shot right now. I could be captured at any moment. This entire building might suddenly explode. Someone could've discovered Kenji and James. We might all die today. The facts are obvious.

But we know we need to take the chance just the same.

Because moving forward is the only way to survive.

The gun is growing slick in my hands, but I hold on to it anyway. My legs are screaming against the pain, but I push them faster anyway. My lungs are sawing my rib cage in half, but I force them to process oxygen anyway. I have to keep moving. There's no time for human deficiencies.

The fire escape in this building is nearly impossible to find. Our feet pound the tiled floors, our hands searching through the bleak light for some kind of outlet, some kind of access to the streets. This building is larger than we anticipated, massive, with hundreds of possible directions. I realize it must have been a *warehouse* and not just a store. Adam ducks behind an abandoned desk, pulling me down with him.

"Don't be stupid, Kent—you can only run for so long!" someone shouts. The voice isn't more than 10 feet away.

Adam swallows. Clenches his jaw. The people trying to kill him are the same ones he used to eat lunch with. Train with. Live with. He *knows* these guys. I wonder if that knowledge makes this worse.

"Just give us the girl," a new voice adds. "Just give us the girl and we won't shoot you. We'll pretend we lost you. We'll let you go. Warner only wants the girl."

Adam is breathing hard. He grips the gun in his hand. Pops his head out for a split second and fires. Someone falls to the floor, screaming.

"KENT, YOU SON OF A—"

Adam uses the moment to run. We jump out from behind the desk and fly toward a stairwell. Gunshots miss us by millimeters. I wonder if these two men are the only ones who followed us inside.

The spiral staircase winds into a lower level, a basement of some kind. Someone is trying to aim for Adam, but our erratic movements make it almost impossible. The chance of him hitting me instead are too high. He's unleashing a mass of expletives in our wake.

Adam knocks things over as we run, trying to create any kind of distraction, any kind of hazard to slow down the soldier behind us. I spot a pair of storm cellar doors and realize this area must've been ravaged by tornadoes. The weather is turbulent; natural disasters are common. Cyclones must have ripped this city apart. "Adam—" I tug on his arm. We hide behind a low wall. I point to our only possible escape route.

He squeezes my hand. "Good eye." But we don't move until the air shifts around us. A misstep. A muffled cry. It's almost blindingly black down here; it's obvious the electricity was disconnected a long time ago. The soldier has tripped on one of the obstacles Adam left behind.

Adam holds the gun close to his chest. Takes a deep breath. Turns and takes a swift shot.

His aim is excellent.

An uncontrolled explosion of curse words confirms it. Adam takes a hard breath. "I'm only shooting to disable," he says. "Not to kill."

"I know," I tell him. Though I wasn't sure.

We run for the doors and Adam struggles to pull the latch open. It's nearly rusted shut. We're getting desperate. I don't know how long it'll be until we're discovered by another set of soldiers. I'm about to suggest we shoot it open when Adam finally manages to break it free.

He kicks open the doors and we stumble out onto the street. There are 3 cars to choose from.

I'm so happy I could cry.

"It's about time," he says.

But it's not Adam who says it.

# THIRTY-NINE

There's blood everywhere.

Adam is on the ground, clutching his body, but I don't know where he's been shot. There are soldiers swarming around him and I'm clawing at the arms holding me back, kicking the air, crying out into the emptiness. Someone is dragging me away and I can't see what they've done to Adam. Pain is seizing my limbs, cramping my joints, breaking every single bone in my body. I want to shriek through the sky, I want to fall to my knees and sob into the earth. I don't understand why the agony isn't finding escape in my screams. Why my mouth is covered with someone else's hand.

"If I let go, you have to promise not to scream," he says to me.

He's touching my face with his bare hands and I don't know where I dropped my gun.

Warner drags me into a still-functioning building and kicks open a door. Hits a switch. Fluorescent lights flicker on with a dull hum. There are paintings taped to the walls, alphabet rainbows stapled to corkboards. Small tables scattered across the room. We're in a classroom.

I wonder if this is where James goes to school.

Warner drops his hand. His glassy green eyes are so delighted I'm petrified. "God I missed you," he says to me. "You didn't actually think I'd let you go so easily?"

"You shot Adam," are the only words I can think of. My mind is muddled with disbelief. I keep seeing his beautiful body crumpled on the ground, red red red. I need to know if he's alive. He has to be alive.

Warner's eyes flash. "Kent is dead."

"*No—*"

Warner backs me into a corner and I realize I've never been so defenseless in my life. Never so vulnerable. 17 years I spent wishing my curse away, but in this moment I'm more desperate than ever to have it back. Warner's eyes warm unexpectedly. His constant shifts in emotion are difficult to anticipate. Difficult to counter.

"Juliette," he says. He touches my hand so gently it startles me. "Did you notice? It seems I am immune to your gift." He studies my eyes. "Isn't that incredible? Did you notice?" he asks again. "When you tried to escape? Did you feel it . . . ?"

Warner who misses absolutely nothing. Warner who absorbs every single detail.

Of course he knows.

But I'm shocked by the tenderness in his voice. The sincerity with which he wants to know. He's like a feral dog, crazed and wild, thirsty for chaos, simultaneously aching for recognition and acceptance.

Love.

"We can really be together," he says to me, undeterred by my silence. He pulls me close, too close. I'm frozen in five hundred layers of fear. Stunned in grief, in disbelief.

His hands reach for my face, his lips for mine. My brain is on fire, ready to explode from the impossibility of this moment. I feel like I'm watching it happen, detached from my own body, incapable of intervening. More than anything else, I'm shocked by his gentle hands, his earnest eyes.

"I want you to choose me," he says. "I want you to choose to be with me. I want you to *want* this—"

"You're insane," I choke. "You're psychotic—"

"You're only afraid of what you're capable of." His voice is soft. Easy. Slow. Deceptively persuasive. I'd never realized before just how attractive his voice is. "Admit it," he says. "We're perfect for each other. You want the power. You love the feel of a weapon in your hand. You're . . . attracted to me."

I try to swing my fist but he catches my arms. Pins them to my sides. Presses me up against the wall. He's so much stronger than he looks. "Don't lie to yourself, Juliette. You're going to come back with me whether you like it or not. But you can choose to want it. You can choose to enjoy it—"

"I will *never*," I breathe, broken. "You're sick—you're a sick, twisted monster—"

"That's not the right answer," he says, and seems genuinely disappointed.

"It's the only answer you'll ever get from me."

His lips come too close. "But I love you."

"No you don't."

His eyes close. He leans his forehead against mine. "You have no idea what you do to me."

"I hate you."

He shakes his head very slowly. Dips down. His nose brushes the nape of my neck and I stifle a horrified shiver that he misunderstands. His lips touch my skin and I actually whimper. "God I'd love to just take a bite out of you."

I notice the gleam of silver in his inside jacket pocket.

I feel a thrill of hope. A thrill of horror. Brace myself for what I need to do. Spend a moment mourning the loss of my dignity.

And I relax.

He feels the tension seep out of my limbs and responds in turn. He smiles, loosens his clamp on my shoulders. Slips his arms around my waist. I swallow the vomit threatening to give me away.

His military jacket has a million buttons and I wonder how many I'll have to undo before I can get my hands on the gun. His hands are exploring my body, slipping down my back to feel the form of my figure and it's all I can do to keep from doing something reckless. I'm not skilled enough to overpower him and I have no idea why he's able to touch me. I have no idea why I was able to crash through concrete yesterday. I have no idea where that energy came from.

Today he's got every advantage and it's not time to give myself away.

Not yet.

I place my hands on his chest. He presses me into the curve of his body. Tilts my chin up to meet his eyes. "I'll be good to you," he whispers. "I'll be so good to you, Juliette. I promise."

I hope I'm not visibly shaking.

And he kisses me. Hungrily. Desperately. Eager to break me open and taste me. I'm so stunned, so horrified, so cocooned in insanity I forget myself. I stand there frozen, disgusted. My hands slip from his chest. All I can think about is Adam and blood and Adam and the sound of gunshots and Adam lying in a pool of blood and I nearly shove him off of me. But Warner will not be discouraged.

He breaks the kiss. Whispers something in my ear that sounds like nonsense. Cups my face in his hands and this time I remember to pretend. I pull him closer, grab a fistful of his jacket and kiss him as hard as I can, my fingers already attempting to release the first of his buttons. Warner grips my hips and allows his hands to conquer my body. He tastes like peppermint, smells like gardenias. His arms are strong around me, his lips soft, almost sweet against my skin. There's an electric charge between us I hadn't anticipated.

My head is spinning.

His lips are on my neck, tasting me, devouring me, and I force myself to think straight. I force myself to understand the perversion of this situation. I don't know how to reconcile the confusion in my mind, my hesitant repulsion, my

266

inexplicable chemical reaction to his lips. I need to get this over with. Now.

I reach for his buttons.

And he's unnecessarily encouraged.

Warner lifts me by the waist, hoists me up against the wall, his hands cupping my backside, forcing my legs to wrap around him. He doesn't realize he's given me the perfect angle to reach into his coat.

His lips find my lips, his hands slip under my shirt and he's breathing hard, tightening his grip around me, and I practically rip open his jacket in desperation. I can't let this go on much longer. I have no idea how far Warner wants to push things, but I can't keep encouraging his insanity.

I need him to lean forward just an inch more—

My hands wrap around the gun.

I feel him freeze. Pull back. I watch his face phase through frames of confusion/dread/anguish/horror/anger. He drops me to the floor just as my fingers pull the trigger for the very first time.

The power and strength of the weapon is disarming, the sound so much louder than I anticipated. The reverberations are vibrating through my ears and every pulse in my body.

It's a sweet sort of music.

A small sort of victory.

Because this time the blood is not Adam's.

# FORTY

Warner is down.

I am up and running away with his gun.

I need to find Adam. I need to steal a car. I need to find James and Kenji. I need to learn how to drive. I need to drive us to safety. I need to do everything in exactly that order.

Adam can't be dead.

Adam is not dead.

Adam will not be dead.

My feet slap the pavement to a steady rhythm, my shirt and face spattered with blood, my hands still shaking slightly in the setting sun. A sharp breeze whips around me, jolting me out of the crazed reality I seem to be swimming in. I take a hard breath, squint up at the sky, and realize I don't have much time before I lose the light. The streets, at least, have long since been evacuated. But I have exactly zero idea where Warner's men might be.

I wonder if Warner has the tracker serum as well. I wonder if they'd know if he were dead.

I duck into dark corners, try to read the streets for clues, try to remember where Adam fell to the ground, but my memory is too weak, too distracted, my brain too broken to process these kinds of details. That horrible instant is one mess of insanity in my mind. I can't make any sense of it and Adam could be anywhere by now. They could've done anything to him.

I don't even know what I'm looking for.

~~I might be wasting my time.~~

I hear sudden movement and dart into a side street, my fingers tightening around the weapon slick in my grip. Now that I've actually fired a gun, I feel more confident with it in my hands, more aware of what to expect, how it functions. But I don't know if I should be happy or horrified that I'm so comfortable so quickly with something so lethal.

Footsteps.

I slide up against the wall, my arms and legs flat against the rough surface. I hope I'm buried in the shadows. I wonder if anyone's found Warner yet.

I watch a soldier walk right past me. He has rifles slung across his chest, a smaller sort of automatic weapon in his hands. I glance down at the gun in my own hand and realize I have no idea how many different kinds there are. All I know is some are bigger than others. Some have to be reloaded constantly. Some, like the one I'm holding, do not. Maybe Adam can teach me the differences.

Adam.

I suck in my breath and move as stealthily as I can through the streets. I spot a particularly dark shadow on a stretch of the sidewalk ahead of me and make an effort to avoid it. But as I get closer I realize it's not a shadow. It's a stain.

Adam's blood.

269

I squeeze my jaw shut until the pain scares away the screams. I take short, tiny, too-quick breaths. I need to focus. I need to use this information. I need to pay attention—

I need to follow the trail of blood.

Whoever dragged Adam away still hasn't come back to clean the mess. There's a steady spattered drip that leads away from the main roads and into the poorly lit side streets. The light is so dim I have to bend down to search for the spots on the ground. I'm losing sight of where they lead. There are fewer here. I think they've disappeared entirely. I don't know if the dark spots I'm finding are blood or old gum pounded into the pavement or drops of life from another person's flesh. Adam's path has disappeared.

I back up several steps and retrace the line.

I have to do this 3 times before I realize they must've taken him inside. There's an old steel structure with an older rusted door that looks like it's never been opened. It looks like it hasn't been used in years. I don't see any other options.

I wiggle the handle. It's locked.

I shift my entire weight into breaking it open, slamming it open, but I've only managed to bruise my body. I could shoot it down like I've seen Adam do, but I'm not certain of my aim nor my skill with this gun, and I'm not sure I can afford the noise. I can't make my presence known.

There has to be another way into this building.

There is no other way into this building.

My frustration is escalating. My desperation is crippling.

My hysteria is threatening to break me and I want to scream until my lungs collapse. Adam is in this building. He has to be in this building.

I'm standing right outside this building and I can't get inside.

This can't be happening.

I clench my fists, try to beat back the maddening futility enveloping me in its embrace but I feel crazed. Wild. Insane. The adrenaline is slipping away, my focus is slipping away, the sun is setting on the horizon and I remember James and Kenji and Adam Adam Adam ~~and Warner's hands on my body and his lips on my mouth and his tongue tasting my neck~~ and all the blood

everywhere

everywhere

everywhere

and I do something stupid.

I punch the door.

In one instant my mind catches up to my muscle and I brace myself for the impact of steel on skin, ready to feel the agony of shattering every bone in my right arm. But my fist flies through 12 inches of steel like it's made of butter. I'm stunned. I harness the same volatile energy and kick my foot through the door. I use my hands to rip the steel to shreds, clawing my way through the metal like a wild animal.

It's incredible. Exhilarating. Completely feral.

This must be how I broke through the concrete in Warner's

torture chamber. Which means I still have no idea how I broke through the concrete in Warner's torture chamber.

I climb through the hole I've created and slip into the shadows. It's not hard. The entire place is cloaked in darkness. There are no lights, no sounds of machines or electricity. Just another abandoned warehouse left to the elements.

I check the floors but there's no sign of blood. My heart soars and plummets at the same time. I need him to be okay. I need him to be alive. Adam is not dead. He can't be.

Adam promised James he'd come back for him.

He'd never break that promise.

I move slowly at first, wary, worried that there might be soldiers around, but it doesn't take long for me to realize there's no sound of life in this building. I decide to run.

I tuck caution in my pocket and hope I can reach for it if I need to. I'm flying through doors, spinning around turns, drinking in every detail. This building wasn't just a warehouse. It was a factory.

Old machines clutter the walls, conveyor belts are frozen in place, thousands of boxes of inventory stacked precariously in tall heaps. I hear a small breath, a stifled cough.

I'm bolting through a set of swinging double doors, searching out the feeble sound, fighting to focus on the tiniest details. I strain my ears and hear it again.

Heavy, labored breathing.

The closer I get, the more clearly I can hear him. It has to be him. My gun is up and aimed to fire, my eyes careful now, anticipating attackers. My legs move swiftly, easily, silently. I nearly shoot a shadow the boxes have cast on the floor. I take a steadying breath. Round another corner.

And nearly collapse.

Adam is hanging from bound wrists, shirtless, bloodied and bruised everywhere. His head is bent, his neck limp, his left leg drenched in blood despite the tourniquet wrapped around his thigh. I don't know how long the weight of his entire body has been hanging from his wrists. I'm surprised he hasn't dislocated his shoulders. He must still be fighting to hold on.

The rope wrapped around his wrists is attached to some kind of metal rod running across the ceiling. I look more closely and realize the rod is a part of a conveyor belt. That Adam is on a conveyor belt.

That this isn't just a factory.

It's a slaughterhouse.

I'm too poor to afford the luxury of hysteria right now.

I need to find a way to get him down, but I'm afraid to approach. My eyes search the space, certain that there are guards around here somewhere, soldiers prepared for this kind of ambush. But then it occurs to me that perhaps I was never really considered a threat. Not if Warner managed to drag me away.

No one would expect to find me here.

I climb onto the conveyor belt and Adam tries to lift his head. I have to be careful not to look too closely at his wounds, not to let my imagination cripple me. Not here. Not now.

"Adam . . . ?"

His head snaps up with a sudden burst of energy. His eyes find me. His face is almost unscathed; there are only minor cuts and bruises to account for. Focusing on the familiar gives me a modicum of calm.

"Juliette—?"

"I need to cut you down—"

"Jesus, Juliette—how did you find me?" He coughs. Wheezes. Takes a tight breath.

"Later." I reach up to touch his face. "I'll tell you everything later. First, I need to find a knife."

"My pants—"

"What?"

"In"—he swallows—"in my pants—"

I reach for his pocket and he shakes his head. I look up. "Where—"

"There's an inside pocket *in* my pants—"

I practically rip his clothes off. There's a small pocket sewn into the lining of his cargo pants. I slip my hand inside and retrieve a compact pocketknife. A butterfly knife. I've seen these before.

They're illegal.

I start stacking boxes on the conveyor belt. Climb my way up and hope to God I know what I'm doing. The knife is extremely sharp, and it works quickly to undo the bindings. I realize a little belatedly that the rope holding him together is the same cord we used to escape.

Adam is cut free. I'm climbing down, refolding the knife and tucking it into my pocket. I don't know how I'm going to get Adam out of here. His wrists are rubbed raw, bleeding, his body pounded into one piece of pain, his leg bloodied through with a bullet.

He nearly falls over.

I try to hold on as tenderly as possible, try to hold him close as best I can without hurting him. He doesn't say a word about the pain, tries so hard to hide the fact that he's having trouble breathing. He's wincing against the torture of it all, but doesn't whisper a word of complaint. "I can't believe you found me," is all he says.

And I know I shouldn't. I know now isn't the time. I know it's impractical. But I kiss him anyway.

"You are not going to die," I tell him. "We are going to get out of here. We are going to steal a car. We are going to find James and Kenji. And then we're going to get safe."

He stares at me. "Kiss me again," he says.

And I do.

It takes a lifetime to make it back to the door. Adam had been buried deep in the recesses of this building, and finding our way to the front is even more difficult than I expected. Adam is trying so hard, moving as fast as he can, but he still isn't fast at all. "They said Warner wanted to kill me himself," he explains. "That he shot me in the leg on purpose, just to disable me. It gave him a chance to drag you away and come back for me later. Apparently his plan was to torture me to death." He winces. "He said he wanted to enjoy it. Didn't want to rush through killing me." A hard laugh. A short cough.

~~His hands on my body his hands on my body his hands on my body~~

"So they just tied you up and abandoned you here?"

"They said no one would ever find me. They said the building is made entirely of concrete and reinforced steel and no one can break in. Warner was supposed to come back for me when he was ready." He stops. Looks at me. "God, I'm so happy you're okay."

I offer him a smile. Try to keep my organs from falling out. Hope the holes in my head aren't showing.

He pauses when we reach the door. The metal is a mangled mess. It looks like a wild animal attacked it and lost. "How did you—"

"I don't know," I admit. Try to shrug, be indifferent. "I just punched it."

"You just punched it."

"And kicked it a little."

He's smiling and I want to sob into his arms. I have to focus on his face. I can't let my eyes digest the travesty of his body.

"Come on," I tell him. "Let's go do something illegal."

I leave Adam in the shadows and dart up to the edge of the main road, searching for abandoned vehicles. We have to travel up 3 different side streets until we finally find one.

"How are you holding up?" I ask him, afraid to hear the answer.

He presses his lips together. Does something that looks like a nod. "Okay."

That's not good.

"Wait here."

It's pitch-black, not a single street lamp in sight. This is good. Also bad. It gives me an extra edge, but makes me extra vulnerable to attack. I have to be careful. I tiptoe up to the car.

I'm fully prepared to smash the glass open, but check the handle first. Just in case.

The door is unlocked.

The keys are in the ignition.

There's a bag of groceries in the backseat.

Someone must've panicked at the sound of the alarm and unexpected curfew. They must've dropped everything and run for cover. Unbelievable. This would be absolutely perfect if I had any idea how to drive.

I run back for Adam and help him hobble into the passenger side. As soon as he sits down I can tell just how much pain he's in. Bending his body in any way at all. Putting pressure on his ribs. Straining his muscles. "It's okay," he tells me, he lies to me. "I can't stand on my feet for much longer."

I reach into the back and rummage through the grocery bags. There's real food inside. Not just strange bouillon cubes designed to go into Automats, but fruit and vegetables. Even Warner never gave us bananas.

I hand the yellow fruit to Adam. "Eat this."

"I don't think I can eat—" He pauses. Stares at the form in his hands. "Is this what I think it is?"

"I think so."

We don't have time to process the impossibility. I peel

it open for him. Encourage him to take a small bite. I hope it's a good thing. I heard bananas have potassium. I hope he can keep it down.

I try to focus on the machine under my feet.

"How long do you think we'll have until Warner finds us?" Adam asks.

I take a few bites of oxygen. "I don't know."

A pause. "How did you get away from him . . . ?"

I'm staring straight out the windshield when I answer. "I shot him."

"No." Surprise. Awe. Amazement.

I show him Warner's gun. It has a special engraving in the hilt.

Adam is stunned. "So he's . . . dead?"

"I don't know," I finally admit, ashamed. I drop my eyes, study the grooves in the steering wheel. "I don't know for sure." I took too long to pull the trigger. It was stiffer than I expected it to be. Harder to hold the gun between my hands than I'd imagined. Warner was already dropping me when the bullet flew into his body. I was aiming for his heart.

I hope to God I didn't miss.

We're both too quiet.

"Adam?"

"Yeah?"

"I don't know how to drive."

# FORTY-ONE

"You're lucky this isn't a stick shift." He tries to laugh.

"Stick shift?"

"Manual transmission."

"What's that?"

"A little more complicated."

I bite my lip. "Do you remember where we left James and Kenji?" I don't even want to consider the possibility that they've moved. Been discovered. Anything. I can't fathom the idea.

"Yes." I know he's thinking exactly what I'm thinking.

"How do I get there?"

Adam tells me the right pedal is for gas. The left is to brake. I have to shift into *D* for *drive*. I use the steering wheel to turn. There are mirrors to help see behind me. I can't turn on my headlights and will have to rely on the moon to light my way.

I turn on the ignition, press the brake, shift into drive. Adam's voice is the only navigation system I need. I release the brake. Press the gas. Nearly crash into a wall.

This is how we finally get back to the abandoned building.

Gas. Brake. Gas. Brake. Too much gas. Too much brake.

Adam doesn't complain and it's almost worse. I can only imagine what my driving is doing for his injuries. I'm grateful that at least we're not dead, not yet.

I don't know why no one has spotted us. I wonder if maybe Warner really is dead. I wonder if everything is in chaos. I wonder if that's why there are no soldiers in this city. They've all disappeared.

I think.

I almost forget to put the car in park when we reach the vaguely familiar broken building. Adam has to reach over and do it for me. I help him transition into the backseat, and he asks me why.

"Because I'm making Kenji drive, and I don't want your brother to have to see you like this. It's dark enough that he won't see your body. I don't think he should have to see you hurt."

He nods after an infinite moment. "Thank you."

And I'm running toward the broken building. Pulling the door open. I can only barely make out two figures in the dark. I blink and they come into focus. James is asleep with his head in Kenji's lap. The duffel bags are open, cans of food discarded on the floor. They're okay.

Thank God they're okay.

I could die of relief.

Kenji pulls James up and into his arms, struggling a little under the weight. His face is smooth, serious, unflinching. He doesn't smile. He doesn't say anything stupid. He studies my eyes like he already knows, like he already understands why it took us so long to get back, like there's only one reason why I must look like hell right now, why I have blood all over my shirt. Probably on my face. All over my hands. "How is he?"

And I nearly lose it right there. "I need you to drive."

He takes a tight breath. Nods several times. "My right leg is still good," he says to me, but I don't think I'd care even if it weren't. We need to get to his safe place, and my driving isn't going to get us anywhere.

Kenji settles a sleeping James into the passenger side, and I'm so happy he's not awake for this moment.

I grab the duffel bags and carry them to the backseat. Kenji slides in front. Looks in the rearview mirror. "Good to see you alive, Kent."

Adam almost smiles. Shakes his head. "Thank you for taking care of James."

"You trust me now?"

A small sigh. "Maybe."

"I'll take a *maybe*." He grins. Turns on the car. "Let's get the hell out of here."

Adam is shaking.

His bare body is finally cracking under the cold weather, the hours of torture, the strain of holding himself together for so long. I'm scrambling through the duffel bags, searching for a coat, but all I find are shirts and sweaters. I don't know how to get them on his body without causing him pain.

I decide to cut them up. I take the butterfly knife to a few of his sweaters and slice them open, draping them around his figure like a blanket. I glance up. "Kenji—does this car have a heater?"

"It's on, but it's pretty crappy. It's not working very well."

"How much longer until we get there?"

"Not too much."

"Have you seen anyone that might be following us?"

"No." He pauses. "It's weird. I don't understand why no one has noticed a car flying through these streets after curfew. Something's not right."

"I know."

"And I don't know what it is, but obviously my tracker serum isn't working. Either they really just don't give a shit about me, or it's legit not working, and I don't know why."

A tiny detail sits on the outskirts of my consciousness. I examine it. "Didn't you say you slept in a shed? That night you ran away?"

"Yeah, why?"

"Where was it . . . ?"

He shrugs. "I don't know. Some huge field. It was weird. Crazy shit growing in that place. I almost ate something I thought was fruit before I realized it smelled like ass."

My breath catches. "It was an empty field? Barren? Totally abandoned?"

"Yeah."

"The nuclear field," Adam says, a dawning realization in his voice.

"What nuclear field?" Kenji asks.

I take a moment to explain.

"Holy crap." Kenji grips the steering wheel. "So I could've died? And I didn't?"

I ignore him. "But then how did they find us? How did they figure out where you live—?"

"I don't know," Adam sighs. Closes his eyes. "Maybe Kenji is lying to us."

"Come on, man, what the hell—"

"Or," Adam interrupts, "maybe they bought out Benny."

"No." I gasp.

"It's possible."

We're all silent for a long moment. I try to look out the window but it's very nearly useless. The night sky is a vat of tar suffocating the world around us.

I turn to Adam and find him with his head tilted back, his hands clenched, his lips almost white in the blackness. I wrap the sweaters more tightly around his body. He stifles a shudder.

"Adam . . ." I brush a strand of hair away from his forehead. His hair has gotten a little long and I realize I've never really paid attention to it before. It's been cropped short since the day he stepped into my cell. I never would've thought his dark hair would be so soft. Like melted chocolate. I wonder when he stopped cutting it.

He flexes his jaw. Pries his lips open. Lies to me over and over again. "I'm okay."

"Kenji—"

"Five minutes, I promise—I'm trying to gun this thing—"

I touch his wrists, trace the tender skin with my fingertips. The bloodied scars. I kiss the palm of his hand. He takes a broken breath. "You're going to be okay," I tell him.

His eyes are still closed. He tries to nod.

"Why didn't you tell me you two were together?" Kenji asks unexpectedly. His voice is even, neutral.

"What?" Now is not the time to be blushing.

Kenji sighs. I catch a glimpse of his eyes in the rearview mirror. The swelling is almost completely gone. His face is healing. "I'd have to be *blind* to miss something like that. I mean, hell, just the way he looks at you. It's like the guy has never seen a woman in his life. Like putting food in front of a starving man and telling him he can't eat it."

Adam's eyes fly open. I try to read him but he won't look at me.

"Why didn't you just tell me?" Kenji says again.

"I never had a chance to ask," Adam answers. His voice is less than a whisper. His energy levels are dropping too fast. I don't want him to have to talk. He needs to conserve his strength.

"Wait—are you talking to me or her?" Kenji glances back at us.

"We can discuss this later—," I try to say, but Adam shakes his head.

"I told James without asking you. I made . . . an assumption." He stops. "I shouldn't have. You should have a choice.

284

You should always have a choice. And it's your choice if you want to be with me."

"Hey, so, I'm just going to pretend like I can't hear you guys anymore, okay?" Kenji makes a random motion with his hand. "Go ahead and have your moment."

But I'm too busy studying Adam's eyes, his soft soft lips. His furrowed brow.

I lean into his ear, lower my voice. Whisper the words so only he can hear me.

"You're going to get better," I promise him. "And when you do, I'm going to show you exactly what choice I've made. I'm going to memorize every inch of your body with my lips."

He exhales suddenly, shaky, uneven. Swallows hard.

His eyes are burning into me. He looks almost feverish, and I wonder if I'm making things worse.

I pull back and he stops me. Rests his hand on my thigh. "Don't go," he says. "Your touch is the only thing keeping me from losing my mind."

# FORTY-TWO

"We're here, and it's nighttime. So according to my calculations, we must not have done anything stupid."

Kenji shifts into park. We're underground again, in some kind of elaborate parking garage. One minute we were aboveground, the next we've disappeared into a ditch. It's next to impossible to locate, much less to spot in the darkness. Kenji was telling the truth about this hideout.

I've been busy trying to keep Adam awake for the past few minutes. His body is fighting exhaustion, blood loss, hunger, a million different points of pain. I feel so utterly useless.

"Adam has to go straight to the medical wing," Kenji announces.

"They have a medical wing?" My heart is parasailing in the springtime.

Kenji grins. "This place has everything. It will blow your goddamn mind." He hits a switch on the ceiling. A faint light illuminates the old sedan. Kenji steps out the door. "Wait here—I'll get someone to bring out a stretcher."

"What about James?"

"Oh." Kenji's mouth twitches. "He, uh—he's going to be asleep for a little while longer."

"What do you mean . . . ?"

He clears his throat. Once. Twice. Smooths out the wrinkles in his shirt. "I, uh, may or may not have given him something to . . . ease the pain of this journey."

"You gave a ten-year-old a *sleeping pill?*" I'm afraid I'm going to break his neck.

"Would you rather he were awake for all of this?"

"Adam is going to kill you."

Kenji glances at Adam's drooping lids. "Yeah, well, I guess I'm lucky he won't be able to kill me tonight." He hesitates. Ducks into the car to run his fingers through James's hair. Smiles a little. "The kid is a saint. He'll be perfect in the morning."

"I can't *believe* you—"

"Hey, hey—" He holds up his hands. "Trust me. He's going to be just fine. I just didn't want him to be any more traumatized than he had to be." He shrugs. "Hell, maybe Adam will agree with me."

"I'm going to murder you." Adam's voice is a soft mumble.

Kenji laughs. "Keep it together, bro, or I'll think you don't really mean it."

Kenji disappears.

I watch Adam, encourage him to stay awake. Tell him he's almost safe. Touch my lips to his forehead. Study every shadow, every outline, every cut and bruise of his face. His muscles relax, his features lose their tension. He exhales a little more easily. I kiss his top lip. Kiss his bottom lip. Kiss his cheeks. His nose. His chin.

Everything happens so quickly after that.

4 people run out toward the car. 2 older than me, 2 older than them. A pair of men. A pair of women. "Where is he?" the older woman asks. They're all looking around, anxious. I wonder if they can see me staring at them.

Kenji opens Adam's door. Kenji is no longer smiling. In fact, he looks . . . different. Stronger. Faster. Taller, even. He's in control. A figure of authority. These people *know* him.

Adam is lifted onto the stretcher and assessed immediately. Everyone is talking at once. Something about broken ribs. Something about losing blood. Something about airways and lung capacity and *what happened to his wrists? Something about checking his pulse and *how long has he been bleeding?* The young male and female glance in my direction. They're all wearing strange outfits.

Strange suits. All white with gray stripes down the side. I wonder if it's a medical uniform.

They're carrying Adam away.

"Wait—" I trip out of the car. "Wait! I want to go with him—"

"Not now." Kenji stops me. Softens. "You can't be with him for what they need to do. Not now."

"What do you mean? What are they going to do to him?" The world is fading in and out of focus, shades of gray flickering as stilted frames, broken movements. Suddenly nothing makes sense. Suddenly everything is confusing me. Suddenly my head is a piece of pavement and I'm being trampled to death. I don't know where we are. I don't know who Kenji is. Kenji was Adam's friend. Adam knows him.

Adam. My Adam. Adam who is being taken away from me and I can't go with him and I want to go with him but they won't let me go with him and I don't know why—

"They're going to help him—*Juliette*—I need you to focus. You can't fall apart right now. I know it's been a crazy day—but I need you to stay calm." His voice. So steady. So suddenly articulate.

"Who *are* you . . . ?" I'm beginning to panic. I want to grab James and run but I can't. He's done something to James and even if I knew how to wake him up, I can't touch him. I want to rip my nails out. *"Who are you—"*

Kenji sighs. "You're starving. You're exhausted. You're processing shock and a million other emotions right now. Be logical. I'm not going to hurt you. You're safe now. Adam is safe. James is safe."

"I want to be with him—I want to see what they're going to do to him—"

"I can't let you do that."

"What are you going to do to me? Why did you bring me here . . . ?" My eyes are wide, darting in every direction. I'm spinning, stranded in the middle of the ocean of my own imagination and I don't know how to swim. "What do you want from me?"

Kenji looks down. Rubs his forehead. Reaches into his pocket. "I really didn't want to have to do this."

I think I'm screaming.

# FORTY-THREE

I'm an old creaky staircase when I wake up.

Someone has scrubbed me clean. My skin is like satin. My eyelashes are soft, my hair is smooth, brushed out of its knots; it gleams in the artificial light, a chocolate river lapping the pale shore of my skin, soft waves cascading around my collarbone. My joints ache; my eyes burn from an insatiable exhaustion. My body is naked under a heavy sheet. I've never felt so pristine.

I'm too tired to be bothered by it.

My sleepy eyes take inventory of the space I'm in, but there's not much to consider. I'm lying in bed. There are 4 walls. 1 door. A small table beside me. A glass of water on the table. Fluorescent lights humming above me. Everything is white.

Everything I've ever known is changing.

I reach for the glass of water and the door opens. I pull the sheet up as high as it will go.

"How are you feeling?"

A tall man is wearing plastic glasses. Black frames. A simple sweater. Pressed pants. His sandy-blond hair falls into his eyes.

He's holding a clipboard.

"Who are you?"

He grabs a chair I hadn't noticed was sitting in the corner. Pushes it forward. Sits down beside my bed. "Do you feel dizzy? Disoriented?"

"Where's Adam?"

He's holding his pen to a sheet of paper. Writing something down. "Do you spell your last name with two *r*s? Or just one?"

"What did you do with James? Where's Kenji?"

He stops. Looks up. He can't be more than 30. He has a crooked nose. A day of scruff. "Can I at least make sure you're doing all right? Then I'll answer your questions. I promise. Just let me get through the basic protocol here."

I blink.

How do I feel. I don't know.

Did I have any dreams. I don't think so.

Do I know where I am. No.

Do I think I'm safe. I don't know.

Do I remember what happened. Yes.

How old am I. 17.

What color are my eyes. I don't know.

"You don't know?" He puts down his pen. Takes off his glasses. "You can remember exactly what happened yesterday, but you don't know the color of your own eyes?"

"I think they're green. Or blue. I'm not sure. Why does it matter?"

"I want to be sure you can recognize yourself. That you haven't lost sight of your person."

"I've never really known my eye color, though. I've only looked in the mirror once in the last three years."

The stranger stares at me, his eyes crinkled in concern. I finally have to look away.

"How did you touch me?" I ask.

"I'm sorry?"

"My body. My skin. I'm so . . . clean."

"Oh." He bites his thumb. Marks something on his papers. "Right. Well, you were covered in blood and filth when you came in, and you had some minor cuts and bruises. We didn't want to risk infection. Sorry for the personal intrusion—but we can't allow anyone to bring that kind of bacteria in here. We had to do a superficial detox."

"That's fine—I understand," I hurry on. "But *how*?"

"Excuse me?"

"How did you touch me?" Surely he must know. How could he not know? God I hope he knows.

"Oh—" He nods, distracted by the words he's scribbling on his clipboard. Squints at the page. "Latex."

"What?"

"Latex." He glances up for a second. Sees my confusion. "Gloves?"

"Right." Of course. Gloves. Even Warner used gloves until he figured it out.

~~Until he figured it out. Until he figured it out. Until he figured it out.~~

I replay the moment over and over and over in my mind. The split second I took too long to jump from the window. The moment of hesitation that changed everything. The instant I lost all control. All power. Any point of dominance. He's never going to stop until he finds me and it's my own fault.

I need to know if he's dead.

I have to force myself to be still. I have to force myself not to shake, shudder, or vomit. I need to change the subject. "Where are my clothes?" I toy with the perfect white sheet hiding my bones.

"They've been destroyed for the same reasons you needed to be sanitized." He picks up his glasses. Slips them on. "We have a special suit for you. I think it'll make your life a lot easier."

"A special suit?" I look up. Part my lips in surprise.

"Yes. We'll get to that part a bit later." He pauses. Smiles. There's a dimple in his chin. "You're not going to attack me like you did Kenji, are you?"

"I attacked Kenji?" I cringe.

"Just a little bit." He shrugs. "At least now we know he's not immune to your touch."

"I *touched* him?" I sit up straight and nearly forget to pull my sheet up with me. I'm burning from head to toe, blushing through my mind, clutching at the sheet like a lifeline. "I'm so sorry—"

"I'm sure he'll appreciate the apology." Blondie is studying his notes religiously, suddenly fascinated by his own handwriting. "But it's all right. We've been expecting some destructive tendencies. You've been having one hell of a week."

"Are you a psychologist?"

"Sort of." He brushes the hair away from his forehead.

"Sort of?"

He laughs. Pauses. Rolls the pen between his fingers. "Yes. For all intents and purposes, I am a psychologist. Sometimes."

"What is that supposed to mean . . . ?"

He parts his lips. Presses them shut. Seems to consider answering me but examines me instead. He stares for so long I feel my face go hot. He starts scribbling furiously.

"What am I doing here?" I ask him.

"Recovering."

"How long have I been here?"

"You've been asleep for almost fourteen hours. We gave you a pretty powerful sedative." Looks at his watch. "You seem to be doing well." Hesitates. "You look very well, actually. Stunning, really."

I have a handful of scrambled words in my mouth. A blush flushing up my face. "Where's Adam?"

He takes a deep breath. Underlines something on his papers. His lips twitch into a smile.

"Where is he?"

"Recovering." He finally looks up.

"He's okay?"

Nods. "He's okay."

I stare at him. "What does that mean?"

2 knocks at the door.

The bespectacled stranger doesn't move. He rereads his notes. "Come in," he calls.

Kenji walks inside, a little hesitant at first. He peeks at me, his eyes cautious. I never thought I'd be so happy to see him. But while it's a relief to see a face I recognize, my stomach immediately twists into a knot of guilt, knocking me over from the inside. I wonder how badly I must've hurt him. He steps forward.

My guilt disappears.

I look more closely and realize he's perfectly unharmed. His leg is working fine. His face is back to normal. His eyes are no longer puffy, his forehead is repaired, smooth, untouched. He was right.

He does have a spectacular face.

A defiant jawline. Perfect eyebrows. Eyes as pitch-black as his hair. Sleek. Strong. A bit dangerous.

"Hey, beautiful."

"I'm sorry I almost killed you," I blurt out.

"Oh." He startles. Shoves his hands into his pockets. "Well. Glad we got that out of the way." I notice he's wearing a destroyed T-shirt. Dark jeans. I haven't seen anyone wear jeans in such a long time. Army uniforms, cotton basics, and fancy dresses are all I've known lately.

I can't really look at him. "I panicked," I try to explain. I clasp and unclasp my fingers.

"I figured." He cocks an eyebrow.

"I'm sorry."

"I know."

I nod. "You look better."

He cracks a grin. Stretches. Leans against the wall, arms

crossed at his chest, legs crossed at the ankles. "This must be difficult for you."

"Excuse me?"

"Looking at my face. Realizing I was right. Realizing you made the wrong decision." He shrugs. "I understand. I'm not a proud man, you know. I'd be willing to forgive you."

I gape at him, unsure whether to laugh or throw something. "Don't make me touch you."

He shakes his head. "It's incredible how someone can look so right and feel so wrong. Kent is a lucky bastard."

"I'm sorry—" Psychologist-man stands up. "Are you two finished here?" He looks to Kenji. "I thought you had a purpose."

Kenji pushes off the wall. Straightens his back. "Right. Yeah. Castle wants to meet her."

# FORTY-FOUR

"Now?" Blondie is more confused than I am. "But I'm not done examining her."

Kenji shrugs. "He wants to meet her."

"Who's Castle?" I ask.

Blondie and Kenji look at me. Kenji looks away. Blondie doesn't.

He cocks his head. "Kenji didn't tell you anything about this place?"

"No." I falter, uncertain, glancing at Kenji, who won't look at me. "He never explained anything. He said he knew someone who had a safe place and thought he could help us—"

Blondie gapes. Laughs so hard he snorts. Stands up. Cleans his glasses with the hem of his shirt. "You're such an ass," he says to Kenji. "Why didn't you just tell her the truth?"

"She never would've come if I told her the truth."

"How do you know?"

"She nearly *killed* me—"

My eyes are darting from one face to the other. Blond hair to black hair and back again. "What is going *on*?" I demand. "I want to see Adam. I want to see James. And I want a set of *clothes*—"

"You're naked?" Kenji is suddenly studying my sheet and not bothering to be subtle about it.

I flush despite my best efforts, flustered, frustrated. "Blondie said they destroyed my clothes."

*"Blondie?"* Blond man is offended.

"You never told me your name."

"Winston. My name is Winston." He's not smiling anymore.

"Didn't you say you had a suit for me?"

He frowns. Checks his watch. "We won't have time to go through that right now." Sighs. "Get her something to wear temporarily, will you?" He's talking to Kenji. Kenji who is still staring at me.

"I want to see Adam."

"Adam isn't ready to see you yet." ~~Blondie~~ Winston tucks his pen into a pocket. "We'll let you know when he's ready."

"How am I supposed to trust any of you if you won't even let me see him? If you won't let me see James? I don't even have my basic things. I want to get out of this bed and I need something to wear."

"Go fetch, Moto." Winston is readjusting his watch.

"I'm not your dog, *Blondie*," Kenji snaps. "And I told you not to call me Moto."

Winston pinches the bridge of his nose. "No problem. I'll also tell Castle it's your fault she's not meeting with him right now."

Kenji mutters something obscene under his breath. Stalks off. Almost slams the door.

A few seconds pass in a strained sort of silence.

I take a deep breath. "So what's *moto* mean?"

Winston rolls his eyes. "Nothing. It's just a nickname—his last name is Kishimoto. He gets mad when we chop it in half. Gets sensitive about it."

"Well why do you chop it in half?"

He snorts. "Because it's hard as hell to pronounce."

"How is that an excuse?"

He frowns. "What?"

"You got mad that I called you Blondie and not Winston. Why doesn't he have the right to be mad that you're calling him Moto instead of Kenji?"

He mumbles something that sounds like, "It's not the same thing."

I slide down a little. Rest my head on the pillow. "Don't be a hypocrite."

# FORTY-FIVE

I feel like a clown in these oversized clothes. I'm wearing someone else's T-shirt. Someone else's pajama pants. Someone else's slippers. Kenji says they had to destroy the clothes in my duffel bag, too, so I have no idea whose outfit is currently hanging on my frame. I'm practically swimming in the material.

I try to knot the extra fabric and Kenji stops me. "You're going to mess up my shirt," he complains.

I drop my hands. "You gave me *your* clothes?"

"Well what did you expect? It's not like we have extra dresses just lying around." He shoots me a look, like I should be grateful he's even sharing.

Well. I guess it's better than being naked. "So who's Castle again?"

"He's in charge of everything," Kenji tells me. "The head of this entire movement."

My ears snap off. *"Movement?"*

Winston sighs. He seems so uptight. I wonder why. "If Kenji hasn't already told you anything, you should probably wait to hear it from Castle himself. Hang tight. I promise we're going to answer your questions."

"But what about Adam? Where is *James*—"

"Wow." Winston runs a hand through his floppy hair. "You're just not going to give it up, huh?"

"He's fine, Juliette," Kenji intervenes. "He needs a little more time to recover. You have to start trusting us. No one here is going to hurt you, or Adam, or James. They're both fine. Everything is fine."

But I don't know if *fine* is good enough.

We're walking through an entire city underground, hallways and passageways, smooth stone floors, rough walls left untouched. There are circular disks drilled into the ground, glowing with artificial light every few feet. I notice computers, all kinds of gadgets I don't recognize, doors cracked open to reveal rooms filled with nothing but technological machinery.

"How do you find the electricity necessary to run this place?" I look more closely at the unidentifiable machines, the flickering screens, the unmistakable humming of hundreds of computers built into the framework of this underground world.

Kenji tugs on a stray strand of my hair. I spin around. "We steal it." He grins. Nods down a narrow path. "This way."

People both young and old and of all different shapes and ethnicities shuffle in and out of rooms, all along the halls. Many of them stare, many of them are too distracted to notice us. Some of them are dressed like the men and women who rushed out to our car last night. It's an odd kind of uniform. It seems unnecessary.

"So . . . everyone dresses like that?" I whisper, gesturing to the passing strangers as inconspicuously as possible.

Kenji scratches his head. Takes his time answering. "Not everyone. Not all the time."

"What about you?" I ask him.

"Not today."

I decide not to indulge his cryptic tendencies, and instead ask a more straightforward question. "So are you ever going to tell me how you healed so quickly?"

"Yes," Kenji says, unfazed. "We're going to tell you a lot of things, actually." We make an abrupt turn down an unexpected hallway. "But first—" Kenji pauses outside of a huge wooden door. "Castle wants to meet you. He's the one who requested you."

"*Requested*—?"

"Yeah." Kenji looks uncomfortable for just a wavering second.

"Wait—what do you mean—"

"I mean it wasn't an accident that I ended up in the army, Juliette." He sighs. "It wasn't an accident that I showed up at Adam's door. And I wasn't supposed to get shot or get beaten half to death, but I did. Only I wasn't dropped off by some random dude." He almost grins. "I've always known where Adam lived. It was my job to know." A pause. "We've all been looking for you."

My mouth is sitting on my kneecaps.

"Go ahead." Kenji pushes me inside. "He'll be out when he's ready."

"Good luck," is all Winston says to me.

1,320 seconds walk into the room before he does.

He moves methodically, his face a mask of neutrality as he brushes wayward dreadlocks into a ponytail and seats himself at the front of the room. He's thin, fit, impeccably dressed in a simple suit. Dark blue. White shirt. No tie. There are no lines on his face, but there's a streak of silver in his hair and his eyes confess he's lived at least 100 years. He must be in his 40s. I look around.

It's an empty space, impressive in its sparseness. The floors and ceilings are built by bricks carefully pieced together. Everything feels old and ancient, but somehow modern technology is keeping this place alive. Artificial lighting illuminates the cavernous dimensions, small monitors are built into the stone walls. I don't know what I'm doing here. I don't know what to expect. I have no idea what kind of person Castle is but after spending so much time with Warner, I'm trying not to get my hopes up. I don't even realize I've stopped breathing until he speaks.

"I hope you're enjoying your stay so far."

My neck snaps up to meet his dark eyes, his smooth voice, silky and strong. His eyes are glinting with genuine curiosity, a smattering of surprise. I've forgotten I know how to speak.

"Kenji said you wanted to meet me," is the only response I offer.

"Kenji would be correct." He takes his time breathing. He takes his time shifting in his seat. He takes his time studying my eyes, choosing his words, touching two fingers to his lips. He seems to have dominated the concept of time. *Impatience* is likely not a word in his vocabulary. "I've heard . . . stories. About you." Smiles. "I simply wanted to know if they were true."

"What have you heard?"

He smiles with teeth so white it looks like snow falling on the chocolate valleys of his face. He opens his hands. Studies them for a moment. Looks up. "You can kill a man with nothing but your bare skin. You can crush five feet of concrete with the palm of your hand."

I'm climbing a mountain of air and my feet keep slipping. I need to get a grip on something.

"Is it true?" he asks.

"Rumors are more likely to kill you than I am."

He studies me for too long. "I'd like to show you something," he says after a moment.

"I want answers to my questions." This has gone on too long. I don't want to be lulled into a false sense of security. I don't want to assume Adam and James are okay. I don't want to trust anyone until I have proof. I can't pretend like any of this is all right. Not yet. "I want to know that I'm safe," I tell him. "And I want to know that my friends are safe. There was a ten-year-old boy with us when we arrived and I want to see him. I need to make certain he is healthy and unharmed. I won't cooperate otherwise."

His eyes inspect me a few moments longer. "Your loyalty is refreshing," he says, and he means it. "You will do well here."

"My friends—"

"Yes. Of course." He's on his feet. "Follow me."

This place is far more complex, far more organized than I'd ever imagined it to be. There are hundreds of different directions to get lost in, almost as many rooms, some bigger than others, each dedicated to different pursuits.

"The dining hall," Castle says to me.

"The dormitories." On the opposite wing.

"The training facilities." Down that hall.

"The common rooms." Right through here.

"The bathrooms." On either end of the floor.

"The meeting halls." Just past that door.

Each space is buzzing with bodies, each body adapted to a particular routine. People look up when they see us. Some wave, smile, delighted. I realize they're all looking at Castle. He nods his head. His eyes are kind, humble. His smile is strong, reassuring.

He's the leader of this entire *movement*, is what Kenji said. These people are depending on him for something more than basic survival. This is more than a fallout shelter. This is much more than a hiding space. There is a greater goal in mind. A greater purpose.

"Welcome," Castle says to me, gesturing with one hand, "to Omega Point."

# FORTY-SIX

"Omega Point?"

"The last letter in the Greek alphabet. The final development, the last in a series." He stops in front of me and for the first time I notice the omega symbol stitched into the back of his jacket. "We are the only hope our civilization has left."

"But how—with such small numbers—how can you possibly hope to compete—"

"We've been building for a long time, Juliette." It's the first time he's said my name. His voice is strong, smooth, stable. "We've been planning, organizing, mapping out our strategy for many years now. The collapse of our human society should not come as a surprise. We brought it upon ourselves.

"The question wasn't *whether* things would fall apart," he continues. "Only *when*. It was a waiting game. A question of who would try to take power and how they would try to use it. Fear," he says to me, turning back for just a moment, his footsteps silent against the stone, "is a great motivator."

"That's pathetic."

"I agree. Which is why part of my job is reviving the stalled hearts that've lost all hope." We turn into another

306

corridor. "And to tell you that almost everything you've learned about the state of our world is a lie."

I stop in place. Nearly fall over. "What do you mean?"

"I mean things are not nearly as bad as The Reestablishment wants us to think they are."

"But there's no food—"

"That they give *you* access to."

"The animals—"

"Are kept hidden. Genetically modified. Raised on secret pastures."

"But the air—the seasons—the *weather*—"

"Is not as bad as they'll have us believe. It's probably our only real problem—but it's one caused by the perverse manipulations of Mother Earth. *Man-made* manipulations that we can still fix." He turns to face me. Focuses my mind with one steady gaze.

"There is still a chance to change things. We can provide fresh drinking water to all people. We can make sure crops are not regulated for profit; we can ensure that they are not genetically altered to benefit manufacturers. Our people are dying because we are feeding them poison. Animals are dying because we are forcing them to eat waste, forcing them to live in their own filth, caging them together and abusing them. Plants are withering away because we are dumping chemicals into the earth that make them hazardous to our health. But these are things we can fix.

"We are fed lies because believing them makes us weak, vulnerable, malleable. We depend on others for our food, health, sustenance. This cripples us. Creates cowards of our people. Slaves of our children. It's time for us to fight back." His eyes are bright with feeling, his fists clenched in fervor. His words are powerful, heavy with conviction, articulate and meaningful. I have no doubt he's swayed many people with such fanciful thoughts. Hope for a future that seems lost. Inspiration in a bleak world with nothing to offer. He is a natural leader. A talented orator.

I have a hard time believing him.

"How can you know for certain that your theories are correct? Do you have proof?"

His hands relax. His eyes quiet down. His lips form a small smile. "Of course." He almost laughs.

"Why is that funny?"

He shakes his head. Just a bit. "I'm amused by your skepticism. I admire it, actually. It's never a good idea to believe everything you hear."

I catch his double meaning. Acknowledge it. "Touché, Mr. Castle."

A pause. "You are French, Ms. Ferrars?"

~~"My mother, perhaps."~~ I look away. "So where is your proof?"

"This entire movement is proof enough. We survive because of these truths. We seek out food and supplies from the various storage compounds The Reestablishment has constructed. We've found their fields, their farms, their animals. They have hundreds of acres dedicated to crops. The farmers are slaves, working under the threat of death to themselves or their family members. The rest of society is either killed or corralled into sectors, sectioned off to be monitored, carefully surveyed."

I keep my face blank, smooth, neutral. I still haven't decided whether or not I believe him. "And what do you need with me? Why do you care if I'm here?"

He stops at a glass wall. Points through to the room beyond. Doesn't answer my question. "Your Adam is healing because of our people."

I nearly trip in my haste to see him. I press my hands against the glass and peer into the brightly lit space. Adam is asleep, his face perfect, peaceful. This must be the medical wing.

"Look closely," Castle tells me. "There are no needles attached to his body. No machines keeping him alive. He arrived with three broken ribs. Lungs close to collapsing. A bullet in his thigh. His kidneys were bruised along with the rest of his body. Broken skin, bloodied wrists. A sprained ankle. He'd lost more blood than most hospitals would be able to replenish."

My heart is about to fall out of my body. I want to break through the glass and cradle him in my arms.

"There are close to two hundred people at Omega Point," Castle says. "Less than half of whom have some kind of gift."

I spin around, stunned.

"I brought you here," he says to me carefully, quietly, "because this is where you belong. Because you need to know that you are not alone."

# FORTY-SEVEN

My jaw is dangling from my shoelace.

"You would be invaluable to our resistance," he tells me.

"There are others . . . like me?" I can hardly breathe.

Castle offers me eyes that empathize with my soul. "I was the first to realize my affliction could not be mine alone. I sought out others, following rumors, listening for stories, reading the newspapers for abnormalities in human behavior. At first it was just for companionship." He pauses. "I was tired of the insanity. Of believing I was inhuman; a monster. But then I realized that what seemed a weakness was actually a strength. That together we could be something extraordinary. Something *good*."

I can't catch my breath. I can't find my feet. I can't cough up the impossibility caught in my throat.

Castle is waiting for my reaction.

I feel so nervous so suddenly. "What is your . . . gift?" I ask him.

His smile disarms my insecurity. He holds out his hand. Cocks his head. I hear the creak of a distant door opening. The sound of air and metal; movement. I turn toward the sound only to see something hurtling in my direction. I duck. Castle laughs. Catches it in his hand.

I gasp.

He shows me the key now caught between his fingers.

"You can move things with your mind?" I don't even know where I found the words to speak.

"I have an impossibly advanced level of psychokinesis." He twists his lips into a smile. "So yes."

"There's a *name* for it?" I think I'm squeaking. I try to steady myself.

"For my condition? Yes. For yours?" He pauses. "I'm uncertain."

"And the others—what—they're—"

"You can meet them, if you'd like."

"I—yes—I'd like that," I stammer, excited, 4 years old and still believing in fairies.

I freeze at a sudden sound.

Footsteps are pounding the stone. I catch the pant of strained breathing.

"*Sir*—" someone shouts.

Castle starts. Stills. Pivots around a corner toward the runner. "Brendan?"

"Sir!" he pants again.

"You have news? What have you seen?"

"We're hearing things on the radio," he begins, his broken words thick with a British accent. "Our cameras are picking up more tanks patrolling the area than usual. We think they may be getting closer—"

The sound of static energy. Static electricity. Garbled voices croaking through a weak radio line.

Brendan curses under his breath. "Sorry, sir—it's not usually this distorted—I just haven't learned to contain the charges lately—"

"Not to worry. You just need practice. Your training is going well?"

"Very well, sir. I have it almost entirely under my command." Brendan pauses. "For the most part."

"Excellent. In the meantime, let me know if the tanks get any closer. I'm not surprised to hear they're getting a little more vigilant. Try to listen for any mention of an attack. The Reestablishment has been trying to pinpoint our whereabouts for years, but now we have someone particularly valuable to their efforts and I'm certain they want her back. I have a feeling things are going to develop rather quickly from now on."

A moment of confusion. "Sir?"

"There's someone I'd like for you to meet."

Silence.

Brendan and Castle step around the corner. Come into view. And I have to make a conscious effort to keep my jaw from unhinging. I can't stop staring.

Castle's companion is white from head to toe.

Not just his strange uniform, which is a blinding shade of shimmering white, but his skin is paler than mine. Even his hair is so blond it can only be accurately described as white. His eyes are mesmerizing. They're the lightest shade of blue I've ever seen. Piercing. Practically transparent. He looks to be my age.

He doesn't seem *real*.

"Brendan, this is Juliette," Castle introduces us. "She arrived just yesterday. I was giving her an overview of Omega Point."

Brendan's smile is so bright I nearly flinch. He sticks out his hand and I almost panic before he frowns. Pulls back, says, "Er, wait—sorry—," and flexes his hands. Cracks his knuckles. A few sparks fly out of his fingers. I'm gaping at him.

He shrinks back. Smiles a bit sheepishly. "Sometimes I electrocute people by accident."

Something in my heavy armor snaps off. Melts away. I feel suddenly understood. Unafraid of being myself. I can't help my grin. "Don't worry," I tell him. "If I shake your hand I might kill you."

"Blimey." He blinks. Stares. Waits for me to take it back. "You're serious?"

"Very."

He laughs. "Right then. No touching." Leans in. Lowers his voice. "I have a bit of a problem with that myself, you know. Girls are always talking about electricity in their romance, but none are too happy to actually *be* electrocuted, apparently. Bloody confusing, is what it is." He shrugs.

My smile is wider than the Pacific Ocean. My heart is so full of relief, comfort, acceptance. Adam was right. Maybe things can be okay. Maybe I don't have to be a monster. Maybe I do have a choice.

I think I'm going to like it here.

Brendan winks. "It was very nice meeting you, Juliette. I'll be seeing you?"

I nod. "I think so."

"Brilliant." He shoots me another smile. Turns to Castle. "I'll let you know if I hear anything, sir."

"Perfect."

And Brendan disappears.

I turn to the glass wall keeping me from the other half of my heart. Press my head against the cool surface. Wish he would wake up.

"Would you like to say hello?"

I look up at Castle, who is still studying me. Always analyzing me. Somehow his attention doesn't make me uncomfortable. "Yes," I tell him. "I want to say hello."

# FORTY-EIGHT

Castle uses the key in his hand to open the door.

"Why does the medical wing have to be locked?" I ask him.

He turns to me. He's not very tall, I realize for the first time. "If you'd known where to find him—would you have waited patiently behind this door?"

I drop my eyes. Don't answer. Hope I'm not blushing.

He tries to be encouraging. "Healing is a delicate process. It can't be interrupted or influenced by erratic emotions. We're lucky enough to have two healers among us—a set of twins, in fact. But most fascinating is that they each focus on a different element—one on the physical incapacitations, and one on the mental. Both facets must be addressed, otherwise the healing will be incomplete, weak, insufficient." He turns the door handle. "But I think it's safe for Adam to see you now."

I step inside and my senses are almost immediately assaulted by the scent of jasmine. I search the space for the flowers but find none. I wonder if it's a perfume. It's intoxicating.

"I'll be just outside," Castle says to me.

The room is filled with a long row of beds, simply made.

All 20 or so of them are empty except for Adam's. There's a door at the end of the room that probably leads to another space, but I'm too nervous to be curious right now.

I pull up an extra chair and try to be as quiet as possible. I don't want to wake him, I just want to know he's okay. I clasp and unclasp my hands. I'm too aware of my racing heart. And I know I probably shouldn't touch him, but I can't help myself. I cover his hand with mine. His fingers are warm.

His eyes flutter for just a moment. They don't open. He takes a sudden breath and I freeze.

I almost collapse into tears.

"What are you *doing*?"

My neck snaps at the sound of Castle's panicked voice.

I drop Adam's hand. Push away from the bed, eyes wide, worried. "What do you mean?"

"Why are you—you just—you can *touch* him—?" I never thought I'd see Castle so confused, so perplexed. He's lost his composure, one arm half extended in an effort to stop me.

"Of course I can tou—" I stop. Try to stay calm. "Kenji didn't tell you?"

"This young man has immunity from your touch?" Castle's words are whispered, astonished.

"Yes." I look from him to Adam, still sound asleep. ~~So does Warner.~~

"That's . . . *astounding*."

"Is it?"

"Very." Castle's eyes are bright, so eager. "It certainly

isn't coincidence. There is no coincidence in these kinds of situations." He pauses. Paces. "Fascinating. So many possibilities—so many theories—" He's not even talking to me anymore. His mind is working too quickly for me to keep up. He takes a deep breath. Seems to remember I'm still in the room. "My apologies. Please, carry on. The girls will be out soon—they're assisting James at the moment. I must report this new information as soon as possible."

"Wait—"

He looks up. "Yes?"

"You have theories?" I ask him. "You—you know why these things are happening . . . to me?"

"You mean to *us*?" Castle offers me a gentle smile.

I try not to blush. I manage to nod.

"We have been doing extensive research for years," he says. "We think we have a pretty good idea."

"And?" I can hardly breathe.

"If you should decide to stay at Omega Point, we'll have that conversation very soon, I promise. Besides, I'm sure now is probably not the best time." He nods at Adam.

"Oh." I feel my cheeks burn. "Of course."

Castle turns to leave.

"But do you think that Adam—" The words tumble out of my mouth too quickly. I try to pace myself. "Do you think he's . . . like *us*, too?"

Castle pivots back around. Studies my eyes. "I think," he says carefully, "that it is entirely possible."

I gasp.

"My apologies," he says, "but I really must get going. And I wouldn't want to interrupt your time together."

I want to say yes, sure, of course, absolutely. I want to smile and wave and tell him it's no problem. But I have so many questions, I think I might explode; I want him to tell me everything he knows.

"I know this is a lot of information to take in at once." Castle pauses at the door. "But we'll have plenty of opportunities to talk. You must be exhausted and I'm sure you'd like to get some sleep. The girls will take care of you—they're expecting you. In fact, they'll be your new roommates at Omega Point. I'm sure they'll be happy to answer any questions you might have." He clasps my shoulders before he goes. "It's an honor to have you with us, Ms. Ferrars. I hope you will seriously consider joining us on a permanent basis."

I nod, numb.

And he's gone.

*We have been doing extensive research for years,* he said. *We think we have a pretty good idea,* he said. *We'll have that conversation very soon, I promise.*

For the first time in my life I might finally understand what I am and it doesn't seem possible. And Adam. *Adam.* I shake myself and take my seat next to him. Squeeze his fingers. Castle could be wrong. Maybe this *is* all coincidence.

I have to focus.

I wonder if anyone has heard from Warner lately.

"Juliette?"

318

His eyes are half open. He's staring at me like he's not sure if I'm real.

"Adam!" I have to force myself to be still.

He smiles and the effort seems to exhaust him. "God it's good to see you."

"You're *okay*." I grip his hand, resist pulling him into my arms. "You're really okay."

His grin gets bigger. "I'm so tired. I feel like I could sleep for a few years."

"Don't worry, the sedative will wear off soon."

I spin around. Two girls with exactly the same green eyes are staring at us. They smile at the same time. Their long brown hair is thick and stick-straight in high ponytails on their heads. They're wearing matching silver bodysuits. Gold ballet flats.

"I'm Sonya," the girl on the left says.

"I'm Sara," her sister adds.

I have no idea how to tell them apart.

"It's so nice to meet you," they say at exactly the same time.

"I'm Juliette," I manage. "It's a pleasure to meet you, too."

"Adam is almost ready for release," one says to me.

"Sonya is an excellent healer," the other one chimes in.

"Sara is better than I am," says the first.

"He should be okay to leave just as soon as the sedative is out of his system," they say together, smiling.

"Oh—that's great—thank you so much—" I don't know who to look at. Who to answer. I glance back at Adam.

319

He seems thoroughly amused.

"Where's James?" he asks.

"He's playing with the other children." I think it's Sara who says it.

"We just took him on a bathroom break," says the other.

"Would you like to see him?" Back to Sara.

"There are other children?" My eyes are as wide as my face.

The girls nod at the same time.

"We'll go get him," they chorus. And disappear.

"They seem nice," Adam says after a moment.

"Yeah. They do." This whole place seems nice.

Sonya and Sara come back with James, who seems happier than I've ever seen him, almost happier than seeing Adam for the first time. He's thrilled to be here. Thrilled to be with the other kids, thrilled to be with "the pretty girls who take care of me because they're so nice and there's so much food and they gave me *chocolate*, Adam—have you ever tasted *chocolate*?" and he has a big bed and tomorrow he's going to class with the other kids and he's already excited.

"I'm so happy you're awake," he says to Adam, practically jumping up and down on his bed. "They said you got sick and that you were resting and now you're awake so that means you're better, right? And we're safe? I don't really remember what happened on our way here," he admits, a little embarrassed. "I think I fell asleep."

I think Adam is looking to break Kenji's neck at this point.

"Yeah, we're safe," Adam tells him, running a hand through his messy blond hair. "Everything is okay."

James runs back to the playroom with the other kids. Sonya and Sara invent an excuse to leave so we have some privacy. I'm liking them more and more.

"Has anyone told you about this place yet?" Adam asks me. He manages to sit up. His sheet slides down. His chest is exposed. His skin is perfectly healed—I can hardly reconcile the image I have in my memory with the one in front of me. I forget to answer his question.

"You have no scars." I touch his skin like I need to feel it for myself.

He tries to smile. "They're not very traditional in their medical practices around here."

I look up, startled. "You . . . know?"

"Did you meet Castle yet?"

I nod, bewildered.

He shifts. Sighs. "I've heard rumors about this place for a long time. I got really good at listening to whispers, mostly because I was looking out for myself. But in the army we hear things. Any and all kinds of enemy threats. Possible ambushes. There was talk of an unusual underground movement from the moment I enlisted. Most people said it was crap. That it was some kind of garbage concocted to scare people—that there was no way it could be real. But I always hoped it had some basis in truth, especially after I found out about you—I hoped we'd be able to find others with similar abilities. But I didn't know who to ask. I had no connections—no way of knowing how to find them." He shakes his head. "And all this time, Kenji was working undercover."

"He said he was looking for me."

Adam nods. Laughs. "Just like I was looking for you. Just like Warner was looking for you."

"I don't understand," I mumble. "Especially now that I know there are others like me—stronger, even—why did Warner want *me*?"

"He discovered you before Castle did," Adam says. "He felt like he claimed you a long time ago." Adam leans back. "Warner's a lot of things, but he's not stupid. I'm sure he knew there was some truth to those rumors—and he was fascinated. Because as much as Castle wanted to use his abilities for good, Warner wanted to manipulate those abilities for his own cause. He wanted to become some kind of superpower." A pause. "He invested a lot of time and energy just studying you. I don't think he wanted to let that effort go to waste."

"Adam," I whisper.

He takes my hand. "Yeah?"

"I don't think he's dead."

# FORTY-NINE

"He's not."

Adam turns. Frowns at the voice. "What are you doing here?"

"Wow. What a greeting, Kent. Be careful not to pull a muscle thanking me for saving your ass."

"You lied to all of us."

"You're welcome."

"You sedated my ten-year-old brother!"

"You're still welcome."

"Hey, Kenji." I acknowledge him.

"My clothes look good on you." He steps a bit closer, smiles.

I roll my eyes. Adam examines my outfit for the first time.

"I didn't have anything else to wear," I explain.

Adam nods a little slowly. Looks at Kenji. "Did you have a message to deliver?"

"Yeah. I'm supposed to show you where you'll be staying."

"What do you mean?"

Kenji grins. "You and James are going to be my new roommates."

Adam swears under his breath.

"Sorry, bro, but we don't have enough rooms for you and Hot Hands over here to have your own private space." He winks at me. "No offense."

"I have to leave right now?"

"Yeah, man. I want to go to sleep soon. I don't have all day to wait around for your lazy ass."

"*Lazy—?*"

I hurry to interrupt before Adam has a chance to fight back. "What do you mean, you want to go to sleep? What time is it?"

"It's almost ten at night," Kenji tells me. "It's hard to tell underground, but we all try to be aware of the clocks. We have monitors in the hallways, and most of us try to wear watches. Losing track of night and day can screw us up pretty quickly. And now is not the time to be getting too comfortable."

"How do you know Warner isn't dead?" I ask, nervous.

"We just saw him on camera," Kenji says. "He and his men are patrolling this area pretty heavily. I managed to hear some of their conversation. Turns out Warner got shot."

I suck in my breath, try to silence my heartbeats.

"That's why we got lucky last night—apparently the soldiers got called back to base because they *thought* Warner was dead. There was a shift in power for a minute. No one knew what to do. What orders to follow. But then it turned out he wasn't dead. Just wounded pretty bad. His arm was all patched up and in a sling," Kenji adds.

Adam finds his voice before I do. "How safe is this place from attack?"

Kenji laughs. "Safe as *hell*. I don't even know how they managed to get as close as they did. But they'll never be able to find our exact location. And even if they do, they'll never be able to break in. Our security is just about impenetrable. Plus we have cameras everywhere. We can see what they're doing before they even plan it.

"It doesn't really matter, though," he goes on. "Because they're looking for a fight, and so are we. We're not afraid of an attack. Besides, they have no idea what we're capable of. And we've been training for this shit forever."

"Do you—" I pause. Flush. "Can you—I mean, do you have a . . . gift, too?"

Kenji smiles. And disappears.

He's really gone.

I stand up. Try to touch the space he was just standing in.

He reappears just in time to jump out of reach. "HEY— whoa, careful—just because I'm invisible doesn't mean I can't feel anything—"

"Oh!" I pull back. Cringe. "I'm sorry—"

"You can make yourself *invisible*?" Adam looks more irritated than interested.

"Just blew your mind, didn't I?"

"How long have you been spying on me?" Adam narrows his eyes.

"As long as I needed to." But his grin is laced with mischief.

"So you're . . . corporeal?" I ask.

"Look at you, using big fancy words." Kenji crosses his arms. Leans against the wall.

"I mean—you can't, like, walk through walls or anything, can you?"

He snorts. "Nah, I'm not a ghost. I can just . . . blend, I guess is the best word. I can blend into the background of any space. Shift myself to match my surrounds. It's taken me a long time to figure it out."

"Wow."

"I used to follow Adam home. That's how I knew where he lived. And that's how I was able to run away—because they couldn't really see me. They tried to shoot at me anyway," he adds, bitter, "but I managed not to die, at least."

"Wait, but why were you following Adam home? I thought you were looking for *me*?" I ask him.

"Yeah—well, I enlisted shortly after we got wind of Warner's big project." He nods in my direction. "We'd been trying to find you, but Warner had more security clearance and access to more information than we did—we were having a hard time tracking you down. Castle thought it would be easier to have someone on the inside paying attention to all the crazy shit Warner was planning. So when I heard that Adam was the main guy involved in this particular project and that he had this history with you, I sent the information to Castle. He told me to watch out for Adam, too—you know, in case Adam turned out to be just as psycho as Warner. We wanted to make sure he wasn't a threat to you or our plans. But I had no idea you'd try to run away together. Messed me the hell up."

We're all silent for a moment.

"So how much did you spy on me?" Adam asks him.

"Well, well, well." Kenji cocks his head. "Is Mr. Adam Kent suddenly feeling a little intimidated?"

"Don't be a jackass."

"You hiding something?"

"Yeah. My gun—"

"Hey!" Kenji claps his hands together. "So! Are we ready to get out of here, or what?"

"I need a pair of pants."

Kenji looks abruptly annoyed. "Seriously, Kent? I don't want to hear that shit."

"Well, unless you want to see me naked, I suggest you do something about it."

Kenji shoots Adam a dirty look and stalks off, grumbling something about lending people all of his clothes. The door swings shut behind him.

"I'm not really naked," Adam tells me.

"Oh," I gasp. Look up. My eyes betray me.

He can't bite back his grin in time. His fingers graze my cheek. "I just wanted him to leave us alone for a second."

I'm blushing through my bones. Fumbling for something to say. "I'm so happy you're okay."

He says something I don't hear.

Takes my hand. Pulls me up beside him.

He's leaning in and I'm leaning in until I'm practically on top of him and he's slipping me into his arms and kissing me with a new kind of desperation, a new kind of passion, a burning need. His hands are threaded in my hair, his lips so soft, so urgent against mine, like fire and honey exploding in my mouth. My whole body is steaming.

Adam pulls back just a tiny bit. Kisses my bottom lip. Bites it for just a second. His skin is 100 degrees hotter than it was a moment ago. His lips are pressed against my neck and my hands are on a journey down his upper body and I'm wondering why there are so many freight trains in my heart, why his chest is a broken harmonica. I'm tracing the bird caught forever in flight on his skin and I realize for the first time that he's given me wings of my own. He's helped me fly away and now I'm stuck in centripetal motion, soaring right into the center of everything. I bring his lips back up to mine.

"Juliette," he says. 1 breath. 1 kiss. 10 fingers teasing my skin. "I need to see you tonight."

Yes.

Please.

2 hard knocks send us flying apart.

Kenji slams open the door. "You do realize this wall is made of *glass*, don't you?" He looks like he's bitten the head off a worm. "No one wants to see that."

He throws a pair of pants at Adam.

Nods to me. "Come on, I'll take you to Sonya and Sara. They'll set you up for tonight." Turns to Adam. "And don't *ever* give those pants back to me."

"What if I don't want to sleep?" Adam asks, unabashed. "I'm not allowed to leave my room?"

Kenji presses his lips together. Narrows his eyes. "I

will not use this word often, Kent, but *please* don't try any fancy secret-sneaking-away shit. We have to regulate things around here for a reason. It's the only way to survive. So do everyone a favor and keep your pants on. You'll see her in the morning."

But morning feels like a million years from now.

# FIFTY

The twins are still asleep when someone knocks. Sonya and Sara showed me where the girls' bathrooms are so I had a chance to shower last night, but I'm still wearing Kenji's oversized clothes. I feel a little ridiculous as I pad my way toward the door.

I open it.

Blink. "Hey, Winston."

He looks me up and down. "Castle thought you might like to change out of those clothes."

"You have something for me to wear?"

"Yeah—remember? We made you something custom."

"Oh. Wow. Yeah, that sounds great."

I slip outside silently, following Winston through the dark halls. The underground world is quiet, its inhabitants still asleep. I ask Winston why we're up so early.

"I figured you'd want to meet everyone at breakfast. This way you can jump into the regular routine of things around here—even get started on your training." He glances back. "We all have to learn how to harness our abilities in the most effective manner possible. It's no good having no control over your body."

"Wait—you have an *ability*, too?"

"There are exactly fifty-six of us who do. The rest are our family members, children, or close friends who help out with everything else. So yes, I'm one of those fifty-six. So are you."

I'm nearly stepping on his feet in an effort to keep up with his long legs. "So what can you do?"

He doesn't answer. And I can't be sure, but I think he's blushing.

"I'm sorry—" I backpedal. "I don't mean to pry— I shouldn't have asked—"

"It's okay," he cuts me off. "I just think it's kind of stupid." He laughs a short, hard laugh. "Of all the things I should be able to do," he sighs. "At least you can do something *interesting*."

I stop walking, stunned. Horrified. "You think this is a competition? To see which magic trick is more twisted? To see who can inflict the most pain?"

"That's not what I meant—"

"I don't think it's *interesting* to be able to kill someone by accident. I don't think it's *interesting* to be afraid to touch a living thing."

His jaw is tense. "I didn't mean it like that. I just . . . I wish I were more useful. That's all."

I cross my arms. "You don't have to tell me if you don't want to."

He rolls his eyes. Runs a hand through his hair. "I'm just—I'm very . . . flexible," he says.

It takes me a moment to process his admission. "Like— you can bend yourself into a pretzel?"

"Sure. Or stretch myself if I need to."

I'm gawking so openly I must be embarrassing myself. "Can I see?"

He bites his lip. Readjusts his glasses. Looks both ways down the empty hall. And loops one arm around his waist. Twice.

I'm gaping like a dead fish. "Wow."

"It's stupid," he grumbles. "And useless."

"Are you insane?" I lean back to look at him. "That's *incredible*."

But his arm is back to normal and he's walking away again. I have to run to catch up.

"Don't be so hard on yourself," I try to tell him. "It's nothing to be ashamed of." But he's not listening and I'm wondering when I became a motivational speaker. When I made the switch from hating myself to accepting myself. When it became okay for me to choose my own life.

Winston leads me to the room I met him in. The same white walls. The same small bed. Only this time, Adam and Kenji are waiting inside. My heart kicks into gear and I'm suddenly nervous.

Adam is up. He's standing on his own and he looks perfect. Beautiful. Unharmed. There's not a single drop of blood on his body. He walks forward with only a slight discomfort, smiles at me with no difficulty. His skin is a little paler than normal, but positively radiant compared to his complexion the night we arrived. His natural tan offsets a pair of eyes a shade of blue in a midnight sky.

"Juliette," he says.

I can't stop staring at him. Marveling at him. Amazed by how incredible it feels to know that he's all right. "Hey." I manage to smile.

"Good morning to you, too," Kenji interjects.

I startle. I'm pinker than a summer sunset, and shrinking just as quickly. "Oh, hi." I wave a limp hand in his direction.

He snorts.

"All right. Let's get this over with, shall we?" Winston walks toward one of the walls, which turns out to be a closet. There's one pop of color inside. He pulls it off the hanger.

"Can I, uh, have a moment alone with her?"

Winston takes off his glasses. Rubs his eyes. "I need to follow protocol. I have to explain everything—"

"I know—that's fine," Adam says. "You can do it after. I just need a minute, I promise. I haven't really had a chance to talk to her since we got here."

Winston frowns. Looks at me. Looks at Adam. Sighs.

"All right. But then we'll be back. I need to make sure everything fits and I have to check the—"

"Perfect. That sounds great. Thanks, man—" And he's shoving them out the door.

"Wait!" Winston slams the door back open. "At least get her to put the suit on while we're outside. That way it won't be a complete waste of my time."

Adam stares at the material in Winston's outstretched hand. Winston rubs his forehead and mumbles something about people always wasting his time, and Adam suppresses a grin. Glances at me. I shrug. "Okay," he says, grabbing the suit. "But now you have to get out—" And pushes them both back into the hallway.

"We're going to be *right outside*," Kenji shouts. "Like five seconds away—"

Adam closes the door behind them. Turns around. His eyes are burning into me.

I don't know how to calm my heart. I try to speak and fail.

He finds his voice first. "I never had a chance to say thank you," he says.

I drop my eyes. Pretend heat isn't fighting its way up my face. Pinch myself for no real reason.

He steps forward. Leans in. Takes my hands. "Juliette."

I peek up at him.

*"You saved my life."*

I bite the inside of my cheek. It seems so silly to say "You're welcome" for saving someone's life. I don't know what to do. "I'm just so happy you're okay," is all I manage.

He's staring at my lips and I'm aching everywhere. If he kisses me right now I don't think I'll let him stop. He takes a sharp breath. Seems to remember he's holding something. "Oh. Maybe you should put this on?" He hands me a slinky piece of something purple. It looks tiny. Like a jumpsuit that could fit a small child. It weighs less than nothing.

I offer Adam a blank stare.

He grins. "Try it on."

I stare differently.

"Oh." He jumps back, a little bashful. "Right—I'll just—I'll turn around—"

I wait until his back is to me before I exhale. I look around. There don't seem to be any mirrors in this room. I shed the oversized outfit. Drop each piece on the floor. I'm standing here, completely naked, and for a moment I'm too petrified to move. But Adam doesn't turn around. He doesn't say a word. I examine the shiny purple material. I imagine it's supposed to stretch.

It does.

In fact, it's unexpectedly easy to slip on—like it was designed specifically for my body. There's built-in lining for where underwear is supposed to be, extra support for my chest, a collar that goes right up to my neck, sleeves that touch my wrists, legs that touch my ankles, a zipper that pulls it all together. I examine the ultrathin material. It feels like I'm wearing nothing. It's the richest shade of purple, skintight but not tight at all. It's breathable, oddly comfortable.

"How does it look . . . ?" Adam asks. He sounds nervous.

"Can you help me zip it up?"

He turns around. His lips part, falter, form an incredible smile. His eyebrows are touching the ceiling. I'm blushing so hard I don't even know where to look. He steps forward and I turn around, only too eager to hide my face, the butterflies racing through my chest. Adam touches my hair and I realize it's almost all the way down my back. Maybe it's time I cut it.

His fingers are so careful. He pushes the waves over my shoulder so they won't get caught in the zipper. Trails a line from the base of my neck down to the start of the seam, down to the dip in my lower back. I can hardly keep myself upright. My spine is conducting enough electricity to power a city. He takes his time zipping me up. Runs his hands down the length of my silhouette. "God you look incredible," is the first thing he says to me.

I turn around. He's pressing his fist to his mouth, trying to hide his smile, trying to stop the words from tumbling out of his lips.

I touch the material. Decide I should probably say something. "It's very . . . comfortable."

"Sexy."

I look up.

He's shaking his head. "It's sexy as hell."

He steps forward. Slips me into his arms.

"I look like a gymnast," I mumble.

"No," he whispers, hot hot hot against my lips. "You look like a superhero."

# EPILOGUE

I'm still tingling when Kenji and Winston burst back into the room.

"So how is this suit supposed to make my life easier?" I ask anyone who'll answer.

But Kenji is frozen in place, staring without apology. Opens his mouth. Closes it. Shoves his hands into his pockets.

Winston steps in. "It's supposed to help with the touching issue," he tells me. "You don't have to worry about being covered from head to toe in this unpredictable weather. The material is designed to keep you cool or keep you warm based on the temperature. It's light and breathable so your skin doesn't suffocate. It will keep you safe from hurting someone unintentionally, but offers you the flexibility of touching someone . . . intentionally, too. If you ever needed to."

"That's amazing."

He smiles. Big. "You're welcome."

I study the suit more closely. Realize something. "But my hands and feet are totally exposed. How's that supposed to—"

"Oh—shoot," Winston interrupts. "I almost forgot." He runs over to the closet and pulls out a pair of flat-heeled black ankle boots and a pair of black gloves that stop right before the elbow. He hands them to me. I study the soft leather of the accessories and marvel at the springy, flexible build of the boots. I could do ballet and run a mile in these shoes. "These should fit you," he says. "They complete the outfit."

I slip them on and tip up on my toes, luxuriate in the feeling of my new outfit. I feel invincible. I really wish I had a mirror for once in my life. I look from Kenji to Adam to Winston. "What do you think? Is it . . . okay?"

Kenji makes a strange noise.

Winston looks at his watch.

Adam can't stop smiling.

He and I follow Kenji and Winston out of the room, but Adam pauses to slip off my left glove. He takes my hand. Intertwines our fingers. Offers me a smile that manages to kiss my heart.

And I look around.

Flex my fist.

Touch the material hugging my skin.

I feel incredible. My bones feel rejuvenated; my skin feels vibrant, healthy. I take big lungfuls of air and savor the taste.

Things are changing, but this time I'm not afraid. This time I know who I am. This time I've made the right choice and I'm fighting for the right team. I feel safe. Confident.

Excited, even.

Because this time?

I'm ready.

# ACKNOWLEDGMENTS

My infinite thanks go to:

My husband, my best friend, my biggest fan, and the only man in the world who understands the inside of my brain. You are the brightest star in my universe.

My parents, who've been cheering for me every minute of my life, never once doubting me, never once discouraging me. You inspire me every single day.

My brothers, because no one knows our stories like we do. Because we stick together. Because you've always believed in me and I will forever believe in you.

Tana & Randa, for everything. For every moment, every word of encouragement, every laugh, every cherished memory. You've been there from the very beginning.

Sarah, who gave me the strength to be brave. You held my hand in the moments I needed it most and I will never forget that.

Jodi Reamer, the most incredible superhuman I've ever known. You've filled my days with shooting stars, and one day I will pluck the moon from the sky and fit it in your mailbox.

Alec Shane, who gave me the one chance that changed my world.

Tara Weikum, the best editor a girl could ask for. It's been such a privilege working with someone who so absolutely understands my story. My characters are safe with you in a way they wouldn't have been anywhere else and I still can't believe I got so lucky. You are unbelievable and I adore you.

A big thank-you to everyone at HarperCollins and Writers House who work tirelessly behind the scenes to make my dreams come true: Melissa Miller, for being nothing less than fabulous; Christina Colangelo, Diane Naughton, and Lauren Flower, for their endless enthusiasm and marketing genius; and Allison Verost, my fearless publicist! Thanks also to Alison Donalty, art director and purse carrier and coffee savior—you are an absolute gem; Ray Shappell, the brilliant man behind the cover design; Brenna Franzitta, whose copy-editing skills are worth millions; Cecilia de la Campa, for her indefatigable efforts in acquiring foreign rights; and Beth Miller, for being one of my first cheerleaders.

To all of my first readers, including Sumayyah, Bahareh, and Saba, as well as my brilliant blog and Twitter friends who make my days so much brighter and infinitely more beautiful: Thank you for sharing my journey and honoring me with your friendship—I hope you know I'm always cheering for you!

And for every reader who picks up this book: Well. Without you, where would we be?

Thank you, thank you, thank you!